FIRST QUIVER

BETH C. GREENBERG

A NOVEL

Enjoy Cupid!

ISOTOPIA
PUBLISHING

FIRST QUIVER
Copyright © 2021 Beth C. Greenberg

ISBN (paperback): 978-1-7359447-0-8
ISBN (hardcover): 978-1-7359447-2-2
ISBN (ebook): 978-1-7359447-1-5

Cover design, illustrations, and Isotopia logo by Betti Gefecht
Edited by Susan Atlas and Dominic Wakeford
Interior design by Domini Dragoone
Family tree background image © sabphoto/123RF.com

ISOTOPIA PUBLISHING
www.isotopiapublishing.com
www.bethcgreenberg.com

First Edition

For Larry,
the truest Love my heart has ever known.

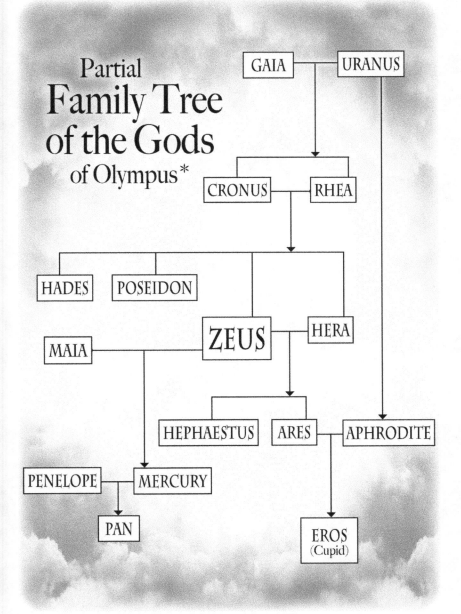

Partial **Family Tree of the Gods** of Olympus*

GAIA — URANUS

CRONUS — RHEA

HADES   POSEIDON

ZEUS — HERA

MAIA

HEPHAESTUS   ARES   APHRODITE

PENELOPE — MERCURY

PAN

EROS (Cupid)

*Names chosen by gods in 480 C.E.

A full listing of divine characters can be found immediately following the story.

Love—Eros—makes his home in men's hearts,
but not in every heart, for where there is hardness,
he departs. His greatest glory is that he cannot
do wrong nor allow it; force never comes near him.
For all men serve him of their own free will. And he
whom Love touches not walks in darkness.

—PLATO, THE SYMPOSIUM

1

THE FALL

It occurred to Cupid as his fingernails slipped off the edge of Mount Olympus that Mother had finally called his bluff. His sandaled feet flipped toward the sky, almost, but not quite entirely, blotting out the grim faces peering down at him. If only he hadn't seen that tear rolling down Aphrodite's cheek, perhaps he could have avoided the sting at the back of his own eyes.

No. He wouldn't give Ares the satisfaction.

He sank like a shuttlecock—head down, feathers up—swifter than he would have thought possible, but then what could a boy with wings know about falling? His attempts to join in when the other boys went cliff diving had always ended with a cowardly, last-minute swoop before reaching the water, but today would be different. He'd resolved to take his punishment like a man.

The sky slapped his cheeks, thrashed his eyes, burned the tips of his ears. He clenched his jaw with determination, but it was no use. Reflexes kicked in, bringing a surge of relief followed by a sharp spike of shame. His wings flexed, lifted, and flapped.

Nothing.

Faster he fell, though his wings beat harder. Flapping then flailing then flipping, an end-over-end freefall. Feathers flew every which way, clogging the sky like a giant pillow fight until there were no more feathers to lose and no way to slow his descent. Wind whistled through the scant folds of his chiton, all that preserved his last shred of dignity.

He sucked in a shallow breath, then another. Blood pounded in his ears. His heart raced as if trying to beat the rest of him to the mountain's base. The vivid colors of Mount Olympus ran together like a smeared oil painting as he tumbled past, dizzy and disoriented and utterly at the mercy of the laws of physics he probably should have paid more attention to at the academy.

His first glimpse of the Great Cloud choked his lungs with dread. The gray vapor formed a chilling likeness to the jaws of Zeus, open to swallow him whole. Breaching the border of the mortal world was expressly forbidden, but he could not have stopped his ghastly tumble to beg entry even if he wanted to. He braced for a crash, but the gate stood wide open.

Cupid dragged in his last breath of Olympian air, committed to memory his final blurry glimpse of the only home he'd ever known, and disappeared into the blinding froth.

The cloud closed around him like a thick, wet fleece. Icy droplets slipped between his lips and clung to his eyelashes. The dense mist slowed his drop to a sufferable pace, more drifting leaf than falling brick. Foam plugged his ears with silence. All he could hear was the wildly erratic beat of his own heart and the thoughts banging around in his head. Suspended between two worlds, he was profoundly alone.

Not even his own mother had stood by him.

Would she still not care if the gods were to decide to torture him? The prospect of physical harm sent a violent shiver through Cupid's body. He had never much concerned himself with the fate of Prometheus, but now he couldn't shake the image of the great Titan chained to a rock while a giant eagle tore away at his exposed liver, day after day for all of eternity.

What if the gods required feats of great strength? He no more possessed the brawn of Hercules than he did the forbearance of Prometheus, thus the ultimate fear: *What if I fail?* He wouldn't be the first fallen god not to see his home again, he recalled with a heavy heart.

Fear worked itself into a knot of bravado. To the Underworld with all of them! He'd run once his feet hit the ground—or drag himself if his legs were too mangled—and not even try to earn back his boring, predictable life. *You'll be sorry then, Mother.*

As if answering for the goddess who'd birthed him, the Great Cloud spat Cupid out with a brutal shove into Earth's atmosphere. The mortals' air tasted bitter, he decided with a smack of his lips. The color palette dulled to muted blues, greens, and browns, as if someone had drawn a curtain over his eyes. He wondered if he'd adjust to this new world or if he'd even want to. A forceful tug cut short his speculation.

Invisible arms dragged him toward the ground with alarming velocity. Earth's gravity, he recalled suddenly, was serious business. His shoulders twitched out of habit but only reminded him he had no landing gear whatsoever.

He fought back terror with the might of three thousand years of faith in his mother's love, though he had to acknowledge he'd sorely tested Aphrodite this time. Cupid was still weighing his mother's heart when the grassy field rose to meet his bottom.

RESURRECTION

If Pan were capable of a heart attack, Mercury's sudden appearance in the weight room might have given him one. Only the wing-footed messenger of the gods could have bypassed the security desk at Pan's gym without notice.

"Greetings from the gods," said Mercury.

Pan carefully lowered his barbell to the floor. "Nice sweatpants, Dad," he said, grinning at his father's attempt to blend in with the mortals. "Did you knock off The Gap on your way here?"

Mercury forced a smile. Never a good sign.

"Oh, shit. Don't tell me they're sending Clotho back down to serve out the rest of her sentence."

Six years ago, Clotho's punishment had run into the kind of nasty snag the gods abhorred, one that drew attention. As the Fate responsible for spinning the thread of life, Clotho's arrival in Tarra had wreaked havoc on the town's fertility rates. The sudden increase in pregnancies might have prematurely forced Pan out of Indiana if the Board of Health hadn't mistakenly correlated the spike with an entirely coincidental increase in the consumption of a certain locally produced bone broth, hence the so-called Bone Broth Baby Boom. Clotho wasn't completely to blame, really. Divine powers didn't translate predictably to earth's atmosphere, as the gods above were well aware. Fortunately for all involved, Clotho was called back to the Mount to reverse an accidental death, returning life in Tarra, Indiana, to its usual monotony.

"No, Clotho's sentence was commuted," Mercury assured him. "Case closed."

"Well, that's a relief," Pan said. Catching the odd expression on Mercury's face, he added, "Isn't it?"

"Yes, of course. Um, I don't know how to tell you this . . ." The hesitation was curious. Since when did his father get emotional about delivering a message?

"Just say it already. You're freaking me out."

"It's Cupid."

"Cupid?" *Freak-out complete.* Every hair on the back of Pan's neck stood on end.

"Yes," said Mercury. "The Divine Council has passed judgment. Nine minutes until touchdown."

"What? Why?"

"You know they don't give me the details, son. Some mischief with his arrows. It is not good."

Pan's thoughts became a montage of Cupid's previous escapades, none of which had ever gotten him exiled before, nor had Pan imagined they ever would. Not with Aphrodite, the High Priestess of Enabling, on deck to clean up her son's messes.

Oh, Q, what have you done?

Pan knew the drill. Managing the paperwork was no problem; the hard part was being resurrected from the ashes of Caesarea every time a new divine fell to earth. And now, because of some dumbass prank, the confrontation Pan had always feared was hurtling directly toward him like one of the mortals' heat-seeking missiles.

"The terrible twosome rides again, hmm?" Mercury's elbow nudge and wistful tone held just enough cheer to make Pan's gut lurch, but he pulled himself together before answering.

"Don't know about the riding. Sounds like Cupid's gotten himself into deep shit with the gods this time."

"And you'll be right here to help him out of it," said Mercury.

"As if that will make up for two thousand years of deception."

Mercury set his hand on Pan's shoulder and squeezed. "We all did what we had to do, son. He'll forgive you."

3

EARTHLING

Considering the chaotic journey and the crash landing, Cupid was remarkably unscathed.

"Huh," he marveled out loud, testing his new voice. It was deeper than his voice on Olympus. Liking the sound of it, he babbled just to hear the rich tones reverberate in the unfamiliar atmosphere. "I made it in one piece, Mother, in case you're worried," he said, tipping his chin skyward and sending up a stiff-handed salute.

He ran his fingertips across his bare chest, expecting to be met by soft flesh, and was shocked to find hard mounds under taut skin and . . . was that actual chest hair? He dropped his gaze to behold the wondrous sight. His fingers had changed too, grown longer and more slender. He flipped his hands over and back, staring as if they belonged to someone else, then applied the foreign fingertips to twin columns of wondrous, muscular ridges he'd only ever seen on bellies other than his own—not that he hadn't tried. He'd even traded favors for training sessions from Hercules, but no matter how much weight he lifted or how furiously he crunched, his body could never respond. And here was the physique he'd always desired without any effort at all.

Emboldened, he pressed his luck—it seemed the day for it— and swept his thumb over the bunched fabric in his lap. A grin widened across his face. Whatever lurked under his chiton was substantially larger now than when he'd left home.

This new body of his would have been cause for jubilation if not for his dire predicament. That he appeared to be freed from the bondage of perpetual puberty only meant the Divine Council had something far worse in store for him.

Saving the more intimate exploration for later, Cupid stretched his legs out along the ground and ran his palms down the thick, muscular ropes of his new thighs, relishing the power he sensed just below the skin. His toes poked out well past the edge of his sandals, a man's feet in a child's shoes. He unbuckled the leather straps and wriggled out of them.

Setting his bare feet beneath him, he pushed off the thick grass floor and stood, a good forty centimeters taller than before. He dusted off his hands, admired his well-developed arms for a moment, then pulled his fingers through his hair. The soft curls of his Olympian form had lost their downy feel; the new hair was fuller, straighter, and coarser. Pondering his missing curls, he drummed his fingertips on his chin.

"What's this?" he inquired aloud, knowing full well he had sprouted whiskers for the very first time. "Great Zeus!" His palms scrubbed merrily up and down the new growth on his cheeks.

He rolled his thickened shoulders back a few times, getting comfortable in his new body. He'd been so distracted by his muscles and his phallus and his stubble, he'd forgotten entirely about losing his wings. While those wings had never burdened him, he couldn't help but notice shedding their weight was a tremendous relief.

He reached back and ran his palm over one shoulder, finding skin instead of feathers. He craned his neck around, fearing a gaping hole, but there was no grisly crater, no scar, not even a nick. Nothing.

Well, not exactly nothing. There seemed to be writing of some sort. He'd have to find himself a looking glass. There was so much about this Earth body he still needed to explore. As if feeling excluded from his considerations, his stomach gurgled and groaned.

The internal noises were answered by a rustling of foliage at the edge of the clearing. Panic filled his chest.

4

REUNITED

As the leaf crunching grew louder, so did a breathy, musical sound that instantly reminded Cupid of home. The low-hanging tree branches gave way, and Cupid did a double take when a man strongly resembling his long-lost best friend Pan advanced toward him.

Cupid stared with wide eyes. A familiar thicket of red hair ran from the top of the man's head, connected to neatly trimmed vines covering both of his ruddy cheeks, and disappeared behind the flute at his chin. Where Pan would have sported two pointy horns, this man had a forehead as human as Cupid's. In place of the satyr's hindquarters, a man's lower body appeared, ending with two human feet in place of hooves. Obscured by clothing, the finer details were uncertain.

The deep-green twinkle from the other man's gaze strummed an unmistakable chord deep within Cupid's soul. But how? This man in front of him was definitely not a satyr, and he was also very obviously alive—unlike Cupid's best friend.

With a lump in his throat, Cupid hazarded a quaky trial of the once-frequent name on his tongue. "*Pan?*"

The redhead nodded once as the flute fell away from his mouth. "Welcome to Earth, Q."

Cupid squinted, though his vision had never been clearer. "Is that really you?"

"I might ask you the same, my friend."

He'd mourned his best friend for the last two thousand years, and all the while, Pan lived and breathed? Confusion and elation took their turns with Cupid. It seemed very little of his previous reality had survived the fall. He wasn't at all sure he minded.

"You're alive!"

"Well, aren't you the observant one." A chuckle accompanied the voice Cupid had known so long and so well.

"I don't understand." Cupid scratched his head and regarded Pan's patient smile. Perhaps the fall had muddled Cupid's mind, but Pan seemed real enough—in fact, more vital than ever. Cupid shook off his doubts and threw his arms around his old friend, bending to adjust for the slight difference in their new heights. "I've missed you so much," Cupid said, tightening his hug. Tears sprang to his eyes.

Pan squeezed him back, his grip as strong as Cupid remembered, then pulled away with a hearty slap on Cupid's back. "It's great to see you too, man."

He inspected Pan's lower half once more, but his eyes had not deceived him. The satyr was a satyr no more. "What happened to your hooves and tail?"

"You didn't pass them on your way down?"

"I don't know. I was too busy falling."

A sudden burst of laughter startled Cupid. "You're still you on the inside, I see," Pan answered, landing a punch on Cupid's arm that, surprisingly, didn't hurt.

"As are you." Cupid was comforted to see Pan up to his old favorite pastime, even if that pastime was teasing Cupid.

"Sorry. I couldn't resist," Pan responded. "I suppose my goat parts are hanging out with your wings at some great Bacchanalia far from here."

"I know. Look at me!" Cupid spun around and waved his arms at every possible angle, celebrating his newfound freedom.

Pan set his fingers onto the base of Cupid's spine and slid them slowly upwards, tracing a line where the wings used to be. "Hmm, what have we here?"

"It says something, right?"

"Indeed. You've got yourself some serious ink, my friend."

Cupid craned his neck to see. "Is it something fashionable?"

Pan chuckled. "Depends on your fashion sense. It's Plato."

"Plato?" Awe hushed Cupid's voice. "What's it say?"

Pan read the message inscribed up Cupid's back. "*He whom Love touches not walks in darkness.*"

"Huh," Cupid said, pivoting to face Pan. "What's that mean?"

"I'm guessing you're supposed to figure that out."

Cupid's open-mouthed gawp melted into a foxy grin. "Do you think this *ink* will make me popular with the girls down here?"

"Yeah, I don't think that's going to be a problem," said Pan while looking Cupid up and down, pausing for what felt like a disproportionately long time on his midsection. "Last time I saw you, the only action you were getting was the five-knuckle slip-n-slide." Pan shook his fist in an obscene gesture. "And now, look at you. You're all grown up and . . ." Pan trailed off with a low rumble at the back of his throat.

"Sculpted?" Cupid could practically see Michelangelo standing beside him, chisel in hand, admiring his masterpiece.

"Yes, Narcissus," Pan replied with a smirk. "When did all this happen?"

"Just now. While I was falling."

"*Just now?*" Pan said, his mouth holding onto the *ow*. "You mean to tell me you've been stuck with that sorry excuse for a willy until *today?*"

Cupid's cheeks heated with mortification. "After all this time apart, we're together again for all of five minutes, and all you can find to talk about is my *willy?*"

"Holy shit. You're still a *virgin.*"

The dreaded v-word still stung, but Cupid's new body revived a long-buried hope. "Maybe not for long."

Pan angled his face toward the sky. "I see you're making this one interesting."

"Who are you talking—*wait*. They know you're alive?"

"Oh, uh . . ." The humor disappeared from Pan's expression. "Don't move. I'll be right back." Pan ducked into the woods, reappearing in the clearing moments later holding a stack of clothes similar to his own. "Here. Everything won't fit perfectly, but it'll be close enough for now. C'mon, get dressed before someone sees you."

"I *am* dressed," Cupid fired back.

"Sorry, pal, but the only people who dress in togas down here are drunken frat boys out for a quick roll in the hay."

"What's a frat?" Clearly, the limited field of Earth-vision afforded by Cupid's bow gaiascope had left some gaps in his understanding of contemporary American vernacular.

Pan huffed. "Basically, an excuse for abusing alcohol and taking advantage of gullible girls."

"That doesn't sound so terrible."

"You've spent way too much time with Dionysus. Do you want lunch, or what?"

Motivated by his belly's demands, Cupid unwrapped his chiton, plucked the stiff blue pants from the pile in Pan's arms, and stepped cautiously into the first leg.

"Whoa. Underwear first."

A pair of white shorts came flying at Cupid's chest, and he flung out his arm to catch them. He stretched the waist opening apart with his thumbs. "You expect me to squeeze myself into this?"

"You'll get used to it. The pouch goes in the front."

A scowl settled on Cupid's face as he arranged himself inside the clingy fabric. "I don't see what the big deal is," he complained, stepping into the pants once again. "Who's to know if I forgo the underwear?"

"*I'll* know, okay?" A twinge of longing radiated from Pan, who hastily fluffed out the red shirt he'd been holding and pushed the neck hole over Cupid's head.

Cupid froze, one arm midway through the sleeve, and caught his old chum's face turning bright pink. Well, that was different.

"Put the flip-flops on," Pan said gruffly, dropping a pair of strange sandals onto the grass.

"Flip *what?*"

"Push your toes under the leather strap, like mine."

As Cupid wriggled his toes into place on either side of the uncomfortable post, Pan took off toward the thicket. "Wait!" Cupid called, clomping with unsure steps over tree roots and forest debris until his toes mastered the grab-and-lift. "You know I'm an abysmal hunter. And I don't even have my bow, in case you've forgotten."

Pan laughed heartily over his shoulder. "Hop in my truck, and I'll show you how the mortals do it."

5

CRIME AND PUNISHMENT

The Salvador Deli would not have been Pan's first choice to pop Cupid's earth-food cherry, but it was a short drive from the drop spot. Relief at finding Pan alive had to give way to resentment sooner or later, and he didn't want the two of them trapped in his Titan when that conversation hit.

Not that sitting across the booth from Beefcake Charlie was so easy either. It was more than the buff body, though. Earth-Cupid was sending out some kind of supernatural, erotic waves that made Pan ache in all kinds of ways he wasn't prepared for and would surely get in the way of facilitating Cupid's punishment, whatever the hell that might be.

"I don't see what giant ants and droopy clocks have to do with food," Cupid said, scanning the bright mural.

"It's a pun. The artist's name is Salvador Dalí."

"Oh." A wide grin broke across Cupid's face, and he even chuckled. *Damn.* Pan had forgotten how easy Cupid was, that uncanny ability of his to find joy in the most ordinary situations—a necessity, Pan supposed, of spending every damn day flying around Olympus with only his arrows for entertainment.

Along came their waitress—a leggy, chesty blonde who lit up like a neon sign as she took in the freshly fallen god studying his menu. Pan couldn't fault the girl for overlooking his own godly gifts; he might have wondered at her judgment if she hadn't.

"Hello, my name is Layla." *Flash, sizzle, pop.* "I'll be taking care of you."

Cupid snapped his head up, registering delight at her obvious interest. "*Yassas!*"

A giggle leapt out of Layla, and Cupid beamed back at her like a fool who had never seen a girl before. "Pickled tomatoes, gentlemen?" Layla leaned forward with the metal bowl, her tits straining at the buttons of her mustard-colored uniform.

"Yes, please." Cupid licked his lips appreciatively.

Her musk surely smelled ten times as potent to Cupid's newly magnified senses. Boxer briefs or not, his brand-new pecker had to be well on its way to a full salute.

"We're ready to order," Pan said.

Drawing her pencil from behind her ear, Layla aimed a suggestive, "What can I get you, hon?" at Cupid.

"He'll have the 'Persistence of Pastrami' on rye with coleslaw and Russian, french fries, and a black cherry soda. And I'll have the 'Surreal Stack'—extra tongue—with a ginger ale. Did you get all that?"

"Mmhmm, extra tongue." Layla barely looked away from Cupid's baby blues to scribble down the order. "I'll put that right in for you," she assured them while tucking the pencil into her mountainous hairdo. Neither man missed the exaggerated sway of her retreating hips.

Pan leaned across the table. "Did you smell that?"

BETH C. GREENBERG

"Does Argus have a hundred eyes? I can hardly breathe." Cupid's nose twitched comically. "What just happened?"

"*That*, my friend, was the full force of your divine charisma amplified by earth's atmosphere, overloading the delicate circuitry of the human sensory receptors."

Cupid squinted hard. "You know I failed physics."

"And took me down with you," Pan said with a booming laugh. No wonder, when the two spent more time on shenanigans than formulas. "We just learned what happens when earth girl meets earth-*you*."

"Wow, really? Are they always that . . .?"

"*Titillated?*" They grinned as they had as two little boys trying out their naughty words on each other. "Nope, but then, the God of Erotic Love has never fallen before. And while we're on the topic, how *did* the favored son of Aphrodite manage to get his ass booted off the Mount?"

"Apparently," Cupid said, chest puffed with self-congratulation, "shooting an arrow into the rump of Cerberus while he was squabbling with Hera was"—Cupid lifted his arms and waggled his fingers toward the tin ceiling tiles—"unacceptable."

Pan's jaw dropped. If he'd been given a week to imagine Cupid's crime, he could not have come up with anything so reckless. "You set the three-headed hound of Hades on the *wife* of the *Supreme Ruler* of Olympus? How exceptionally stupid of you."

"Yeah, perhaps I didn't think that through. Hades wasn't amused either."

"He's not exactly renowned for his sense of humor—or his forgiving spirit."

Cupid leaned forward, a familiar mayhem dancing in his eyes. "You should've seen it, Pan. The horny mutt attached himself to Hera's leg and humped her all the way to Zeus's palace."

"Cerberus left the gates of the Underworld unguarded?"

"He was in love." Cupid freed the gleeful smile he'd bitten back so far and batted his eyelashes like a Saturday morning cartoon character. The poor fool was way too pleased with himself about all this.

"Let's see. With a single arrow, you managed to piss off Hades, Hera, and *Zeus*? You do like to poke the beast."

"Ha!" Cupid slammed his palm down onto the table. "Everyone knows Zeus would be relieved to have a willing volunteer to service the old cow—"

Pan flew out of his seat and clamped his hand over Cupid's mouth before he could dig them both an even deeper hole. Cupid struggled against the gag until Pan pointed a finger skyward. Only after Cupid nodded did Pan release his grip and settle into the booth again.

"Your mother must've gotten quite the earful from those three." A smirk grew and died on Pan's lips; he was far more comfortable in the role of accomplice than guardian, but his job allowed zero wiggle room.

"Oh yes," Cupid said, finally sobering a bit, "and don't forget Father."

"*Fuck me*," replied Pan. Of course Ares wouldn't miss the chance to escalate a bit of mischief into a full-blown war, especially when his bastard son was the battleground.

Cupid cleared his throat and impersonated Ares's stern, gravelly voice with an accuracy that made Pan's skin prickle. "I told you something like this would happen one day, Aph. You've always been too soft on the boy."

Despite the passage of time and the change of venue, Pan felt as if he and Cupid might have picked up the conversation where they'd left off just yesterday, not two thousand years of yesterdays. "I'm a fairly open-minded guy, and I couldn't imagine Cerberus lusting after me."

Cupid winked. "I could arrange a little tryst for the two of you, if you'd like."

"Not without your golden arrows, you can't, hotshot."

Cupid's cocky grin vanished. Nothing humbled a guy like impotence.

Layla delivered their drinks along with two straws plucked from her apron pocket. Cupid rattled off a thank you, sending Layla away in a full-on swoon.

"You're getting that waitress all worked up."

"Am I not supposed to use manners?"

Pan tore the wrapper off his straw, rolled it into a tight ball, and popped it onto his tongue. Cupid watched in disbelief as Pan stuffed the wad into the tip of his straw, raised the shooter to his lips, and blew. Cupid's hand flew up and deflected the spitball sailing toward his nose.

"I see you're still ten."

Shrugging off the insult, Pan plucked a green tomato from the bowl. "You need to try one of these." He sank his teeth through the thick skin and slurped at the seeds. Cupid watched until curiosity or hunger got the better of him, then reached for a tomato of his own, took one bite, and promptly spat the whole thing into his hand.

"This is horrid." Cupid scowled and sucked down half his soda. An entertaining fit of coughs and burps ensued. "Are you trying to burn my innards with rotten fruit and painful drink?"

"I like this stuff."

"Of course you do," Cupid said, crossing his arms. "You're a goat."

"Not anymore," Pan replied swiftly. "And you should probably be nice to me. I'm your only friend down here, maybe your only friend in the cosmos right now."

Cupid picked up the spitball sitting on his placemat, the

edges of his mouth forming a rare frown as he rolled the wad between his fingers. *Crap.* Newly fallens were always vulnerable to culture shock, anguish, and despair. Given Cupid's unhealthy bond with his mother, he'd require an especially close watch.

"Talk to me, Q."

"Mother didn't even try to stop them from throwing me off Mount O."

"Ouch."

"Right." Cupid let out a shaky sigh. "And she said I couldn't come home until I'd made things right with love."

"Oh, is that all?" Pan huffed, a knot tightening in his belly. "And did she happen to mention how you are supposed to do that?"

"Not a clue," Cupid said with a shrug of his shoulders. Then, reminded they weren't carrying the weight of his wings, he rolled them again.

Layla swished to the table and set Cupid's plate down in front of him.

"Uh, miss?" Pan waved his hand back and forth under her nose.

She plunked down Pan's plate and returned her adoring gaze to Cupid just in time to watch his tongue wrangle a loose flap of pastrami hanging over the side of his sandwich.

"Mmm. Now, *this* is gooood," Cupid gushed.

"So glad you like it," Layla gushed back, as if she'd cured the meat herself.

"Hallelujah," said Pan, when the waitress finally left Cupid's side. "She was one second away from climbing into your lap and feeding you by hand."

"Do you think she would?" Cupid's smirk forced a blob of pink dressing to the corner of his mouth.

"See? This is why people don't like you."

"Oh yeah? I think I just made a new friend," Cupid said, jerking his chin toward the kitchen.

"Fine. Go see if your new friend wants to help you earn your wings back."

Cupid paused mid-chew, and Pan could see the gears clicking into place as Cupid seemed to grasp that Pan was his only way home. "How did you find me anyway?"

Pan tensed. "How do you *think*?"

Cupid put on his thinking face and pondered Pan's question, which was only his own question turned back on itself. He dragged two fries through a coleslaw river before delivering them to his mouth.

"You're doing that wrong." Pan reached across Cupid's plate and snatched one of his fries.

"Doing what? Hey!"

"I'm sorry, but I cannot sit idly by and watch while you drown another french fry." Relieved he had diverted Cupid's attention, Pan swirled the french fry around the little white cup of ketchup on the side of Cupid's plate. "*Ketchup*"—he paused to bite off the doused end and savor the taste on his tongue—"is the perfect combination of sweet and tart to complement the salty taste of the fry without turning it into a handful of mashed potatoes. Shall I demonstrate again?" Pan reached for another fry, and Cupid batted his hand away.

"Maybe I *like* mashed potatoes." Cupid deliberately pressed one of his fries like a sponge into the milky puddle on his plate, then ate it with a theatrical moan to prove his point.

"That is truly disgusting."

Cupid shot him a defiant smile.

Layla appeared just then to see if they were "still enjoying everything." When Pan asked for the check, she replied, "Sure thing," sweet as honey, and slid the handwritten slip to the middle of the table with her bright red fingernail before retreating again. Pan pulled out his wallet and tossed two twenties onto the table.

"That's the currency here?"

"Yes. Much easier to carry than a sack of coins." Pan gave him the dime tour of his plastic: debit, credit, driver's license, memberships. "If you're eating in a restaurant, add twenty percent for a tip. Remember your percentages?"

"Yes. We passed that class."

"Barely," Pan replied with a snort. "That reminds me"—Pan pulled out his phone and aimed the camera at Cupid—"say cheese."

"Why?"

Pan rolled his eyes and showed Cupid the photo he'd just snapped. "You look like you're about to hit the high note at a karaoke bar. Just smile, will ya?"

Still bewildered, Cupid flashed a smile long enough for Pan to capture it. In a few seconds, the photo was on its way to Pan's local documents specialist.

Layla stopped by to scoop up the check. "I'll be on break. *Out back*," she added for Cupid's benefit. With a big, goofy smile plastered across his cheeks, Cupid watched Layla's backside disappear behind the swinging kitchen doors.

"I'm not sure if you realize what's going on here, Q, but if you're game for turning in your v-card, you seem to have an eager partner."

"Of course I'm game." Cupid bounced off the banquette and would have bolted for the door had Pan not grabbed his arm.

"Whoa there, loverboy," Pan said with a chuckle. "Not so fast."

"Fast? My whole life, I've watched from the sidelines while everyone around me fornicated with anything that moved—and plenty that didn't."

"Easy, dude. I'm not gonna cockblock you." Pan poked into his wallet again, pulled out a condom, and slid it over to Cupid, using Layla's one-finger method. "Allow me to introduce you to the condom."

"What's that?"

"Think of this as a petasos for your pecker."

Cupid glowered at the package. "You want me to hood my phallus *now*?"

"Do you want to sit here arguing with me or go see what Layla has for you *out back*?"

Pocketing the condom, Cupid scooted out of the booth. "*Yasou!*"

"Meet me at the truck when you're finished, and don't tell her it's your first time."

6

EARTH GIRL

Cupid had no trouble locating Layla in the back alley; her scent called to him like a musk deer attracting its mate. It also didn't hurt that she was standing right in front of the fire door when he bolted through it.

Her eyes widened as she took in his full height. "Wow, you're even better standing up." She shook her head as if flummoxed by the words leaving her own mouth.

"You're very sweet . . . and very pretty." And he was so very eager.

A powerful pregame thrum coursed through his new human body. Cupid had no interest in prolonging the chase. Part of him still expected to wake from this dream to find himself back in his safe, boring, old bed, imprisoned in his useless body.

Layla's gaze drifted downward and settled between his legs. Cupid felt an intoxicating jolt: *want*. His concentration faltered as he paused to curse Pan and the tight fabric restricting his inflamed desire, but if all went according to plan, he would be free soon enough. Though his body was uninitiated, erotic love was Cupid's realm. Natural instinct, countless years of observation, and—*what was it Pan had called it?*—his "divine charisma" all kicked in. He was as ready as any being who'd ever lived.

He stepped in closer, his toes nearly touching her shoes, and released the clip at the top of Layla's head. The tight knot of hair unfurled and tumbled over her shoulders. "So soft," he whispered, hypnotizing both of them as his fingers gently swept through her hair.

The pencil fell away and clattered to the pavement, shaking Layla out of her stupor. "I'm not sure what's come over me. I've never done anything like this before."

"Neither have I." He smiled at her; she nodded back.

Cupid's fingertips brushed the delicate skin behind her ear. Layla shuddered and sighed as her eyelids fluttered closed.

Touch; response. How very gratifying.

Dipping his face to the hollow of her neck, Cupid left a first, gentle kiss. Her supple skin trapped his voice, turning it into a soft murmur. "*Mmm, so warm.*"

She sucked in a quick breath; so did he.

The back alley reeked of garbage from the nearby waste bin, but Layla smelled of jasmine and heavily applied creams and powders. Cupid wanted to sample her mouth—hard, sloppy kisses had always seemed so exciting—but he couldn't bear the thought of tasting the thick paste on her lips and instead skated his kisses downward. *Wise choice,* he concluded as his mouth met the plump pillows of her cleavage, a location that lived up to a long lifetime of unfulfilled dreams. The flesh tasted all the sweeter for having been off limits until just now.

With sudden urgency, Layla gripped Cupid's head, grasping handfuls of wavy hair and clutching his face to her chest. He reached around her back and tugged her forward, grunting when their hips collided. Impatient for more, he explored the enticing curve of her bottom and slipped his hands under the hem of her uniform.

Cupid's head snapped up as his palms met bare flesh. "You're not wearing underwear." Oh, was Pan going to get a piece of his mind.

Layla's cheeks brightened. "I *was* while I was working. I swear."

Realizing his mistake, Cupid gave her fleshy bottom a squeeze. "No, I like it."

Cupid guided her backward into the brick wall and wedged his knee between her thighs. She opened for him like the palace gates. His fingers penetrated her entrance with delicate caresses. Layla let out a surprised squeak, which melted into a low, needy moan.

"Holy hell, what are you doing to me?" Swooning off-balance, she locked her arms around Cupid's neck and tucked her face just above his collar. "Don't stop."

"Gods, you are dripping with desire," said Cupid. Her answering whimper thrilled him.

Cupid wanted more than his fingers inside her though. This new manhood of his demanded its turn. He fumbled at his exasperating buttons, but one hand was not enough to manage the job.

Layla was quick to help, and he happily relocated his hand to a more satisfying location—inside the top of Layla's dress—while she worked open his pants and tugged them over his hips. "Did you bring protection?" she whispered in a heated frenzy.

Just before his pants cleared his knees, Cupid retrieved the condom Pan had forced on him. Layla tore open the packet while Cupid took a half step back to push down his undershorts. Uncaged at last, his heavy erection sprang from the elastic and slapped impressively against the bottom of his T-shirt.

"Wow!" Cupid exclaimed, gripping himself with a tight fist. He'd doubled in length and girth since before meeting Layla.

Layla licked her lips. "Are you planning to share that, or would you two prefer to be alone?"

Being alone happened to be one thing the God of Erotic Love definitely did not need more of. "No, thank you."

Layla's eyes opened wide as she reached for him. With one final tug, Cupid surrendered his shiny new toy. His reward was immediate—the snug embrace of Layla's palm, radiating ripples of pleasure outward from the bullseye of his groin. A hiss escaped him as he rocked back onto his heels. Before this moment, Cupid might have fooled himself into believing another's hand was no different than his own—but never again.

"Shame to cover this up," Layla said as she rolled a cool, slippery sheath down the length of his erection with a fluid flick of her wrist. Though he bristled at first, Cupid set aside his objections when Layla clenched his torso within her powerful thighs, clambered onto his hips, and pulled him inside her, centimeter by blessed centimeter.

Her ankles locked behind his back, drawing him deeper. Her walls gripped him everywhere at once. Consumed with the novelty, the friction, and, admittedly, the pride afforded by his Earthly member, his head swirled with pleasure. Cupid dropped his forehead to her chest while they thrust together vigorously into nearly synchronized, mutual oblivion.

It all made sense now: the treacherous, all-consuming pursuit of this exhilarating release, the Bacchanalia, the chasing of nymphs through wooded forests, marriage and extramarital affairs. As Cupid caught his breath, he lamented all his wasted, sexless days.

Layla released a contented sigh, scratching her long fingernails along his scalp. He lifted his face from her cleavage and returned her dreamy smile. He didn't need to ask if she'd enjoyed herself, and that made his happiness complete.

"My break's over," she said with a wistful lilt. "Back to reality."

He took the hint and gingerly lifted her out of his lap and returned her feet to the ground. While Layla straightened her uniform, Cupid shoved the condom toward the end of his spent, yet still impressive penis. A pocket of sticky fluid spilled onto his fingertips. Cupid thrust the messy sock into the nearby dumpster with a muffled curse, pulled up the dreaded underwear, and refastened his pants.

"Here." Layla pulled a small scrap of paper from her apron and slipped it into Cupid's front pocket.

"What's that?" he asked.

"Whatever spell you just cast over me, I wouldn't mind falling under it—and you—again sometime. Call me. *Anytime*."

Cupid knew enough to pretend he understood. He smiled and nodded. "Thank you."

Layla drank in every detail of Cupid's body with one last, long ogle that made him glow with self-satisfaction. She shook her head and chuckled softly as if accepting she could not solve this puzzle, then started toward the door.

When her hand met the latch, Layla halted and craned her neck around. "What's your name anyway?"

Well, this was a first. Where he came from, everyone knew everyone.

"Cupid."

Layla grinned broadly, and he heard her giggle as she stepped inside. "Yeah, right. And I'm Cleopatra."

7

DEBRIEF

A freshly fucked Cupid climbed into the passenger seat, wearing the biggest, dumbest grin Pan had ever seen. Chuckling, Pan rolled down the windows lest they both choke on the stench. "Well, well, well. Looks like Layla eased your worried mind."

Cupid side-eyed him. "Huh?"

"It's an Eric Clapton song. You need to catch up on pop culture if you're going to fit in down here."

"Oh. Speaking of *fitting in*, I barely did."

"How nice for the two of you." Pan really didn't need reminding of his friend's endowment after sitting alone in his truck doing little more than picturing Cupid burying his bone in that waitress.

"It was. You know how people say size doesn't matter?"

Pan snorted. "Nobody's ever said that to me, but I get your drift."

Waggling his eyebrows, Cupid leaned in to share his big secret. "They were lying."

"You're an idiot, Q. That stuff's not about you; it's about pleasing the girl."

"Huh." Cupid stared ahead, deep in thought. "Oh. Layla gave me something at the end."

"What, like a kiss?"

"Gods no. I couldn't." Cupid's mouth twisted in disgust. "She was nice and all, but she had so much lip paint . . . I had to keep ducking."

Pan brushed his fingers across his mouth to hide his amusement. "What did she give you?"

Cupid reached into his pocket, pulled out the torn-off piece of a check, and studied the writing on one side. "Some numbers. She said I should call her."

Whatever Layla was, Pan would have bet his last nickel she wasn't Cupid's endgame, which meant that little tryst was nothing but the upward *click-click-click* of the roller coaster. By now, Pan had a pretty solid understanding of what happens to things that go up.

"That girl has no idea who she's dealing with," said Pan.

"But she does. I told her."

Fantastic. That's what he got for letting Cupid get jiggy with the natives before they'd worked out his cover story.

"And what did she say?" asked Pan, forcing his words out in a straight, steady line.

"She joked about being Cleopatra."

Pan released a heavy breath as he turned the key in the ignition. The pickup roared to life. "Fasten your seat belt."

"Yes, Mother." Cupid pulled a face as the buckle clicked in. "Straps and girdles and cocks wearing sleeves . . ." He twisted under his belt to round on Pan. "*Re!* Layla was not wearing underwear."

Pan had to do a double take, but yes, Cupid was definitely glaring at him. "Sorry, why are we unhappy about that?"

"Not that she wasn't. That I *am*."

"You'll get used to it," Pan answered. *Soon enough, buddy, you'll wish your boxers were your biggest problem.*

Easing the truck onto the two-lane highway, Pan kept one eye on Cupid, whose head swiveled from his side window to the windshield and back again as the downtown streets rolled under their wheels. How foreign the trappings of modern America always struck the newly fallen, and no god was more insulated from the realities of life on earth—or anywhere, really—than the untouchable prince of Aphrodite's palace. Cupid could meddle in twice as many lives in a day as his quiver could hold arrows and be welcomed home each night with a clear conscience and his favorite dishes waiting at his place at the table.

Pan's own descent wasn't nearly the shock to his system. Earth life in the year 15 was not so different from life on the Mount. The mortals had yet to solve the myriad challenges of so-called "civilization"—communication, transportation, waste disposal, commerce. Pan had plodded through these "advances" along with his fellow earthlings in painful, slow-moving centuries, in sharp contrast to the recent, warp-speed explosion of technologies both helpful and toxic, with the distinction between the ends of the spectrum growing blurrier by the day.

"Driving looks like fun. Can I try?"

Pan's gaze shifted toward the request, and Cupid sat up taller in his seat, as if being measured for a new suit. "We'll see," Pan answered warily. "These earth roads require more skill than just avoiding the occasional chariot in the sky." He proved his point by signaling a lane change, pulling past three cars, and cutting back into the right lane, making it all look very treacherous.

"This is the United States of America, right?" Cupid asked.

"Yep, the good old American heartland."

"Have you been here the whole time?"

Pan slanted his head at Cupid, but to be fair, it wasn't easy keeping track of the years when your own history never changes. "This wasn't here when I, uh"—*died*—"left, remember? I kicked around the Roman Empire for a few centuries and went from kingdom to kingdom in South Asia after that."

Cupid folded his arms over his chest, intent now on getting answers. "Why didn't I ever see you?"

"There are quite a few people down here, in case you hadn't noticed," Pan said, a nervous laugh escaping him.

"I would have found you in a sea of billions, Pan, and you know it."

Pan let out a heavy sigh. "Hephaestus fixed the gaiascope on your bow to block me from your view."

"Just you?"

"No. I travel among a system of thirty-three divine penal colonies across the globe, and your scope won't find any of them." A stark reminder, not that Pan needed it, of his very own brand of prison.

"Penal colonies?" Cupid blinked hard. Yep, it was starting to sink in now.

"That's right. This one happens to be in the state of Indiana, but I move from one Tarra to another about every ten years." Failing to age made Pan stick out like a giant ginger-bearded sore thumb after a while, which necessitated frequent moves even in the absence of any cosmic disturbances. As a creature of the woods, Pan appreciated the variety—new people, new flora and fauna. It certainly wasn't any attachment to this particular Tarra that had kept him here for the last twelve years, more like inertia.

Cupid's eyes flew open with an emotion approaching the appropriate amount of horror. "*Tarra*? As in, *Tartarus*?"

"Exactly. Earth is a convenient way station between Mount O and Tartarus, a perfect spot for the Divine Council to exert control over their prisoners while keeping a close watch from above."

"Why don't I feel like I'm in prison?" Cupid squinted out the window as if the dungeon of torment and suffering were waiting to reveal itself—and it absolutely would, on the gods' schedule, but not the way Cupid imagined.

Don't get too comfortable, friend. Click-click-click.

"Trust me, pal," Pan said. "You're not here to play Tiddly Winks."

Cupid swallowed hard, his Adam's apple bouncing like a basketball. "What about all these mortals? Are they being punished too?"

"You mean like that poor girl who had to have sex with you?"

"Very funny. She quite enjoyed herself."

Pan guffawed. "I should certainly hope so, *God of Erotic Love.* And no, these are basically random humans just trying to grind out a living and find someone to cuddle when the mood strikes."

Poor sons of bitches caught in the crossfire is what they were. The gods didn't hesitate to use mortals as pawns. Collateral damage was always a concern, but Pan's marching orders rarely placed humans at the top of his priority list.

"What do the mortals know about the gods living among them?"

"Not a thing," replied Pan. "The gods of Olympus have long been forgotten—*if* the mortals ever believed we were anything more than fanciful tales recorded by lost civilizations."

"It's all because of the Romans, inventing new names for all of us and jumbling up our stories and confusing everyone," groused Cupid with a familiar refrain.

Zeus had tried to take back the narrative after the fall of Rome, but by then, it was too late to win back the mortals. His so-called "Great Syncretism," the Greco-Roman mash-up resulting in one unified canon, did score big points with the other gods, though, when He allowed everyone to choose which name to keep. For Pan, the decision was a no-brainer; he was all too happy to expunge Faunus—aka "Phallus"—from the records, and good riddance to that one.

"The Romans didn't help matters," said Pan, fully aware there was more than confusion to blame, "but the days of awe and respect from the mortals are long gone."

"If Zeus wants awe and respect, why not just throw down a bunch of thunderbolts? That always kept the ancients in line."

"Believe me," Pan said, "the Big Guy makes all kinds of messes down here—Poseidon, too. The issue is, most moderns tend to put their faith in people called 'scientists,' who explain things like thunder and tsunamis and rainbows and time, and those explanations don't include us."

Watching Cupid process the information gave Pan the sense of a *Freaky Friday* reboot, where Cupid's childhood brain had migrated, at long last, into his adult body. "Huh," Cupid said. "How do they explain love?"

"Oh, love's still a big, fat mystery," answered Pan with a chuckle. "Thing is, the gods aren't in it for awe and respect anymore. I don't need to tell you it's boring as fuck up there on that little mountain, seeing the same faces day after year after century. Humans, on the other hand, provide an endless, rotating cast of extras for the gods' entertainment. Think about it; the gods can pull whatever strings they want up there, and someone down here gets blamed for it. All the fun and none of the consequences."

"So Zeus doesn't want the mortals to know we're up there?"

"Right, which is why you can't use a name that screams 'God of Love.'" Pan lifted both hands off the wheel to illustrate.

"Then what name will I use?"

"How about 'Q'?" Pan suggested. The simpler the better.

"But that's just a letter."

"If anyone pushes, tell 'em it's short for Quentin. That's a very trendy name right now."

"Quentin. *Quentin*." Cupid practiced rolling the name off his tongue, varying his tone each time until the next question occurred. "Is it really necessary to use a condom?" Of course Cupid would be stuck on his new favorite topic—that bright, shiny toy between his legs. Truth be told, Pan's thoughts hadn't traveled as far as they should have from the very same spot.

"Earthlings carry diseases . . . and babies. Trust me, you don't want either," said Pan. "I'd say the love glove is a small price to pay for that new cock you're so proud of. You don't get to take that with you when you leave, you know."

Cupid's eyes narrowed. "I don't?"

"Nope. Learned that lesson the hard way. Remember the first time I was sent?"

"Of course. You chased down the wrong nymph that day."

"Hey, was it my fault Syrinx wouldn't give me a roll in the moss?" Funny how a visit from home could bring back the sting of rejection as if it were yesterday. Surely, Pan's sexual prowess in the intervening millennia as an earth dweller had more than made up for the centuries of rejection on Olympus.

"You did have a nasty habit of sneaking up on unsuspecting nymphs in the woods."

"Maybe if the guy with the golden arrows had helped a brother out once in a while . . ."

"Have you forgotten how much trouble we got into when you talked me into shooting Pitys for you?" Yes, there was that.

"My *point* is," Pan said, "they gave me this smokin' hot earth-bod when I got tossed off the cloud, and I foolishly assumed my hooves and tail were ancient history. The cruelest punishment of all was ascending to Mount O and becoming half goat again."

"That is rotten," Cupid said, adding, "no offense."

"I could almost bear living as a satyr before I experienced the glory of human legs, but it was a low moment in my existence when I felt that tail hanging from my ass again."

"I see your point."

"So you can understand why I asked for a Permanent Descent." *And away we go.*

Cupid's mouth fell open. "You're allowed to do that?"

"I found a way to make myself useful to the gods, and they arranged a convenient cover story."

"Your death." There was no way not to hear betrayal in Cupid's voice.

The old, familiar guilt reared its ugly head. Pan had never been keen on the hunting accident ruse, but what choice had they given him? "I'm so sorry about all of that, Q. Silence was part of my deal."

"But why?"

Pan had practiced this response all morning, yet the words tasted wooden on his tongue. "You can see where . . . *others* might start breaking the rules to try to earn themselves a one-way ticket to earth, right?"

"I guess so," Cupid began, "but if you're the only god catcher—"

"I prefer 'Concierge to the Divine.'"

"*Concierge,*" Cupid repeated with a thick French accent. "Isn't that one of those proper gentlemen who bring people tea and press their trousers?"

"That would be a *butler.*" Considering Cupid's whole world was about to crash down around him, Pan let the indignity slide. "My job is to smooth the transition of fallens from Mount O to earth."

"And how many divines have fallen while you've been down here *concierging?*"

"I stopped counting when I hit triple digits." Over time, as the early Olympians diluted the gene pool by mating with anyone they pleased, each new generation seemed more inclined to test the authority of the Divine Council, hence more fallens for Pan to acclimate.

"Triple digits," Cupid repeated, muttering to himself as he shook his head. "Hundreds of fallen divines and part-divines have kept your secret all this time?"

"Pretty much," answered Pan, bracing for impact.

"But how is that possible? Nobody can keep a secret from anybody on Mount O."

They'd come too far to walk it back now. "Aphrodite can be most persuasive."

"*Mother* is behind this?" Cupid's shoulders shuddered as if calling on his wings to carry him away, but there was no escaping this terrible truth, not for Cupid and not for Pan. "But why would she want to keep me from knowing you were alive and well?"

"I believe she was afraid of losing you."

Cupid slumped against his seat in disbelief, aiming his comments toward the floor. "I mourned my best friend every day for two thousand years while my own mother stood by and watched." His voice, broken and rough, sent a shiver down Pan's spine.

"I'm so sorry, Q. You know I would have told you if I could have." Of all the shitty things Aphrodite had done to Pan, this was the most despicable, dealing the permanent blow to the friendship she'd always scorned.

Cupid's head snapped up, his moist eyes meeting Pan's. "Of course I know that." Maybe Mercury was right; they'd get through this. "But you did choose this life over me." *And there it was*, Cupid's innocence taken for real this time—and not in a good way—by his own mother and his best friend.

The air inside the truck closed in around Pan, hot and thick, choking the breath from his lungs. Sweat rolled out of Pan's pores like earthworms tunneling to the surface after a hard rain. He took the coward's way out, fixing his gaze dead ahead through the windshield while Cupid's eyes lasered two holes into Pan's right cheek. With great effort, Pan forced out the words he'd rehearsed for the last 2,005 years, hoping he'd never have to say them but also fervently hoping he might.

"I want you to know, I never planned any of this. I'd been kicked off the cloud for the third time, and I wasn't any too eager to go home and start the cycle all over again. Let's face it, I wasn't winning any popularity contests up there." Pan chanced a look at Cupid, whose tightly clenched jaw offered no reassurance. "So, while I was down here serving my sentence, I came up with a win-win-win scenario: the gods have their dependable servant on earth, the nymphs can roam freely on Mount O, and I get all the action I can handle down here."

"It wasn't a win for me," Cupid said flatly, chaining Pan forever inside his hideous betrayal with the *blink, blink, blink* of those trusting blue eyes.

"I know, man. You're right. And this is the lamest apology ever, two thousand years too late, and I wouldn't blame you if you hated me for the rest of my stupid, eternal life . . . but I really hope you won't. I'm being one hundred percent honest when I tell you, you're the only reason I almost didn't do it. I've missed you, Q. So fucking much." If not for the driving, Pan would have dropped to his knees and kept right on begging.

"I could never hate you, Pan. You're my best friend. That hasn't changed since we were seven years old, and it never will." Pan's heart rejoiced, even if he couldn't quite reconcile their childhood oath with Cupid 2.0's deep, sexy voice.

"I know I'm a selfish motherfucker to even think of asking, but do you think you could ever forgive me?"

"Hmm, that depends. Will you take me to meet more earth girls?"

Pan's booming laughter bounced off the truck's interior. "Hell yeah, I will."

They really needed to hug this out, but Pan settled for reaching over and squeezing Cupid's shoulder. Cupid grinned his beautiful, uncomplicated grin, and all was right in the cosmos—not counting whatever the gods had in store for Cupid.

8

HOME

"Home, sweet home."

The truck slowed to a roll up the driveway, and Cupid glimpsed Pan's home for the first time. A symmetrical pair of windows on either side of the front door interrupted the otherwise unbroken stone facade of the one-story building. Not exactly the home Cupid would have imagined for the god of the hunt, but then, what indoor dwelling would have been?

Pan touched a button over his head, and a door squawked and rattled its way to the top of a set of tracks, revealing neat rows of garden tools and bicycles lining the walls. Cupid surveyed the space with awe as Pan pulled the truck inside.

"All this is yours?"

Pan's laughter cheered Cupid. "If you're this worked up about the garage, wait till you see inside."

Cupid slipped his fingers behind the latch, pushed open his door, and lunged. A sharp pinch at his shoulder snapped Cupid back against the seat. "Go to the crows! Wretched human restraints."

"Your curses don't translate well," chuckled Pan. "We're gonna have to work on that."

The clip-clop of Pan's sandals led Cupid through the doorway and into a large open space capped off by a flat, white ceiling that blocked out the sky.

"These humans do love their walls, don't they?"

"We live a very interior life down here," said Pan, "especially when the weather is uncooperative."

"That must've been quite the adjustment for you."

"I am outside every chance I get, but it's not the same."

"Do you ever miss your life as a satyr?"

Pan answered swiftly. "No." Neither would Cupid miss all the palace rules or judgy eyes. "Well, *mostly* no," Pan added. "I do miss a spirited mountain climb, but these human legs can give me a decent enough run in the woods. I'll take the trade-off any day. Ready for your tour?"

"Sure." Artificially lighted hallways led to two smaller rooms designed for sleeping, each with its own accommodations for bathing. Cupid was relieved when they found their way back to the airy main room again. "This is where you bring all the fallens?"

"No. I keep a couple apartments on the south side of town."

Cupid's heart sank. "Oh. Is that where you're going to leave me?"

Pan hooked his elbow around Cupid's neck. "Not a chance, Q. You're staying here with me."

"Really?" Were the two old friends finally going to have the sleepover Aphrodite would never condone? *Oh, my darling son, the goat is your outdoor friend.*

"'Course. Make yourself at home."

"In that case . . ." Cupid took off at a dead run and leapt onto the inviting couch, the deep cushions swallowing him.

Pan shook his head, chuckling. "I've been invaded by an

English Mastiff. How about a beer?" He disappeared into the kitchen, returned with two bottles, and twisted off both caps at once.

Cupid peered suspiciously into the depths of the amber opening. "Why's it so dark?"

"It's ale. Try it." Pan clinked Cupid's bottle—"*Yamas!*"—then sucked down half the bottle in one go and sank to the couch with a loud sigh.

An experimental sip coated Cupid's tongue with bitter-tasting foam. "Ugh," he cried, swiping the back of his hand across his mouth. "Dionysus would have your balls for serving this swill. I wouldn't feed this to our sheep."

"As if anyone would trust you to care for the livestock."

"Truly, Pan, how can you drink this donkey piss?"

"Eh, you do what you gotta do to blend in."

"I don't know if I can manage the food and drink, but at least I *look* like I blend in."

"Sure," Pan answered, his beard following his smile up the sides of his cheeks. "You look like every other guy who's a walking orgasm, dipped in a vat of chocolate, drizzled in warm honey, and rolled in sugar." A dense bouquet of lust barreled straight up Cupid's nose.

Cupid's cheeks flared with heat. He'd never thought of his friend that way before, but now that the idea had thrust itself upon him, *why not?* Cupid took a good, hard look at Pan, the man. The solid upper torso was pleasingly familiar: broad, thick shoulders, an abdomen rippled with hard ridges and valleys, and the same trim waist Cupid had always envied. His gaze traveled lower, to the swells of Pan's muscular thighs, straining against his pants. He imagined Pan's Earth body filling out the soft folds of a chiton—even better, running free in his natural wooded surroundings, wearing nothing at all. How exciting a romp with the god of the wild would be. Hard angles colliding, like meeting like, forged iron yielding to pleasures of the flesh.

As if sharing Cupid's fantasy, Pan pumped out a fresh wave of arousal. Cupid's groin obliged with an intrigued twitch that quickly readied for action. Never mind that he was still sticky from his encounter with Layla.

"Dammit, Q. Cut that out."

Cupid didn't need to ask what Pan meant, and they both knew it. "Why?"

"Fuck," Pan said with a frustrated groan. "Because *that* is not happening."

Rejection already, a first for Earth-Cupid. "I thought you wanted me too."

Pan's feral gaze snapped to Cupid's. "Oh, I want you."

"Then what's the problem?"

"The problem . . ." Pan chuckled darkly. "The problem is you're in big trouble, and it's my job to help you out of it. A joyride on your old bestie ain't part of the deal."

The more Pan slipped out of Cupid's grasp, the harder Cupid reasoned. "But I just . . . joy rode with Layla, and no harm has come of it."

"Oh, my innocent friend, while I'd love nothing—and I do mean *nothing*—more than to"—Pan shot him a glance riddled with such longing, Cupid swelled to the point of discomfort—"ride you, I know better than to engage in such reckless activity with one of my charges."

Cupid sensed Pan knew what he was talking about, but the conclusion didn't ease his disappointment, and it certainly didn't take the edge off his hunger. The two men forced their eyes away from each other's until the thick suggestion of sex dissipated from the air, and pulses returned to normal.

"You need to chill." Pan pointed a wand toward a big screen hanging on the wall, and a basketball contest roared to life.

"Wow. It feels like they're playing right there on your wall."

"Yep, and here's the remote. If you don't feel like watching basketball, just keep pressing the up arrow until you find something you like."

The image changed with each tap of Cupid's finger: sports, talking, cooking, music, movies . . . a fascinating, endless array of choices. He'd worked his way through hundreds of channels when he caught a snippet of someone calling out Aphrodite's name.

"Look what they've done to Mother!" Cupid could hardly bear to look at the scantily clad, buxom Aphrodite stretched across the laps of three boys—also barely dressed—who could not have been any older than Cupid's Earth age.

"Ah, *Xena*," Pan said with a smirk. "Always entertaining."

"Those boys are rubbing her feet and . . . and touching her . . . *everywhere*." Cupid wailed. "And she *likes* it."

"Q—"

"My mother is smart," Cupid said through tightly clenched teeth, "and she doesn't dress like a harlot."

"Like I said, the mortals don't really know what to make of us." Pan hopped up and clicked off the TV. "Why don't you take a nice, hot shower and put on some fresh clothes, and we'll go out and meet some more Earth girls, hmm?"

Slightly conflicted about abandoning his mother's honor, Cupid gave him a reluctant nod. The shower was unexpectedly pleasant, considering it was indoors, and Cupid emerged feeling both renewed and relaxed.

Adapting as best as he could to the customs of his new world, Cupid fastened the shirt buttons up to his neck and painstakingly smoothed the long tails inside the snugger, darker jeans Pan had left on his bed. Threading the dreaded belt through the appropriate loops, Cupid buckled himself in tight, though that seemed counter to the purpose of their outing. The shoes waiting for him by the bedroom door were already laced; all Cupid had to do was wriggle his feet inside them. It was odd to look down and find his feet swallowed up to his ankles, but the shoes made walking far easier than the flip-flops.

Pan was leaned against the kitchen counter waiting for him, amusement curling his lips as he surveyed Cupid's outfit.

"What?"

Pan strode over to him and deftly unfastened the top two buttons of Cupid's shirt. "We need to loosen you up." Before Cupid could lodge a complaint, Pan yanked the shirttails out of his pants.

"*Re!*" Cupid protested, swiping away Pan's hands. "It took me forever to arrange that."

"Nobody tucks. You'll look ancient."

"What's the point of the belt if nobody can see it?"

"It's the style. Stop whining. You look hot."

"Oh." Cupid brushed his hand over the sudden tingling in his scalp. "Thanks?"

"For crying out loud." Pan placed a firm hand on Cupid's chest and pushed him away. "That wasn't a proposition."

Cupid shoved his hands in his pockets, and his eyes darted away from Pan, settling on his own shoes for several long seconds.

"Look, Q, this . . . thing between us is not your fault, not mine, and definitely not something we need to dwell on. We'll both find someone else to tickle our fancies tonight, okay?"

"Okay."

"Great. Here's your wallet. Everything you need is inside. Tuck it in your back pocket until you decide to hit the dance floor, then move it to the front. Got it?"

"Sure."

"Super. Next . . . your phone."

Cupid opened his hands in time to catch the thin device flying at his belly. "What do I do with this?"

"Same deal. Keep it close; guard it even more carefully. Go ahead and type in your password, 2222."

Cupid obediently tapped in the numbers. The screen came to life in his hands, small colorful tiles jumping into the black space. "Oh. A game!"

Pan swiped the toy from Cupid's grasp.

"*Kopsto!*" shouted Cupid.

"*You* cut it out," Pan replied. "I need you to pay attention. Your fate might depend on it."

Duly chastised, Cupid mumbled, "Fine."

They spent the next ten minutes at the kitchen counter, Pan teaching Cupid how to answer the phone, place a call, and send a text message to the only programmed number—Pan's.

"All right. Now that you've got the basics down, I have a little treat for you." Pan tapped the screen a couple of times, and a racetrack appeared. "You said you wanted to learn how to drive."

Six sleek cars rumbled and hopped to life at the starting line. It took Cupid mere seconds to master the necessary finger motions.

"C'mon, you can practice in the truck."

Without taking his eyes from the screen, Cupid rose and followed Pan's voice. Only Cupid's godly reflexes saved him from tripping down the step between the house and garage while navigating the on-screen Lotus through its first hairpin turn. Cupid vaguely heard Pan remind him about his seat belt, sigh loudly as he shut Cupid's door, and mutter something about "kids today."

The backward motion of Pan's truck disoriented Cupid, and his Lotus went careening off the next cliff in a spectacular display of flames. "*Noooo!*"

"Fender bender?" Pan teased.

"I made it to checkpoint two," Cupid said with great pride.

"When you make it around the course six times without killing anyone, we'll talk."

Time passed unnoticed as Cupid's race car climbed the winding cliff roads of Monte Carlo. As he managed a sharp curve near the peak, the phone hummed and vibrated in his hands. Cupid made the split-second decision to answer the call. He pressed the flashing button on the screen, then being caught off guard over what might be the appropriate greeting, he stumbled.

"Present," he said timidly, startled when his voice reverberated around the interior of the truck.

Pan's loud snort boomed immediately after. "You're supposed to say hello."

Cupid jerked the phone away from his ear, ended the call, and scowled at Pan. "I was just about to clear level four."

"Way more importantly, you passed your first test. I need to know I can trust you in an emergency."

Irritation quickly turned to dread. "Do you think something terrible is going to happen to me?" Pan paused long enough to confirm Cupid's fears. "*Pan?*"

"Look, at some point, you're gonna get whatever's coming to you. Frankly, when that time comes, the whole Trojan Army won't be able to save you. Until then, this phone will help me keep you out of any trouble you might kick up with the humans."

Hearing his fate delivered with such certainty left Cupid feeling like he'd driven the Lotus off the cliff and into the craggy valley below.

"We're here."

Cupid hadn't realized the truck had stopped, had no idea, in fact, how long he'd been sitting in stunned silence.

"They've got a great steak here," Pan said, reaching over and pushing the bright orange button releasing Cupid's seat belt.

"Mutton?" His spirits lifted slightly.

Pan chuckled and gave his friend a light pat on the cheek. "Come on. Let's go inside and have some fun."

Cupid heard the unspoken "while we can," but the promise of female companionship lured him out of the car. He pushed his phone into his back pocket and followed Pan inside.

9

GOGGLERS

The silky techno beat wrapped its tentacles around the two men, drawing them smoothly across the crowded room and straight into the heart of the buzz. Pan strode in rhythm to the pounding bass as he led Cupid to the thick slab of dark mahogany forming a U-shaped bar.

Pan allowed himself to enjoy the pleasant thrum of anticipation snaking through his system. Whether the pendulum between Pan's legs had swung back to boys in general or just for his impossibly hot friend with his singular charms, Pan couldn't be sure. *I am an evolved being*, Pan reminded himself. He would deal with these new stirrings—somehow. If he couldn't have Cupid for himself, he'd take the next best thing: riding shotgun with his best friend in the driver's seat. Heads were turning, and Pan didn't blame them.

He recognized the well-endowed but otherwise petite, brown-haired bartender from his many trips to The Stagecoach, and on a normal night, Cheri might've recognized Pan too, but by the time she got around to noticing Pan, she was already good and dazzled.

"What can I get you boys tonight?" she asked, dropping two cocktail napkins onto the bar.

"Not beer," Cupid answered, punctuating his statement with a crinkled nose and a finger pointed at Pan.

"Well, that narrows it down a little," Cheri replied with a smile.

"What would you recommend?" Cupid asked her. Pan doubted whether Cupid even had a clue how his eyelids closed halfway, giving off that "come hither" look, or how his voice took on a rough, husky quality around a pretty girl. Cheri was a goner.

"That depends. You got ID, honey?" Cheri may have been spellbound, but she needed her job.

"Yes," Pan answered before Cupid had a chance to cock his head and ask for a definition.

Knocking knees with Cupid under the bar, Pan snagged his wallet and thumbed out his ID onto the bar in front of them, and Cupid followed suit.

Cheri shot Pan a suspicious look before picking up Cupid's ID. "Quentin Arrows?" she read, then lifted her eyes from the picture to Cupid and back again.

"Yes," Cupid replied with a solemn nod.

Pan had to admit, he was pretty darn impressed with Cupid's smoothness—no widened eyes, no lip biting, no nervous twitching. But then, his new name wasn't exactly a lie. Pan tuned out whatever followed Cheri's, "Are you in the mood for something sweet?" and spun on his stool to survey the scene.

Cupid's entrance had clearly been noticed. The ranks were closing in gradually but surely: girls angling their bodies so they could be first in Cupid's field of vision if he happened to glance their way, maraschino cherries tugged seductively from stems, straws teased by tongues that would rather have been wrapped around something else—something of Cupid's. Some of the men subtly rocked their shoulders, sipping at bottles, sizing up the newcomer. Pan huffed, idly calculating which of Cupid's left-overs he might score for himself.

"And for you, Panthino?"

Cupid thumped him on the knee. "Yes, Pan*thino*, what are you drinking? More donkey piss?" Cupid offered an apologetic palm to Cheri. "No offense. I don't like beer."

"None taken. I wouldn't drink the stuff if you sat on my lap, pinned my hands down, and poured it down my throat. Oh dear, did I say that out loud?"

Cupid's brow jumped right up to his hairline as he barked out a happy chuckle. "Except for the force-feeding, that sounds interesting."

She giggled and pivoted back to Pan. "Hon, you better give me your drink order before I get myself into serious trouble here."

"Too late," both men answered in unison, causing the three of them to break up again. "I'll take a Heineken and a couple of dinner menus while you're at it, please."

"Be right back, guys."

"So, what drink did you and Cheri decide on?" Pan asked Cupid.

"A yelling orgasm or something."

"Nice."

Cupid settled into a rhythmic sway equal to the insidious bass, his head bobbing like the hula girl that lived on Pan's dashboard during the sixties. "Is this more of that Clapton person?"

"Nope, this is pure sex music. Feel that throbbing beat?"

"Is sex all you ever think about, Pan?"

"Look who's talking. What are *you* thinking about, the *Iliad*?"

Cupid's eyes twinkled despite the diffuse lighting. "I was thinking about Cheri's breasts, to be honest."

"You're such a dick."

"Goat."

"Here we are . . . a Screaming Orgasm for the dick, a Heineken for the goat, and a pair of menus. I'll be back in a few to take your orders." Cheri gave both men a smirk before skittering away.

"Shoot, do you think she heard what I said about her breasts?" Cupid asked, lowering his voice this time.

"Probably, but she didn't seem offended."

"Oh, look. They have french fries."

Pan chuckled at his friend. "Don't you want to try something new?"

Cupid held up his drink and said, "I'm about to have a screaming orgasm. Doesn't that count?"

"It sure does in my book," said a female voice behind them.

Cupid whipped around as one of the goggling ladies boldly insinuated her hand onto Cupid's arm and worked it up to his shoulder.

"You've really never had one before?" she asked, adding extra breath on the "had." The girl had just assaulted Cupid with 150-proof alcohol directly into his divine olfactory system, but he didn't even flinch. Her friends tittered over her audacity, egging her on so they could enjoy the vicarious glow of Cupid's sexy gaze.

Cupid soaked up the attention like a thirsty sponge, answering with the greatest of ease. "Not in a glass with ice."

A ripple of exaggerated laughter rang out, and more fingers chanced the trail up Cupid's blue and white pinstripes. Pan was tortured by a vision of the women hoisting Cupid onto their shoulders and carting him away like a rock star riding a mosh pit.

Cheri returned to the spectacle, took stock of the unwelcome competition, and captured Cupid's attention with a slightly desperate, "Know what you want, hon?"

"Yes, I'll have the cowboy steak and french fries."

"How'd you like that cooked?"

"Medium rare." Pan answered for him while Cupid directed his attention to the girls tussling over who would treat him to his next orgasm.

Pan used his one-on-one time with Cheri industriously, capitalizing on his opportunity to cash in on the residual sexual energy Cupid had churned up. Pan poured on the charm, reorganizing the probabilities for Cheri until she'd calculated that the certainty of Pan ranked higher than the increasingly unlikely possibility of Cupid.

She straightened the menus with a tap on the bar, gave Pan a meaningful tip of her chin, and winked. "I'll put that right in for you."

And I'll happily do the same for you later, he beamed back with unspoken ardor.

Goggler Two crowded in too close to Cupid's face. "You must be new around here."

"Mmhmm," he hummed back.

"Do you have a name?"

"I have a letter," he answered. "Q."

"'Q' as in 'quadriceps'?" asked the one behind him, laying her hand on Cupid's knee and sliding it north.

Pan had reached his limit. Grabbing his beer, he tapped Cupid's arm with the bottle and leaned in close. "I'm going to take a leak. Don't do anyone I wouldn't do."

Leaving his friend among the growing sea of admirers, Pan moseyed to the bathroom, took a leisurely piss, and paused to check himself in the mirror on the way out. Cupid had a point; Pan was no slouch, himself—not that anything could ever happen between the two of them. Pan shook off the buzzkill and yanked open the bathroom door.

Tossing his head back to finish off his beer, he collided with a pair of tatas belonging to none other than his favorite bartender, who latched onto Pan's wrist to regain her balance. Chivalrously pulling Cheri to safety against his chest, Pan gazed into her startled eyes, down her shirt, and into her eyes again.

"Why, Cheri, are you following me?"

"No! I was taking a quick bathroom br—"

"Easy, doll," Pan said, smiling sweetly to put her at ease. "I was only teasing."

"Oh." Cheri shook off her embarrassment.

Pan curled his fingers around Cheri's waist and brought his lips to her ear. "What time do you *get off* tonight?"

10

HARD TO GET

After the second Orgasm, Pan convinced Cupid to switch to beer, assuring him the taste would be tolerable now and he'd be grateful in the morning. With a pleasantly full belly and a nice buzz from the cocktails, Cupid took his last bite of steak and swiveled around to check out the dance floor. That's when the girl with the flame-colored hair caught his eye.

She was spectacular. *Fluid*—the word lodged in his mind as he watched her move under the lights. With her back to him at first, she had the appearance of a sea nymph, her curly, red-orange hair swishing gently across her bottom, her hips rolling as if performing an underwater ballet. When she raised her crossed wrists over her head, Cupid hopped off his stool and pushed through the crowd, seeing no one but her. He followed her siren song single-mindedly as it called him to the floor, close enough to breathe her in, close enough to touch—but he didn't.

She spun in place, absorbing Cupid's presence behind her with a sexy, unrushed assurance. Her dance was a hand-delivered invitation to feast his eyes, and did he ever. While he was at it, Cupid drew in her intoxicating endorphins, the *swish* of the skirt swirling at her thighs, the sparks popping in the air around her, electrifying every hair on his body.

She roused and fed his appetite at once, tipping her head back, exposing her lovely neck, offering the sexy dip at its base that begged for his tongue—or was it his tongue begging for the dip? Cupid couldn't sort any of it out, especially when her pouty mouth dropped open ever so slightly, a juicy peach he could already taste on his lips. The more he was offered, the greater his hunger.

The blue lights cast a garish glow, but still, he could make out the tiny bronze speckles on her porcelain cheeks and the dazzling aquamarine of her eyes. Mesmerized, Cupid failed to notice he'd started moving along with her. As loose as she was, Cupid was twice as tense—coiled and ready to spring.

A crowd of spectators closed in tight, their collective body heat and desire pulsing through the two dancers at the center. Wordlessly, the girl floated closer and dropped her linked arms over Cupid's head. His fingers itched to touch her, but he couldn't trust himself to stop once he started. He knew enough about the ways of Earthlings to understand intimacy as a private act, not some wild Bacchanalia, but this dance confused him. This *girl* confused him.

She leaned back suddenly, a dead weight around his neck, and he lurched forward to catch her, his pulse pounding in his ears as his fingers met bare skin where her short top left off.

"Whoopsie," she whispered with a cunning grin, her lips so close he could feel her breath on his chin.

His voice came out in a raspy growl. "I need to kiss you."

"Yes," she replied.

Cupid closed the miniscule gap and pressed his mouth over hers. Pleasure buzzed through him. *More.* When the lip-to-lip could no longer satisfy, he found her tongue and kissed her until his knees went weak. She kissed him back with a fervor that surprised him, considering how restrained she'd been until that point.

Cupid crashed against her, and she crashed back. Her thighs pressed against his sides—teasing, rhythmic taps on either side of him. He slid his fingers up her back, needing more skin, more heat, more friction. He strained against his blue jeans.

The music pounded up through the floor, hammered at his feet, and reverberated up his legs. Sex beat, Pan had called it, and now Cupid understood as his hips pulsed against the dancer even though a powerful instinct nagged at him to stop. It didn't help his self-control when she arched her back and offered her ripe, full breasts for the taking.

A firm hand clapped Cupid high on his back. "Come with me," bellowed an urgent voice.

Cupid blinked, startled out of his lusty fog. There stood Pan, and he wasn't messing around.

"Bring your girl."

No conversation was necessary. Cupid took her by the hand and led her from the dance floor. The two of them trailed behind Pan's broad shoulders as he cut a path through the dense crowd and out the door. Outside, the bartender was waiting, and Pan bent to kiss her on the lips. "Sorry about that." From her dazzled response, it appeared all was forgiven.

Flashing a charming smile to both women, Pan said, "Would you ladies excuse us for a moment, please?" before dragging Cupid out of their earshot. "Are you bringing her home?" Pan asked.

"I just met her."

"You two were one hump shy of getting tossed out."

"I don't know what happened. One second, I was on my

stool, and the next . . . I was drawn to her, and I lost control. I don't even know her name."

"She's hot. She's also the only girl in the place not waving her tits in your face."

Cupid's shoulders sagged. "You think she doesn't want me?"

Pan reached his arm around Cupid's shoulders and drew him close. "Oh, she wants you, trust me. She's playing hard to get."

Cupid's forehead crinkled in confusion. "Why would she do that?"

"Because she's smart. Guaranteed she wants you every bit as much as everyone else inside the place, but this one gave you a little space for you to want her back."

"Huh, it worked."

"Usually does. Go close the deal." The two old friends grinned at each other. Pan released Cupid, stalked right over to Cheri, and hoisted her over one shoulder. She answered his deep growl with a cascade of laughter.

Cupid sidled up to his dance partner and buried his hands in his front pockets. "Hello again."

Her sweet, rosy lips lifted into a smile. "Hi." The quiet, restrained voice left Cupid believing she used it only rarely but otherwise let her body do the talking.

Up close, with the benefit of the streetlight and a clearer head, Cupid could discern all the usual signs of attraction: the soft blush on her cheeks, the hesitation to meet his eye, the subtle offering of her open shoulders, the enticing scent of her own natural musk outstripping her hair and body wash. Earth-Cupid's charms hadn't failed him.

"What's your name?" he asked.

"Rory, but you can call me 'Rho.'"

It tickled Cupid that her name was a letter too. "Mine's Q."

Pan spun around quickly, causing Cheri to wobble on his shoulder and flail for something to grab onto. "You two coming or what?"

Rho's cheeks turned a deeper pink, and she wrung her graceful, delicate fingers together in front of her skirt.

Cupid reached over suddenly and took both her hands in his. "Would you?"

Her gaze dropped to Cupid's feet, and she answered with a simple but enthusiastic, "Yes."

As they laced their fingers together and headed to Pan's truck, Cupid marveled at how this intriguing creature next to him, who'd danced and kissed him with such wild abandon, now blushed madly just from holding his hand. He considered her game of pretending not to be interested in him and how it drove him nearly out of his mind with want. Staring out into the black of the night sky with Rho's head on his shoulder, Cupid realized he had an awful lot to learn about the mortal heart—and perhaps even his own.

11

WORKING OUT

"On a strangulation scale from zero to ten, these shorts would be an eleven," said Cupid, peering over his shoulder at his ass in the mirror. "I can't complain about how they look, though."

Pan could have complained plenty about how Cupid's ass looked in those shorts, but focusing on it wouldn't help any. Instead, he reached over and yanked the tags off. Those were keepers.

"Which shirt are you going to wear?"

Cupid carefully considered his choices, finally deciding on the gray *Train Like a Boss* tee, and Pan snapped off that price tag too. "Throw on your sweats and sneakers while I pay."

Pan tossed the plastic bag onto the rear seat where it landed atop the accumulated treasures of the morning—jeans, boots, shirts, and a generous pile of new underwear. Cupid fastened his seat belt without being reminded and set to work on his driving app with impressive dedication. Since Cupid had cleared level six on the way to lunch, Pan had assigned him the racetrack through suburbia. In no time at all, Cupid would be driving himself around. The thought of his imminent independence hung over Pan like a storm cloud, leaving him uncharacteristically melancholy.

Pan enjoyed his job well enough—though the high-risk, high-reward nature of his employment had earned him more than his fair share of agita—but he rarely took his assignments personally. Divines fell; they suffered. They figured it out; they ascended. Pan moved on. With Cupid, everything was different, had been right from the start. If Pan were being honest, he rather enjoyed the responsibility of taking care of Cupid, relished the chance to prove himself worthy of Cupid's faith and easy forgiveness. When the time came to push the bird from his nest, Pan would set aside his own complicated feelings for his best friend and facilitate Cupid's destiny with the utmost gravity and care. No matter that Cupid's "freedom," however the gods defined it, would tear an even bigger hole in Pan's heart.

The Titan pulled neatly between the painted lines of the parking lot in front of the gym. "We have arrived at our destination," Pan announced grandly, pulling Cupid's intense concentration from his game. "You'll need your membership card."

Pan led him through the turnstile and into the locker room. Cupid watched and mimicked Pan's routine, stowing his sweats in a locker, grabbing a towel, taking a pre-workout leak, and following him through the heavy metal door to the weight room.

The sea of heads swiveled to gawp, Pan noticed with great amusement. If Cupid had the inclination and the stamina, he could've easily had his way with every girl in the room and a good portion of the men to boot. The air around them clotted with sexual energy, and Pan resigned himself to another wait in the truck.

"Why is everyone running inside on machines and going nowhere?"

Pan chuckled. "Temperature-controlled environment, pre-dictable routine, cushy running surface, all the comforts of the locker room, and a whole lot of mutual eye-fucking," Pan explained with a waggle of his eyebrows. "It's also easier to get a whole-body workout this way. You go straight from aerobics to free weights, then over to the floor to stretch. Here. Hop on, and I'll show you." Pan slung his towel over the treadmill next to Cupid's and demonstrated how to start the interval workout.

"Can you imagine Hercules on this contraption?" Cupid imitated their muscle-bound friend with a deep voice. "Am I a mouse chasing its supper around in circles?" Cupid broke into giggles, and Pan couldn't help doing the same.

They warmed up with a slow jog. *Damn*, Q was a thing of beauty, running with the grace of a gazelle, long legs kicking out from under those tight shorts, quads popping and rolling. Their belts picked up speed, forcing them into a brisk run. Pan pushed his earbuds into place and shifted his focus to the soccer match on TV.

It wasn't long before he was in the zone, that runner's high buzzing through his system like the good ol' days of romping through the wooded hills of Olympus. Unlike the humans who came to the gym to whip their bodies into shape, Pan's earth-phy-sique did not require sculpting or aerobics. If he ever packed a few extra pounds onto his frame, Pan would revert within a day or two to his "factory settings," whether or not he lifted a finger or his heart rate in the interim. Not surprisingly, there had been stretches during his sojourn on earth where Pan had tested—if not abused—this predictable cycle with jags of overindulgence in food and drink and long absences from productive activity. While his body always bounced back, his state of mind wasn't always as resilient. In the end, Pan worked out for the endor-phin rush, whether that was to be found on the treadmill, under a barbell, or in the arms of one (or more, on a good day) of his fellow gym–goers.

"Pan. Pan! PAN!" The last repetition included the sharp snap of a towel against Pan's arm.

"OW! Fuck!" Pan tugged on the soft wire hanging at his chest and the earbuds popped out. He swung his head to the left. "*What?*"

Pan's annoyance changed to fright as he caught sight of Cupid's pained expression and the hand clutching at his heart. Pan flailed across the handles and smacked the emergency button on Cupid's treadmill but couldn't stop his own before losing his stride.

"Get off!" Pan yelled, thrashing his arms and legs and fighting to right himself while somehow keeping an eye on Cupid. Mercifully, Pan found his balance, slapped the stop button, and rode the slowing belt to the rear of the machine. He hopped off and knelt by Cupid, now lying flat on his back.

"What is it, Q? Are you in pain?"

"It's my heart."

Pan tried to quell his terror, having realized too late he'd simply assumed Cupid's earth-body operated on the same principles as his own. *I will never forgive myself.* He placed a soothing hand on Cupid's shoulder. "I'm going for help. Keep breathing."

Pan started to bolt, but Cupid yanked on his arm so hard the socket clicked. "Ow! Hey!" Pan protested, but the anxiety in Cupid's eyes drew him up short.

"I don't need that kind of help," Cupid forced out through clenched jaws.

"Huh?"

Cupid rubbed harshly at his chest. "Someone just shot me."

"*What?*" Pan, beyond perplexed, spun around to locate the smoking gun he surely would have heard.

Cupid grabbed a fistful of Pan's shirt and tugged him so close, Pan could feel Cupid's words on his nose. "I've been pierced by one of my gold-tipped arrows."

"*Fuck me.*" Pan peered at Cupid's chest for an arrow he knew damn well he wouldn't see. An arrow launched from Cupid's bow on the Mount would become imperceptible the moment it reached the Great Cloud. "Are you sure?"

Cupid stared up at Pan with a pained impatience. "If there's one thing in this cosmos I know, it's the sting of my arrows. There's a distinctive humming noise. The heart vibrates at a high frequency inside the rib cage."

Pan listened as hard as he could. "I don't hear anything."

Cupid rolled his eyes. "And I can't tell a ram from a ewe in a dark forest. Do you really doubt me on this?"

Pan sighed heavily, wanting to believe his friend was not in cardiac arrest, yet his explanation made no sense. "To state the obvious here, I'm looking at the only guy alive who can shoot one of those gold-tipped arrows. So how could you have—?"

Of course. The truth hit Pan so hard, it knocked him onto his ass.

"Q, I need you to think really hard now. Do you remember *anything* else about that scene with your parents yesterday morning?"

Cupid's mouth twisted into a grimace as he forced his mind back to their quarrel. "They argued. Mother cried. Father invoked Oedipus. Mother snapped back that maybe he had his own mommy issues to deal with. Father stormed off."

"And?"

With a shrug, Cupid remembered the rest. "Just before she pushed me over the edge, Mother said, 'Follow your heart, son.'"

Pan's own heart filled with dread. "Motherfucker."

12

THROBBING

If ignorance really could have offered Cupid bliss, he would gladly have run from his fate, but there was something absolutely unignorable about a total assault on a vital organ.

"Would you care to elaborate on that profanity?"

No, Pan's sad green eyes conveyed, *I truly would not.* Pan leaned back onto his palms and sighed heavily. In response to Cupid's furrowed brow, Pan's mouth flattened into a straight line.

Wow. Cupid couldn't remember ever seeing his friend so morose, and they'd been in plenty of tough scrapes together. "By the gods, Pan, you are scaring me."

"Sorry." Pan sprang forward and met Cupid's gaze. "Okay, from what I can understand, it appears your heart's been booby-trapped by none other than the Goddess of Love. Whatever punishment she's got cooked up for you seems to be centered right here." Pan reached forward to tap Cupid's chest. His fingertips recoiled as if they'd touched hot coals. "Shit. Sorry."

"It doesn't hurt on the outside. Just feels like the sons of Uranus are wrestling a herd of wild boars inside my chest."

"Oh, is that all?" Pan attempted a smile, but only one side of his mouth lifted.

"So, this squeezing, pounding, crushing war going on inside my heart is my punishment?"

Pan shrugged. "You know how the gods love their poetic justice, so much the better when delivered with a heavy dose of irony."

"Oh. Ha, ha, ha." Cupid railed on, lifting his eyes toward Olympus. "Inflaming Cupid's heart is ironic. I get it. Are we finished now?"

"How's that working for you?" Pan's calm voice interceded, a gentle but effective bridle to Cupid's runaway jabbering.

"Still throbbing," Cupid said in a defeated whisper.

"Is it very painful?"

Concentrating on his innards, Cupid pinpointed the sensation. "Not exactly. It's more like an agitation, like I need to go *do* something, or maybe *find* someone."

Pan opened his mouth as if to speak and then closed it again. Was Pan really going to start holding back *now*, of all times?

Cupid leveled his friend with a frustrated glare. "*What?*"

"Okay, thinking out loud here. Wouldn't a victim pricked with your gold-tipped arrow fall in love with the first person he sees?" Pan's gaze darted behind, above, all around Cupid—anywhere but meeting his friend's eyes.

For one eternal moment, Cupid studied the man in front of him and allowed for the possibility that Pan might be the object of the invisible arrow. Setting judgment aside, Cupid studied his heart with renewed purpose, stared long and hard into Pan's face, and concluded that the exact same feelings as before were present—deep, abiding friendship and an erotic curiosity they'd mutually agreed to repress.

"It's not you," Cupid said, sensing more than a twinge of

disappointment on Pan's part. Cupid bit back the apology Pan would have been furious to receive.

Pan's cheeks puffed up as a long, heavy breath escaped. "Good. That could've been awkward."

"No kidding. Moving on . . ."

"Right. The good news is your signal appears to be very clear. 'Follow your heart' is not usually a literal command. In your situation, though, it appears your heart was pre-programmed to guide you . . . like a compass, or what moderns would call a GPS."

"What's that?"

As Pan explained satellite signals bouncing from vehicle to sky and back again, Cupid's face twisted with horror. "You're saying I have one of these machines inside me?"

"Not exactly. What I think you have is more of a '*Cardiac Positioning System*'—a CPS, if you will."

"Doesn't seem like I have much of a choice." Cupid pressed his fingertips more forcefully into his chest, offering all the support he could for his besieged organ.

Pan rubbed one hand down his thick beard, and Cupid braced for bad news. "Nope. You gave that up when you shot your last arrow. You're here to learn a lesson, and I'm afraid you're going to feel it right where you live, old buddy." Truth be told, Cupid already suspected as much, but the confirmation of his worst fears didn't stop him from flinching.

"Hey," Pan said, "messing with the gods is risky business, and you went straight to the top. Your little prank pissed off no fewer than six Majors, and let's face it, Ares has been waiting *eons* for an excuse to tan your hide. That said, we both know you hold a special place in Aphrodite's heart. The sooner you accept your punishment and accomplish the mission, the sooner your ache will recede."

Pan's gentle cajoling was reassuring. Cupid wasn't the first god to fall; in fact, almost all had already fallen at some point. Generally speaking, punished deities were returned to Olympus, and life on the Mount went on.

"Okay. Now what?"

"Now, my friend," Pan answered, "we follow that signal."

Drawing and releasing a deep breath, Cupid gave Pan the weary nod he seemed to have been waiting for, and his friend gave him one last encouraging squeeze.

"You're gonna be okay, Q. I've got your back." With that, Pan stood and offered Cupid a hand up.

Cupid moaned softly as his internal engine stirred with new life. Pan stepped aside to let him lead, following protectively at Cupid's elbow, and he couldn't remember ever being more grateful for their friendship. Heads lifted as Cupid passed, but he wasn't interested in pursuing anything but his heart's destination.

The pulsations increased and picked up intensity as the two chased the signal down the long corridor, past spinning cyclists following orders loudly barked over pounding music that reminded Cupid of the sex beat. Cupid mused briefly over the mortals' love for abusive noises, while his own ears were calibrated to the gentle caresses of lutes and harps. Was it his imagination, or did he actually hear the tinkling of harp strings right now? The insistent beating of the rumbling buffalo stampede in his chest gave way to the airy tapping of a swarm of butterflies. Cupid bounced more than walked to the last door on the left, his palm rubbing furious circles over his chest. His head felt light, and a fine sheen of perspiration dampened his forehead.

Cupid thought he might vomit, but he'd never felt a more powerful urge in his life than the one now compelling him to open the door and discover whatever was waiting for him on the other side. He reached for the handle. Pan halted him with a tight grip on Cupid's elbow.

"You sure you're okay?"

"I have no idea, but I have to go in there."

After a vigilant once-over, Pan drew back his hands and gave Cupid a tight nod. "Good luck, man."

13

HOT YOGA

A wall of heat slammed into Pan as Cupid opened the door to the dim studio. Hypnotic music provided a stark contrast to the hard-driving rock beat of the rest of the gym—not that Cupid was anywhere near relaxed. In fact, Pan couldn't remember ever seeing him this keyed up. As Cupid followed the signal like a bloodhound on a fresh trail, Pan could only hope this story would somehow end up more Penelope-and-Odysseus than Orpheus-and-Eurydice.

"Oh my Zeus," Cupid mumbled under his breath, then crossed quickly to the far corner of the room where the instructor crouched in front of the sound system.

Pan berated himself for failing to discuss with Cupid how he might approach the girl, but the time for intervention had passed; there was no stopping the God of Love now. Senses on full alert, Pan followed as closely as possible while attempting to blend his six-and-a-half-foot, red-bearded frame into the white, plaster wall. While not exactly built for stealth, Pan had noticed he'd become somewhat invisible since Cupid's arrival on earth.

He looked on helplessly as Cupid wrung his hands, bounced unproductively on his toes, and tugged his fingers through his hair. Fortunately, the cause of his distress—engrossed in her volume knobs and track selections—was entirely oblivious to the display.

Cupid's impatience finally reached a peak, causing him to blurt out, "You're the one."

Pan angled his face toward the Mount in private exasperation. *Satisfied now?*

The girl glanced up. Her forehead creased with confusion at first, but her expression cycled rapidly to delight. The gods meting out Cupid's punishment had damn good taste in women, at least. Soft, brown hair framed a symmetrical, heart-shaped face that equaled the perfection of her body, which Pan could truly appreciate as she unfolded to her full height.

"I'm the one for what?" she asked, smiling at Cupid as if desperate to know every detail of him, inside and out. And how could Pan feel superior when Cupid had exactly the same effect on him?

"For me."

Oh, to have the confidence of Cupid, Pan mused, though Cupid had simply answered her with complete honesty. She *was* the one for him, even if none of them understood what that meant quite yet.

A mere mortal might've earned a "fuck off" with such a cheesy pickup line, but not Cupid. The girl drank him in, *Train Like a Boss* tee and all. Her nipples pulled into sharp peaks, visible through her sweat-soaked top if one happened to be looking, and Pan sure as shit was. The scent of her arousal twined with Cupid's in the oppressive, humid air and powered up Pan's nostrils like an electric drill.

"You're new here," she said to Cupid.

"Yes. Just arrived yesterday."

The mating dance played out before Pan's eyes, as ancient as the constellations and as fresh as this pair meeting for the very first time. The sole of her bare foot slid up her calf to the edge of her black yoga pants, and her head tipped at a flirty angle. Cupid leaned in closer with every cell in his body. Pan couldn't have said which of the two of them was more lost to desire.

"Ever done hot yoga before?" she asked.

"What?"

Pan laughed out loud and quickly covered his mouth with his hand. He would have wagered his worldly goods that Cupid had absolutely no idea he was standing in a yoga studio with at least a dozen other people who'd filed in for class, let alone that they were all melting like popsicles left out in the sun.

She exaggerated her words, enunciating as if speaking to a foreigner. "Have you EV-er taken any kind of YO-GA class?"

Stupid with awe, Cupid shook his head. He was the love-struck cartoon skunk, heart bursting from his chest on an over-worked spring, eyes popped out and spinning in dizzying circles. All he lacked was the tongue unfurling to the floor. Pan almost felt sorry for the guy, but only *almost* because without a doubt, Cupid would get this girl. It was simply a matter of time—and not very much of it, from the way these two were slobbering over each other.

"I'm Mia," she told him, "and you are . . .?"

"Cup—"

"Q," Pan answered over Cupid's near gaffe, startling them both with his appearance.

"Q?" Mia cast a doubtful glance at Cupid.

Pan babbled on, stalling until Cupid could regain his senses. "Yes, it's short for Quentin. My name's Pan. I've done yoga before, but it's his first time."

"Ah. In that case," Mia said, turning to her eager novice, "I'll need *you* right up front, so I can keep a careful watch. Take off your socks and shoes and grab a mat and a couple of bricks from the closet."

Cupid nodded obediently and floated behind Pan to the closet.

"How's your heart?" Pan asked.

"Lighter than air. Isn't she perfect?" Cupid's longing gaze was locked on Mia as Pan loaded Cupid's arms with supplies.

Pan shook his head and chuckled to himself. "Don't hurt yourself, okay? This stuff's harder than it looks, although I have a feeling you'll be getting plenty of *personal* attention."

Cupid bounded to the front row and plopped down his mat right in front of Mia. The ladies on either side of him happily obliged, sliding over to make space. Pan knew better than to count on the same accommodation. He settled for a spot along the perimeter.

Once class began, Cupid took the instructions seriously, even closing his eyes for the Pranayama exercises while Pan kept a vigilant watch for him on Mia's form. So vigilant was Pan, in fact, he could have graphed the rise and fall of Mia's chest as she emptied her mind and filled her pipes with each new breath. He wasn't masochistic enough to entertain any thought beyond appreciation now that Cupid had his hooks in her, but Pan enjoyed the scenery just the same—the scantily clad, sculpted body flowing like liquid into all kinds of improbable positions.

Damn if Cupid wasn't impressive too—the model pupil, earnestly pushing each stretch and pose to his full potential. Pan had to admit his friend moved with a flexibility and grace belying the novelty of his human physique. Mia fulfilled her promise to keep an eye on him, even adding a solicitous hand or two, but there was certainly no deficiency in Cupid's form requiring assistance.

Nope, there was nothing at all deficient about Cupid's form.

Pan's heart rewound to that awkward wait while Cupid had considered whether Pan might be "the one." Damn Aphrodite for raising Pan's hopes for that split second; would she ever stop torturing him for winning Cupid's loyalty? While Pan harbored mixed feelings about being Cupid's potential punishment, he certainly didn't hate the prospect of Cupid regarding him with that helplessly lost, incurably infatuated, desperate need, which was now aimed full force at Mia.

The boys were Year Ones at the academy the first time Cupid, then called Eros, brought Pan home after school—the day the prince of Aphrodite's palace declared they would be best friends forever, the same day Pan understood he would never be good enough.

Pan had been well warned by his father not to mix with the full-gods, and for the first several weeks of school, Pan had quite contentedly heeded the advice. What did he care, anyway, about a bunch of entitled brats? A precocious seven-year-old, Pan was dealing with a more consuming problem—a confusing but thrilling sensation that started as a tickle between his legs and bloomed into an ache whenever one of those sweet-smelling, bare-breasted nymphs came anywhere near him. Sadly, those exotic creatures, who seemed engineered for the sole purpose of tempting him, were as repelled by Pan as he was drawn to them. He chased; they fled. The all-male gym class became his only relief from his nonstop libido, though the wrestling unit presented a formidable challenge that confused Pan even more. He might have been too innocent to fully understand the jolts of pleasure that came when his groin met the behind of a classmate on hands and knees, but he knew enough to wrap an extra band of material between his legs on wrestling days. So it happened that Pan found himself actually looking forward to the first day of the track unit, as much as he could have been said to look forward to anything that happened at the academy. Running, at least, was not a contact sport.

Pan already knew he was a natural before the boys took off for their first lap. He pulled easily into the lead, his powerful hind quarters giving him a ridiculously unfair advantage over the other boys—a first inside the academy walls. He galloped around the track until he lapped the slowest of his classmates. *I'll show them all,* Pan was thinking as he pushed toward the heart of the pack, prepared to whizz past every boy who'd scored higher on an exam or given an impressive answer in class, and that's when he caught wind of the mocking and laughter.

At the center of the clump, a set of dove-white wings appeared and disappeared in brief, spastic spurts. None other than *Eros.* Of all the divines to steer clear of, this kid's pedigree topped the list: bastard child of the Goddess of Love and the God of War, grandson of Zeus, Himself. *Keep on running,* common sense told Pan, and arguably, his path would have been easier if he had listened.

But Pan was a creature of instinct, and his instincts told him to do something. His hooves kicked up a cloud of dust as he penetrated the mean crowd with their taunts of "Mama's boy" and "Flybaby" and all manner of creative suggestions of where Eros could stick his magic arrows. Pan pulled up right next to Eros and matched his pace. This was the closest Pan had ever been to the winged archer, and he was more than a little surprised to see Eros's odd gait for what it was: not a child of privilege using his wings to cheat the assignment, but rather the exact opposite. Every time his shoulders lifted and the wings would try to flap, Eros would set his jaw and drive his hands toward the ground. With his startlingly blue eyes set dead ahead, he'd force one foot in front of the other. He clearly wasn't built for running, but he didn't seem to know how to give up.

It was the boy's legs furiously fighting the wings, caught between running and flying, that aroused Pan's pity. He knew what it was to be made of two halves that didn't quite form a whole.

Eros puffed out raspy breaths while sweat rolled down his red cheeks in fat rivulets. The strain was obvious, and still the kids mocked him, right up until Pan bellowed at the top of his lungs, "LEAVE HIM ALONE!" His voice shook the ground. They all stopped dead in their tracks, their faces twisted in awe and fear, covering their ears in case he got the bright idea to scream again. Pan scanned their stricken expressions, and he figured his own probably looked about the same. Their gazes met, and the boy blinked up at him. Pan blinked back, holding his breath. Eros's mouth curled into a huge, contagious smile. A friendship was sealed.

Eros thought nothing of inviting his new friend home that day. Pan had never been invited anywhere, let alone the royal palace of Aphrodite. Pan's dad had it all wrong about the gods, and he couldn't wait to set him right. The cook set out a dizzying feast, and Pan was busy enlightening Eros as to the finer points of olive pit–spitting technique when Aphrodite came upon them in the dining room.

"Mother, look what my new friend taught me!" Eros raised his chin and launched a pit high into the air. Three heads followed its flight from one end of the dining table all the way across to the opposite edge, where it skidded to a stop. Beaming with excitement, Eros said, "My best yet, wouldn't you say, Pan?"

"Very impressive, indeed," Pan said, as both boys turned for the mother's approval.

Pan had never forgotten the look of contempt on Aphrodite's face. She yelled for the sentries to "put the livestock outside," and locked Eros in his room for five days straight. After that, the boys were inseparable. So what if Pan had to sneak through the mouse-infested cellar and dark passageways of the palace just to hang out with his best friend? All of Aphrodite's blatant and brutal efforts to drive a wedge between the two had only strengthened their bond. The Goddess of Love could be a raging fire breather, but Cupid was worth it. *Still was.*

Pan angled his body so he could watch Cupid's Savasana pose, certain his friend would be restless and disruptive. When had Q ever sat still in class? Cupid surprised him again by completely settling into the hypnotic meditation as Mia guided the group through full-body relaxation and mindful focus. Pan wondered if Cupid had matured over the years they'd been apart or if his love interest provided sufficient motivation to conquer his tendency toward perpetual motion. Whichever the case, Cupid was disturbingly corpse-like.

Pan felt like a voyeur watching the shared "Namaste" between teacher and newest disciple, sensing the act of mutual honoring reached a far more intimate level for the two of them than anyone around them might suspect. As they lifted their bowed heads and beamed at each other, Pan saw Cupid's smitten expression, and he wondered at Aphrodite's diabolical scheme.

14

ASK HER

Cupid couldn't say if it was the heat, the intense workout, or the breathtaking girl, but he was adrift in a euphoric haze when Pan came up behind him at the supply closet and slapped him on the shoulder. Cupid stacked the last of his exercise bricks on the bottom shelf, turned to face Pan, and burst out laughing.

"*What?*" Pan demanded.

"You look like a drowned rat—a redheaded, red-bearded, drowned rat."

"I guess you haven't looked in a mirror lately."

Following Pan's gaze, Cupid took in his own sweaty shirt. "Oh. I'm disgusting too."

Pan jerked his head toward Mia. "So? What's the deal with you two?"

Cupid spun around to gawk at Mia, who was busy with a line of students battling for her attention. Just then, perhaps sensing his intense gaze, Mia glanced up and caught Cupid's eye, filling him with a giddy rush.

Cupid's long and aimless life had a clarity of purpose he

had never known before, a simple and pure truth that answered every question that ever stretched out behind or ahead of him. "I'm in love with her, Pan."

There was no doubt in his mind; this was that experience that had always been denied him. This drive, *Love*, transcended the urgent physical need he'd felt with Layla, though certainly Mia stirred his passion. This mystery, *Love*, was not Rho's confusing game, though Mia was a wondrous world to be discovered.

"Okay," Pan said with a simple nod that filled Cupid with relief. Cupid was right about the arrow, even if he couldn't quite work out how he'd been nicked, but he wasn't prepared to convince Pan of something he barely understood himself. "How's the heart feeling now?"

"It still feels like a chariot race is going on inside me, but that agitation settled down. It feels like I'm in the right place."

Pan tossed a clean towel to his friend. "You should go talk to her. Ask when you can see her again."

"*Again?* You mean we have to be parted?" His hand flew to his sweaty shirt and he clutched at his chest.

Pan frowned, leaned in closer, and made his voice very soft. "Q, you don't know her life. She might be . . . or . . ." Pan sighed loudly, giving his head a sad shake. "Just go ask her, all right?"

"Yeah, okay."

"One more thing, and this is important, so listen up. *I* know you're in love with her, and *you* know you're in love with her, but it's best if you don't mention it to Mia right away."

"Why?"

"Because people don't go around telling people they just met that they're in love. It's not normal, and you're gonna seriously freak her out."

His reasoning didn't make much sense to Cupid, but Pan seemed emphatic. "Okay."

"Good," said Pan. "I'll be right outside if you need me."

"Sure," Cupid answered solemnly, playing along with the fantasy of Pan—or anyone—actually being able to help.

His heart felt ten times heavier as he made his way through the cluster of Mia's admirers. *By the gods, she was beautiful.* Her belly glistened with sweat between the skimpy top and tight-fitting bottoms. The mortals' love of body-hugging clothing was beginning to make sense. A trickle of perspiration spilled from her hair, rolled down the length of her long, graceful neck, and meandered into the valley between her breasts. He wanted to find it with his tongue and lick it all the way back to where it started.

"I think you lied to me."

"Sorry?" Cupid's attention snapped to the angelic voice above the cleavage, and Mia smiled sweetly back at him.

"That wasn't really your first yoga class, was it?"

"Yes," he answered urgently, lest she think him insincere. "I never lie."

Mia placed her hands on her hips and took in his serious expression. "All right."

She believed him. His shoulders relaxed. He made a quick visual sweep of the room, quite pleased when he realized they were alone in the studio.

"Have you had any water? Shame on me. Your first time in class, and I didn't make sure you were hydrated. Here. Drink." She pressed her plastic bottle into his hand, and without a moment's hesitation, Cupid took a long, cool drink, smacking his lips loudly when he'd finished.

"Thanks. I guess I was thirsty."

"So, what'd you think?"

"It was cold," he answered, handing the bottle back to her. "Thank you."

She giggled. "Not about the water, about the class. Will you come back and see me again?"

"When's your next class?" he asked eagerly.

"In ten minutes."

This wasn't so hard. "Sure."

Mia cocked her head. "Where did you say you're from again?"

Cupid sensed Mount Olympus would not be the correct answer, but he didn't know what else to say without lying. "I didn't."

"Mystery man, eh?" Eyes narrowing, Mia asked, "You're not a fugitive or anything, are you?"

He was more a prisoner than an escapee, but Cupid kept this tidbit stored away as well. "Nope."

"Axe murderer, rapist, child molester?"

"Gods, no."

Raising both eyebrows, she picked up speed. "Deadbeat dad? Philanderer? No-good sonofabitch?"

"Mia, I'm not a bad guy. I promise."

"And everybody knows bad guys'll tell you." She released a cleansing breath, leaned in abruptly, and startled him with one last demand. "Just tell me you're not married."

"I'm not married." Caught off guard by her question, Cupid didn't even think to ask it back.

With a sigh, she glanced over his shoulder before meeting his gaze again. "My next class is about to start."

"Should I get my mat out again?" he asked.

"I really don't think that would be wise."

His heart plummeted. "Oh."

"No, it's just . . . it wouldn't be safe for you to take another class right now."

He brightened. "Then when *can* I see you again?"

Her eyes seemed to delve right into his soul, and Cupid was confident she'd find only the most honorable intentions, not counting the sweat licking. "Oh heck, this is crazy." She trailed off with a confused shake of her head.

"What?"

"I have this insane urge to cook dinner for you tonight."

"Why is that insane? Do you not know how to cook?"

Another giggle burst forth from Mia. She drew her hands—and consequently, Cupid's gaze—to the swath of bare midriff.

Mia's confession dragged his attention back to her puzzled expression: "I don't invite strange men to my house—like *ever*—but I feel like there's something different about you. Crazy, right?"

"Yes," Cupid answered, worried his heart might burst if she revoked the invitation now, "but I feel the same way about you." And he meant it, too, with a desperation he had never felt before.

Mia squinted a bit and studied him some more, or perhaps she was searching herself for an explanation of her own baffling behavior. For some reason, she seemed determined to resist Cupid's charms. He held his breath until, to his enormous relief, she relented.

"Do you have any food allergies?"

"I don't like green tomatoes very much." His nose crinkled at the painful memory.

"I'm pretty sure I can work around that." Mia dug a pen and a scrap of paper out of her bag, scrawled out her phone number, and pushed it into Cupid's hand. "My last class ends at six. Give me some time to clean up, call me, and if I haven't come to my senses by then, I'll tell you where I live."

Cupid smiled so hard his cheeks hurt. "I'll clean up too."

15

DRIVING LESSONS

"The bus stop is outside, Ginger."

Pan spun toward the blonde who'd worked out next to him in class. "Just waiting for a friend, thanks."

Undeterred, the girl slid the end of her high ponytail between two fingers, finishing it off with a suggestive twist. "Would that be a female friend?"

If the girl was dead set on showing him something, Pan couldn't see the harm in looking; he had time to kill. Easing his shoulders into the wall behind him, Pan treated his eyeballs to a leisurely jaunt down her well-toned body. As usual, the nipples caught his attention first—two little spears punching through her drenched, bright pink sports bra—and his gaze landed right back there after a quick trip south. This girl smelled as ripe as they come, a tantalizing bouquet of sweat and desire.

"No. He's definitely not female." *And he's why you're prowling for something between your legs right now.*

"Mmm. In that case, maybe you and I could go"—she sidled closer and thrust those nipples closer to Pan's eyeballs—"find a place to cool down together?"

A twitch inside Pan's compression shorts flashed a bright green light in his brain, but the wiser part of him shut it down. "That's definitely a tempting offer, um—" The girl gasped at Pan's large hand on her delicate shoulder.

"Veronica," she offered with a hopeful lilt.

"—*Veronica*, but I'm afraid I have something I need to take care of right now."

Pan's rejection penetrated Veronica's lusty fog, and her breasts retreated as reality dawned. "Have a blessed day," she muttered.

Pan shook his head at the swish of Veronica's ponytail as she skittered away. He could survive missing out on a romp or two. Regret might sting for a second, but it was no match for the vengeance the gods might inflict if Pan wandered from his post.

The door of the studio burst open, and Cupid tumbled out in a cloud of steam. "You have to teach me how to drive."

"And hello to you too."

Cupid passed him without slowing down—a god on a mission.

"What happened?" Pan asked, chasing him down the narrow hallway.

"She invited me over for dinner, which is why you need to teach me how to drive." Cupid tore a straight line for the turnstile.

"Hold your horses, bro. We have to get our pants." Pan led his edgy friend back to the locker room. "Need the bathroom?"

"No, Mother, but thanks for asking."

Pan shook his head with a huff. Aphrodite was the last being in the cosmos Pan aspired to be mistaken for, and he had no doubt the feeling was mutual.

"You didn't drink enough water," Pan answered, a twinge of neglect nagging at his conscience.

A goofy grin crossed Cupid's face. "Now you sound like Mia." "First your mother, now your new girlfriend? Would I piss standing up if I were one of your females?" Pan let loose his stream in the urinal as Cupid busied himself with his sweatpants. "Now what's all this about dinner?" Pan asked as the two made their way outside.

"She's going to cook for me at her home."

"Her home? That was quick." That was *Cupid*. "Here, hop in—the *passenger* side," Pan added when Cupid opened the driver's door. "I'm not ready to unleash you on the good citizens of Tarra quite yet."

Pan opened all the windows while Cupid jogged to the other side. There would be no way to divert Cupid to a shower until he'd perfected the art of driving.

"Okay. You've got the rules of the road down, and you're pretty decent at driving a phone. All we need to do is translate your skills to the mechanics of an actual car. Gas. Brake. Drive. Reverse. To start the truck, place your foot on the brake and push here."

"Got it," Cupid responded, soaking up everything Pan taught as easily as he'd mastered the yoga moves.

By the time they reached the outer parking spaces of the Fortuna Mall parking lot, Cupid had catalogued every motion and was raring to go. Pan could barely scramble out of the way as Cupid muscled into the driver's seat.

Cupid made quick work of the seat controls, set the mirrors to Pan's specifications, and gave his instructor a pleading smile. "Can I turn it on now?"

"Sure."

Cupid pumped the gas pedal a couple times, and the V-8 growled and trembled under the hood. His delighted laughter filled the cabin. "I could fly circles around Helios in this thing!"

Now, *there* would be a sight to behold: Pan's Titan spinning doughnuts around the sun as it arced across the sky. "That's hardly a fair contest, my friend. You'd have a three hundred eighty-six-horse advantage."

"Wow. Really?" Cupid revved the engine twice more. *Boys will be boys.*

Given the improbability of his own potentially hooved hypothetical offspring ever operating a car, Pan was nearly moved to tears by the father-son-ish moment. "Are we driving or just sitting here making noise?"

Cupid lunged for the gearshift. "Let's go!"

"Wait!" Pan's protective instincts kicked in fully, and he grasped Cupid's wrist with a firm grip.

"What?"

"This is not a video game. If you crash, it's for real. My truck doesn't pop up brand new at the starting line again. And, perish the thought, if you hit a human, the damage is permanent. Understand?"

"Isn't that decided by the Fates?"

"The timing, yes, but you don't want to be the direct cause. Feel me?"

Cupid blinked several times at Pan's sobering message. "Yes." Convinced he'd been heard, Pan released his grip. "Does that mean you and I are mortal down here?"

"I'm not positive, to be honest," Pan replied. "I've broken most of my bones at some point, and that shit hurts, but they've always healed at god-speed. Obviously, I'm not aging. I assume we're immortal down here, but it's not a theory I'm eager to test, hence the seat belts."

"Okay, got it."

"Good. Take us around this lane."

Cupid exhaled, closed his fingers around the gear knob, and coaxed the truck into Drive. With his right hand returned to the wheel, he pulled out of the space with a skill level far outstripping his experience. Pan's tense grasp of his right thigh relaxed as Cupid proved himself both masterful and appropriately vigilant.

"Pull the truck over there," Pan said, directing Cupid to the tire center. "I'll be right back."

He hopped out of the pickup and snagged two orange traffic cones from a stack against the building. Pacing off twenty feet between the two cones, Pan set up a makeshift parking space while firing instructions at Cupid through the open window.

"If you hit a cone, you start over. We do it until you don't have to think."

As if recording an instructional video on parallel parking, Cupid lined up alongside the forward cone, shifted into reverse, cut a flawless curve into the spot, and straightened the wheel. Pan could not have scripted the execution with more precision.

"I didn't think," Cupid announced without an ounce of guile or arrogance.

As far as the recently fallen god knew, perfection was a simple matter of course. Though Pan recognized Cupid's razor-sharp instincts behind the wheel as exceptional even for an Olympian, he wasn't about to let up on his student.

"Not bad for your first time. Again." Pan ordered Cupid through the cones three more times until beginner's luck was entirely ruled out. "Let's see you reverse around the lot and back into that spot over there."

Brimming with pride, Pan observed his protégé's effortless backward glide through the training course and into the angled parking space. Pan strolled over to the passenger side and climbed in.

"Solid."

Cupid's bright smile animated his entire being. "Am I unleashed?"

"Sure. But don't tell Mia you just learned today. It's not exactly *human* to learn to drive so quickly. Know what I mean?"

"Mmhmm." Cupid hummed, his gaze traveling to his side window and into the distance.

"What is it, Q?"

When Cupid turned back, his carefree grin was nowhere to be found. "I'm in love with her, Pan. I can't mess this up. I have no idea how to do a date. And I don't understand earth girls at all."

"Nobody understands earth girls. Not even other earth girls."

"Great," Cupid said with a discouraged moan.

"I can give you a few pointers."

"Yeah?" Cupid beseeched him with an expression so charged with hope and trust, Pan felt a lump rise in his throat. Romance wasn't exactly Pan's specialty, but his best friend was a clean slate, and Pan was the only stick of chalk around.

"All right. Start with a bottle of nice wine. Oh, and flowers are a classy touch."

"Wine and flowers, got it." Cupid tucked each detail away with the same care as memorizing the driving instructions.

"And don't be the first to roll out of bed afterwards."

Cupid answered with a tight, "Great. Thanks."

Pan searched his brain for something beyond lame clichés, but he was fresh out. The truth would have to do. "Look, Q, you're in this thing whether you want it or not. The best advice I can share is what your mother already told you: follow your heart."

Cupid flinched at the reminder. Could his love-addled mind somehow have erased the circumstances that had led him to Mia? The piteous son of a goddess was in for a rough tumble.

Cupid gathered his disappointment into a highly effective glare. "That's it? The extent of your vast experience is to follow Mother's advice?"

Pan shrugged. "I also emphatically recommend a shower."

16

TULIPS

Three hours and a long shower later, Cupid shuffled into the great room, outfitted head to toe in proper-sized clothing plucked from shopping bags strewn across his bed. His most tender regions were nestled inside a pair of silky boxer briefs—a compromise between Pan's dogged insistence on the godforsaken garment and Cupid's demand for comfort. Between the post-yoga soreness and the elephants marching in his chest, Cupid's crotch was pretty much the only part left unscathed—though he suspected that, too, would be swollen later tonight.

Pan glanced up from the couch and blew a whistle through his teeth. "Let me see the back," he commanded, adding a twirl of his finger to get Cupid started.

Cupid rolled his eyes. "You'll see the back when my front walks out the door."

Pan chuckled. "Fine. Belt?"

Cupid raised the hem of his shirt until it cleared the leather belt.

"Condoms?"

Cupid tapped his front pocket, and Pan shot him a grin. "Got your phone?"

With an exasperated sigh, Cupid answered, "Yes and yes, and I have gone to the bathroom. May I go now?"

"Go, already. Flowers and wine are on the counter. Keys are in the car. Drive safe."

This being Cupid's maiden voyage, he especially appreciated the well-lit, high-tech interior of Pan's Barcelona Red Prius, which more closely matched the video game than did Pan's truck. Besides, he had no intention of greeting his date bearing the stench of sweat still hanging thick in the cabin of the Titan. Even in the diminishing daylight, Cupid's vision and reflexes were acute, and his confidence was high, bolstered further by the bouquet of yellow tulips and Pan's best Cabernet lying on the passenger seat.

The robotic orders issuing from the car's GPS provided a certain reassurance though Cupid's internal system had begun tugging at him the moment he stepped out of the shower. A move in any direction other than directly toward Mia had cost him a twinge of discomfort. As Cupid sped toward his date, it became clear his heart functioned "as the crow flies," whereas the Prius, sadly, was at the mercy of the maze of Tarra's streets. This mismatch in guidance mechanisms led to a rapidly building tension within him, an escalating pleasure as he drew closer to his heart's destination, interrupted by random, painful, corrective chest spasms when the roads forced him to steer away from Mia. Fortunately, the two systems eventually harmonized a few blocks from her door, and the good feelings overtook the agony.

Cupid backed the Prius into a tight parallel spot on the street with an economy of shifting that would have made Pan proud. Gifts in hand, he skipped up the walk, humming to himself as he approached a cheery window box with bright pink petunias spilling over the sides. No need to double-check the address before ringing Mia's bell; Cupid's heart left little doubt he was on the right stoop.

"Coming!"

As the clatter of Mia's footsteps drew nearer, Cupid's heart vibrated wildly in his chest. The door opened, and Cupid was met not only by the freshly scrubbed—though sadly, more fully clothed—version of Mia but also by the most enticing swirl of aromas wafting from her kitchen.

Momentarily stunned by the onslaught of sensory input, Cupid took a second to come out with even a simple, "Hello."

"Hello," she answered, dark green flecks dancing in her eyes. "Are those for me?"

"Yes." Cupid offered the tulips to her with one hand and the wine with the other. "So is this."

The cellophane crinkled in her hand as she pulled the flowers to her chest. "Thank you. I love tulips. Come on in. Let me put these in water."

Mia spun away and strode with purpose toward her kitchen. Cupid's gaze slipped to the firm, apple-shaped bottom rocking side to side beneath her tight jeans. *Slim jeans*, Cupid had recently learned, were the most beloved of all the varieties, and now he fully understood why, though it still baffled him why the gaping holes in the material increased their value.

He remembered he was supposed to be following Mia inside and skipped to close the gap between them. She rounded the kitchen counter, rose onto her tiptoes, and reached toward the top shelf, groaning when her fingertips stopped short of the target.

Cupid rushed to her side and set down the wine. Placing one hand on her waist—purely for balance—Cupid stretched to easily reach the vase. "Here you go," he said, his voice cracking a bit as her hair brushed his cheek.

"Thank you."

His hand lingered on her waist until there was no excuse to keep holding on. Still, he stood close enough to feel the heat coming off her cheeks, to note the pink at the tips of her ears as she filled the vase with water.

"Should we open your wine, or would you like something else to drink?"

Cupid relaxed against the counter next to her, unable to tolerate any distance between them. "Whatever you like. Your house smells amazing, by the way. What did you make?"

"Oh, it's a spicy lemongrass soup with tofu. I hope you like it."

Having never tried lemongrass or tofu, he answered with authority. "I'm sure I will."

"I specifically omitted the green tomatoes from the recipe."

Overwhelmed by Mia's kindness, Cupid gave her a tender smile. "Thank you."

She shook her head and giggled gently while pulling a pair of scissors from the top drawer. Cupid watched, transfixed, as Mia snipped each stem and lovingly positioned the flowers into the vase, one at a time, as if welcoming each new guest to the party. Mia studied the arrangement with a tilt of her head that reminded Cupid of the goddess Flora, fussing over her weekly deliveries to the palace. *Mother would be impressed*, Cupid realized with an unexpected stab of homesickness.

"There," Mia said, fluffing the tulips one last time. "Now let's open that wine."

She replaced the shears and pulled out a metal gadget resembling a one-legged woman. Handing the device to Cupid, Mia asked, "Would you like to do the honors?"

"Sure, if you'll show me how to use this thing."

"You've never used a corkscrew before?"

"No, but I'm a quick learner."

"Don't worry, this is way easier than yoga." Stepping into his side, she gripped the neck of the bottle with her free hand. "Okay, so . . ." Mia tilted her face toward Cupid, and he snapped to attention. His Earth repertoire was growing in leaps and bounds. "You're supposed to cut away this little strip, but I usually skip that part and poke this really sharp tip right here into the middle of the cork—just watch your fingers on the point—and then twist."

As she illustrated the twisting, her body swiveled into his— again and again and again. Cupid held his ground, reveling in the close contact of their bodies and the fire blazing between them like two dry sticks rubbed together. Mia cranked the head of the corkscrew around and around, plunging the coiled spike deeper and deeper into the cork with each revolution until the arms were pointing almost straight up.

"Your turn," she said.

"What do I do?"

"Slowly push those levers down until the cork pops out."

"All right."

Mia wedged herself directly in front of Cupid. When he reached around to grasp the metal arms, Mia was caged between his body and the counter. The alluring scent of grapefruit filled Cupid's lungs, and it required all his effort to resist trailing his lips down her neck. Mia's head dropped back against his shoulder, and her hands slid to his forearms while he painstakingly lowered the levers. The tip of the cork burst through the foil and continued to rise until the last of the cork broke free of the bottle's rim with a satisfying *pop*.

Slowly, so as not to jostle the girl in his arms, Cupid lowered the corkscrew to the counter and folded his hands over Mia's belly. His body was a live wire, buzzing from head to toe.

Placing his lips against the soft shell of her ear, he murmured, "Now what?"

She released a rocky sigh. "Now, we let it breathe."

"Breathing is good," Cupid said dreamily, grateful to the genius wine makers for building in a respite after all the drama.

"Mmhmm."

The vibration of Mia's hum against Cupid's chest tipped him over the line he'd been toeing since his arrival. He spun Mia in his arms and gasped when he met a gaze as shot with longing as his own surely had to be. Cupid bent and inched toward her lips.

"Mia," he whispered, "may I kiss you?"

She smiled gently, nodded, and—when he'd smiled back but not yet kissed her—added, "Yes, *yes*."

His heart thudded as he pressed his lips to hers. So *this* was a kiss.

Every single thing Cupid thought he knew flew out of his head to make room for the singular experience of kissing Mia. Her lips were full and soft and gentle and tasted sweeter than the gods' finest nectar. As Mia's arms closed around his back, Cupid purred like a kitten lapping at the purest cream, and if her moans were any indication, Mia's need rivaled his own. She was everything his heart desired. It was disorienting, this overwhelming connection, one Cupid had only imagined in his fantasies of love and lust.

So dazed was Cupid, when Mia tore herself from his lips, he could have sworn she uttered, "Jonah?"

Giving his head a little shake, Cupid attempted to reengage his mental faculties. "Sorry?" He craned his neck when he noticed Mia's gaze was focused over his shoulder.

"Mommy?"

17

MONSTER

Crud on a cracker, Joe! Now? Really? So much for keeping her boys
out of this.

Q spun an about-face, his stunned gaze blinking from
mother to son and back again, and Mia could hardly blame the
guy. Jonah's surprise appearance had splattered shards of sap-
phire around the edges of Q's already dazzling blue eyes. He
deserved an explanation, but Mia could barely think.

"Can you give me a minute?"

Q answered with a wooden nod as his hands fell away from
her back. She tingled where his fingers left her, felt chilled where
his lips had warmed her in a way she hadn't been warmed in far
too long. *Wow.* Maybe Jonah's interruption was the universe hitting the pause button so Mia could get a grip on herself before
she did something they might all regret.

She stepped around Q's hard, eager body and crouched to
pull Jonah into her arms. Heavy with exhaustion, Jonah wilted
over her shoulder like a sack of rice.

"C'mon, little bug. Let's tuck you back in."

"The monster came again, Mommy," he whined into Mia's neck.

"It's okay, baby. Mommy's gonna get rid of him." She rubbed soothing circles into Jonah's back, the planets and stars of his big-boy pajamas clinging to his clammy skin. Afraid to meet Q's gaze, Mia felt his eyes on her back as she wore the familiar path to the boys' room and prayed he'd stick around long enough to let her explain.

"He's under my bed."

"Shh, *shhhh*, we don't want to wake your brothers," she whispered, squatting until both their faces were level with the space under his bed.

"Look, Joe. Nobody here but Merlin." Damn cat doing his damn nocturnal patrols, chasing dust-bunny mice. *Why do I let him sleep in the boys' room again?* Oh yes, because their father is a miserable ass, and these boys need all the love they can get.

"Mommy, do the spell."

Mia put on her serious voice and waved her hand in a mysterious circle. "Subsistam, monstrum!"

A tentative breath shook out of Jonah's chest. "Did it work?" he whispered, his trusting little hands pinching deep wells into Mia's shoulders.

"Hold on; let me check." Mia squeezed her eyes closed and listened for any stray noises in the night that might spook him again. "Yep, all gone. Now, it's back to Sleepyland for you, J-man."

Mia peeled Jonah from her body, settled him gently inside the crumpled bedding, and smoothed the top sheet and blanket across his chest. His perfect little face made her breath hitch, as it often did—thick brows perched like two little awnings over soulful, brown eyes, a sturdy nose, and a pair of full, cherry-pink lips. It wasn't Jonah's fault he'd inherited his father's handsome features, but sometimes Mia worried for him and all the hearts he might break. She, unlike her mother-in-law, would not raise her boys to be assholes.

Perched at the edge of the bed, she pushed the damp hair off Jonah's forehead and bent to leave a kiss on his soft cheek.

Jonah yawned and drilled his fists against his eyelids. "Who is that man you were kissing in the kitchen?"

Mia's heart stuttered. How much did her five-year-old son need to know? She was deliberating between "one of Mommy's yoga students" and "a new friend" when a soft voice behind her took them both by surprise.

"I'm Q."

Heart in her throat, Mia craned her neck to the doorway where Q stood, hands in his front pockets. In the faint illumination of the glow-in-the-dark stars on the ceiling, Mia could make out Q's astonishment as he fully digested the scene: Lucas asleep in his crib, quietly sucking his pacifier; Eli curled up in a fetal ball just beyond the bed rail; and a now wide-awake Jonah, sitting up in bed, peering around Mia to get a better look at the stranger.

"Hi, I'm Jonah."

"Hi." Q smiled at Jonah, then looked to Mia for direction. Her first response should've been anger. She'd asked Q to wait, though to be fair, she wasn't specific about staying in the kitchen. And honestly, shouldn't she have been at least a little freaked out? She'd just exposed her boys to this stranger she'd risked inviting into her home—and vice versa.

Funny thing, in the brief time she'd known this man with the odd name and mysterious past, "should" didn't seem to apply at all. If it had, Q wouldn't even be here right now. Inexplicable, irresistible sex appeal aside, there was something about the man's aura that had fast-forwarded Mia's strict timeline. He had a disarming manner that relieved her, at least temporarily, of the burdensome chainmail she'd worn since the shmuck walked out on all of them. Without seeming to try, Q made Mia trust him.

And *want* him. *God*, how she wanted him. *I'm no better than Merlin with his catnip.*

She hadn't been with a man in—how old was Lucas?—nine months, plus eight and a half more, give or take. There was only so much companionship a vibrator could provide. After the post-abandonment cooling off period, once Mia's resentment of all penis-bearing humans had more or less subsided, she simply hadn't had any time to pine for what she didn't have. Exhausted on every level, Mia would hit her own mattress as soon as the boys were tucked in and steal as much sleep as two young boys and a pregnant body—and later, a newborn—would allow. Working and breastfeeding and surviving had sapped all of her physical strength and choked off any sexual desire she might've dredged up. After a while, sex quietly dropped off her radar—until Q had walked into her studio and awakened her senses like a smoke detector in a forest fire.

How Mia had muddled through that class without hurting herself, she'd never know. At least she could breathe again once Q left the studio, but she had spent the rest of the day distracted in the best possible way. By the end of her last class, Mia had given herself permission to cash in the universe's IOU and indulge in a little pleasure.

And now there he was, leaning against the doorjamb, waiting for her decision to either invite him into her life for real or send him away for good. As she took in Q's unassuming form, it wasn't desire Mia felt so much as relief he was still there, even if it meant Jonah was now impossibly awake.

Rewind. Q had just seen the three sons she'd neglected to mention, and he hadn't run out of there screaming. Either the guy had a serious craving for lemongrass and tofu soup, or he was seriously hard up for sex.

Or maybe I've become a cynical witch.

In any event, the cat was out of the bag—all three boys plus the actual cat. Why banish Q now? Besides, there was a part of her, far enough north to be trustworthy, that sensed Q's innocent, childlike openness might reach Jonah in a way she could not. And so, she risked it.

Praying she wouldn't regret this choice, Mia scooted closer to Jonah and patted the blanket on her other side, an invitation Q accepted with a humble nod. He tiptoed over to the bed and sat down next to Mia.

"Is it true there was a monster in here?" Q whispered across her body.

"Yeah," Jonah replied, wide eyes blinking at the curious turn of events, "under the bed."

Q hastily retracted his feet and peered over the edge of the bed. "Is it still there?"

"No," Jonah assured him. "Mommy spelled him away."

"Oh, good." Q leaned back onto his palms. "I don't like monsters very much. *Especially* when I'm trying to sleep."

"You have a monster too?" Jonah scooted back against his headboard, so enthralled with Q, Mia would've guessed she was all but forgotten.

Q leaned toward Jonah. "I used to. It was the ugliest, most grotesque creature who ever walked . . . the earth."

"What did it look like?" Mia's antennae rose as Jonah pressed for details—details that might make Q's monster all too vivid.

Q launched into a description that raised the hairs on the back of Mia's neck. "And would you believe it had not one, not two, but *three* heads? A goat, a lion, and a snake." *Super. Jonah's second-biggest anxiety.*

"Whoa. Really?"

"Mmhmm. And did I tell you about the fire breathing?" *Ah, the trifecta.*

Jonah sucked in a sudden gasp and dragged the blanket up to his neck. "*Fire?*" he echoed. Q couldn't have picked more terrifying qualities for his monster if he'd been trying.

"Yes," Q said solemnly. "It was terrible. Just terrible." He punctuated the extra terribleness with a grave shake of his head. Mia resisted the urge to pull Jonah into her arms.

"What happened to it?" Jonah asked breathlessly.

"I got rid of her."

Jonah shot Q an incredulous stare. "Your monster was a *girl?*"

"Yes," Q answered, flashing a painfully intimate look at Mia. "Sometimes girls are scary."

"How'd you get rid of her?" Jonah asked, eyes wide and eager.

Q favored Mia with a wink before answering. "I have a very special mother, just like you."

Mia's heart leapt into her throat. *Damn, he's making me the hero?*

"You do?" Sweet Jonah, so hungry for a decent male role model. He was eating this up like a hot fudge sundae.

"Yes. When I was a little boy, she gave me a very special arrow for keeping monsters away. If it's okay with your mommy, I can pass it along to you."

Jonah tipped his head, and the reverence on her son's face just about broke Mia's heart in two. "What about you? Don't you need it?"

Q reached over and ruffled Jonah's hair with his fingers. "I already used it once. That's all it takes."

"Mommy?" Jonah turned his soft, questioning eyes on Mia, and Q's followed.

"Sure, honey."

Jonah's little body twisted toward Q. "She said yes!"

"Great." Q beamed another of his *trust-me* smiles at Mia before taking Jonah's hand. "Okay, we need to stand up for this."

Q hopped off the bed, and Jonah bounced up to his feet on the mattress. Mia bit her tongue; if the ritual involved jumping on the bed, so be it. She just hoped they wouldn't wake Luke and Eli.

"Close your eyes," Q told him, and Jonah immediately obeyed. "Put your arms out. Okay, Sir Jonah . . .?"

Q shot Mia a questioning glance, and she filled in the blanks. "Walker Barnes."

"Nice," Q said under his breath. "I hereby award thee, Sir Jonah Walker Barnes, the Invisible Arrow of Valor, to be used to slay the fierce bed monster of 136 Elm Street. Are you ready, sire?"

"Yes."

Q brushed his fingers across Jonah's outstretched hands, then curled the boy's hands into fists. With his bigger hands surrounding Jonah's, Q leaned in and whispered, "Okay, Jonah. You can open your eyes."

Mia's awe exceeded her son's as Jonah slowly opened his eyes and beheld the wonder of his invisible monster-slaying arrow. His face became one giant smile. "Thank you, Q."

Q released his hands and bowed with a formal flourish. "You won't need it tonight, of course, but the arrow is yours now. If I were you, I'd tuck it under your pillow."

Jonah dropped to his knees and slid the arrow under his pillow exactly as Q had suggested. Mia pulled the blankets up to her son's shoulders, bent over, and kissed him on the cheek. "Night, Joe."

"Night, Mommy. Night, Q."

"G'night, Jonah. Sleep well, now."

"I will."

Mia couldn't detect a trace of fear in her son's voice. She walked to the door with Q trailing close behind. As soon as they rounded the corner, Mia grabbed Q's hand and interlaced her fingers with his.

18

SOUP

Despite their slow saunter back to the kitchen, Cupid's thoughts were racing. Was he shocked to learn Mia had kids? Of course he was. The possibility had never entered his mind. But why would it? How could it? He'd pursued her with a single-minded determination that left no room for wondering who else might need her.

"You were kind of awesome in there," Mia said, jiggling their joined hands.

As this new dimension of Mia seeped into Cupid's understanding of her, he realized how very little he knew about this woman who had become the center of his existence, and on the heels of that realization, how none of it changed anything. The mysterious pull in his chest had brought Cupid here, and he seemed to have no choice but to stay as close to Mia as possible though he had no idea what he was supposed to say. A deafening stillness followed them back to the spot of their miraculous kiss.

"I know you have questions," Mia said, placing her palm over Cupid's thundering heart. "Can we talk over dinner . . . and wine? Please?"

Cupid wanted to cover her hand with his and quell the tempest brewing inside, but the gesture didn't feel genuine. Suddenly, he was hungry and very much in need of a drink. "Sure."

Mia slipped away from him and handed him the open wine bottle and two glasses. "Can you take these to the table while I get the soup?"

By the time Mia returned to the dining room, Cupid had lit the candles and poured the wine nearly to overflowing. Mia had obviously put some effort into setting a nice table for the two of them, and the smells coming from the soup bowls made his mouth water.

"Where do you want me?" he asked, causing a fresh blush to color Mia's cheeks.

"Wherever," she said. "I never sit out here, so . . ."

Cupid settled Mia into her chair before sitting down beside her. She lifted her wine glass; he did the same.

"Here's to a wonderful evening." Mia's toast felt more like a plea as they clinked goblets. "I hope you like the soup," she said, her voice fraught with anxiety. "It's been a while since I've cooked for anyone other than myself and the boys."

Cupid took a roll from the basket, tore off a corner, and dipped it into his soup. Placing the soup-soaked bread onto his tongue, he hummed with pleasure at the mixture of exotic tastes competing for his attention. "It's delicious. You really made this yourself?"

Mia grinned while Cupid scooped two more spoonfuls of the broth into his mouth without a break. "Yes, I gave the scullery maids the night off."

Cupid nodded and drew in another mouthful while Mia shook her head. He stopped eating only long enough to ask, "Aren't you hungry?"

Dragging the spoon through her soup in thoughtful circles,

Mia's green eyes locked onto Cupid's and held his gaze far longer than his question warranted. "Yeah, actually, I'm starved."

His spoon froze in midair. "You should eat."

Neither of them moved for the next few seconds, Cupid having remembered, half a bowl too late, it was impolite to eat everything in sight before one's hostess took her first bite. He hoped this wasn't one of those moments he was being watched from above. Hephaestus wouldn't have a clue about table manners, but Mother sure wouldn't be impressed.

Mia lifted her spoon to her mouth. As Cupid looked on like a jealous lover, a flash of pink tongue shot out for one tantalizing second, curled under the hot broth, and disappeared again. Cupid cleared his throat and reached for his wine glass.

Having taken part in enough Bacchanalia in his day to know the nectar of the vine tended to work at odds with one's nobler self, Cupid sipped with moderation. Mia, however, tipped the wine between her lips, closed her eyes, and swallowed until half the glass was gone.

"Ahh. Much better." She sighed heavily and folded her hands on the table.

Cupid watched her closely, spinning the thin stem of his goblet between his fingers. Words still eluding him, he took another sip.

"So, yeah, I have kids." Mia delivered the news with a flinch, as if waiting to be struck by one of Zeus's thunderbolts.

Cupid held his tongue and offered Mia an encouraging smile. She spilled forth.

"I'm really sorry for springing all this on you. I was sort of hoping we could . . . that I'd . . . *ugh*."

Cupid's attention was drawn to the unfortunate napkin Mia was shredding to bits as she searched for the right words. He scooted his chair closer, then covered her hands with his own and soothed her with one of her own phrases from yoga class. "Find your center, Mia."

She pulled in a practiced breath and released it in deliberate puffs. Her grimace relaxed. "Thanks."

Cupid nodded, entwining his fingers with hers.

When Mia spoke again, guilt dripped like lead weights from her confession. "I wanted to make sure you liked me first."

"I do like you, Mia. Very much." His response could not have been more emphatic or heartfelt.

"Q . . ." She paused again and shook her head, and for one awful moment, Cupid wondered whether she'd ever be able to tell him what plagued her so, but she managed to pull herself together. "I'm lonely," she said, twisting their joined hands.

Cupid's heart swelled anew. "That's hardly a crime."

"I should've warned you about the kids, but I was afraid I'd scare you away."

A new, terrifying idea occurred to him. "Are there more?"

"Because raising three boys alone isn't enough?" A harsh bark rose from the depths of her throat.

Cupid shrugged, unsure of what else to say.

"No, that's all. Just the four of us."

Drawing on a boldness born of absolute necessity, Cupid asked, "What about the boys' father?"

"He's out of the picture."

Cupid had not been on Earth long enough to understand exactly what she meant, but he remembered the mortal custom of wearing wedding bands and cursed himself for not being more observant earlier. He definitely detected metal under his palm, and with a lump in his throat, he lifted his hand to inspect Mia's jewelry. Two rings on the right hand.

She continued, saving him from the pain of asking. "We're divorced. Fifteen months, two weeks, and three days."

"*Fifteen months?*" Cupid was well aware of the gestation period for human babies, even if deities sprang forth in unpredictable ways from all sorts of body parts. "How old is the baby?"

"He's nine months." Mia tortured her napkin again. "Yeah, I know. I was three months along when the final papers came through." Her voice floated away on a river of regret. "Anyway, the asshole is gone, and he stopped going through the motions of visiting more than a year ago, and we're all better off for it. Actually," she added, "I've heard he's gained twenty pounds, and his hair is falling out." A smile curled the edges of her lips.

Cupid sensed he should leave this thread of conversation on that relatively light note, but he was stuck on the math. "He's never met his youngest son?"

"Nope. And yes, he knows about Lucas. Knew I was pregnant when we signed the papers."

A sadness settled over Mia, and Cupid lifted the bottle and refilled both their goblets.

"From what I can see, it seems you're doing great on your own," he said.

"I do the best I can for my boys. I take on as many classes as they'll give me down at the gym, and it helps that they offer free childcare, but the only break I get is the occasional night my mother can watch them. We make do. *Anyway* . . ." Mia flicked her hand as if batting away a housefly. "You don't need to hear my problems. This is why I didn't want to tell you all the gory details. Now you're looking at me with 'those eyes.'"

"What eyes?"

"Pity."

Cupid searched every chamber of his heart, but all he could find was love. "No, Mia. What you're seeing is admiration."

Mia's eyes brimmed with tears. "Just so you know, Q, you're the first guy I've invited into my home since the asshole left. I've actually never taken a chance like this." Mia downed half the new pour, eyeing Cupid with suspicion, as if she weren't quite sure what kind of magic he'd worked on her. Cupid might have wondered the same about Mia if not for the gods pulling the strings from above.

"Maybe you were waiting for me," Cupid said.

She let out a soft sigh. "You know, you really don't have to be so damn perfect. Your chances are really, really good tonight."

"My chances?" Cupid felt Mia searching his eyes for something, and he held stock still until she found it.

She nudged her chin toward his soup bowl. "Eat. You're going to need your strength."

19

DESSERT

Mia swapped her empty dessert dish for the steaming mug of coffee waiting on the side table and drew her feet up beneath her on the love seat they were sharing. "You must be a fan of Greek mythology."

Q's dessert spoon halted suddenly, sending one of the blueberries tumbling over the edge and into his lap, causing Mia unclean thoughts. "Why do you say that?" he asked.

"Your vivid description of the chimera earlier. I swear you had me looking right through your eyes at the monster."

Leaning in closer, Q asked, "You know the chimera?"

"Not personally," Mia said, shaking her spoon in his direction. "Not like you, apparently."

A cloud of panic seemed to cross his face but blew over just as quickly. "Oh. Yeah." Mia watched the berry with envy as Q plucked it off his jeans and popped it into his mouth.

"I guess I've always been a little fascinated by those stories," she said. Q studied her wordlessly as she continued. "A rainbow appears in the sky one day and *poof!* Iris, the messenger, appears on the scene. Must be nice—you have a problem you can't solve or a phenomenon you can't explain, you invent a god or two, and it all makes sense. Those ancient poets sure were a creative bunch, huh?"

"I suppose," he said guardedly. "Is that how most mort—people view the gods?"

"As opposed to what?"

Q shrugged and scraped at the raspberry seeds stuck to the side of his dish as if he were mining diamonds. Mia couldn't help but notice the blush that crept up his cheeks.

"Wait, you're not saying you believe those myths?" she asked.

Q took a long drag from his coffee mug. "Some of the stories feel quite vivid to me."

There he went again, displacing Mia's center of gravity with his profoundly simple worldview. She reached over and rubbed Q's knee through his jeans. He watched uneasily at first, but after several strokes Mia could sense the tense cables of his thigh relaxing. "I find that incredibly romantic for some reason."

Q tipped his chin up, finally peeking at Mia from beneath those inhumanly long, coal-colored lashes. He blinked slowly, seeming to measure her comment. His lips inched up into a cautious smile. "I'm romantic?"

Though Q's easy confidence was heady, it was his shy uncertainty that made Mia's heart lurch. "Mmhmm," she hummed, setting her mug out of the way for what she hoped he'd do next.

Q did not disappoint. Cupping his hand behind Mia's neck, he drew her closer and leaned in to meet her lips. They fell right back inside their perfect kiss from earlier, testing and tasting slowly at first, then devouring each other with renewed urgency.

Was she imagining that tug again, the musky rope binding her to this stranger? Had it been so long she'd forgotten what it felt like to be with a real man? No, this wasn't something forgotten; this was a brand-new experience, so much desire pulsing through her. Between kisses, his tumbled-out "Gods, Mia" sent a shiver down her spine. She leaned into Q's hard angles.

If he noticed Mia's desperation, he was too much of a gentleman to let on, even as she opened her legs around his knee. Q responded with a low grunt and pushed his tongue further into her inviting mouth. She'd basically made up her mind at the gym, but every word since, every gentle act of kindness had cemented her decision. How much lovelier that she really liked this man, that he surprised her at every turn. There was no way she could deny herself this exquisite treat.

He startled when she stood, but his features softened immediately when she reached for his hand. "Not out here," she whispered, adding a directed arch of her brow as understanding dawned from deep within his hooded bedroom eyes.

Q hopped up from the sofa, giving Mia the distinct impression he would've followed her to the end of the earth. There was only one place she wanted him right now, though, needed him more than even she'd realized. His hand glided across hers, and their fingers linked as if they'd held hands forever. She steered him away from the berry-stained custard dishes and soiled soup bowls in the sink, away from the boys sleeping across the hall, away from the backbreaking yoke of providing and worrying and hoping.

She reached around him and softly closed the bedroom door. He was riveted to her—watching, waiting, wanting. Q's otherworldly aura seemed to vibrate and glow brighter as the two of them approached the inevitable, as if he were somehow designed solely for this purpose. Ridiculous, but then again, she had no clue how he'd suddenly materialized in her life, whether he had three wives, or if he'd been lying earlier when he'd promised he wasn't a serial killer.

"Mia." Q's fingers skittered up Mia's bare arms and disappeared under the billowy short sleeves of her top. "Where'd you go?"

Her attention snapped to his dazzling gaze, and she rattled her head to shake out the crazy. There had been no indication he meant her any harm, and if the guy was after loot, good luck to him.

"I'm right here," she mumble-sighed into his striped shirt, letting his magic seep into her bones. His heartbeat pounded firm and quick against her cheek.

"I need to see you," came his gruff reply. He slipped his fingers into the sliver of space between her jeans and her top. "Please?"

Mia had never been shy. Genetically gifted and painstakingly toned, she was used to being admired at the front of class, later in the locker room, and—though not in a good long while—in the bedroom. So it surprised her that her hands were trembling as she opened the button at the back of her neck and that they continued to shake as she started the blouse upward.

Q's lips trailed after the disappearing fabric, pressing soft kisses into her belly and higher while Mia wriggled out of her blouse. He unclasped the bra hooks at her back and slid the lace straps down her arms. She handled the rest, revealing and then removing the matching pink panties edged with a tiny black lace ruffle while Q repeated, "So perfect," like a mantra. At the time, her purchase had seemed wishful and extravagant. It was all worth it for tonight, for the way Q's tongue swiped across his lips, the way he looked at her as if she were his oxygen.

His shirt buttons gave way, uncovering the muscular chest she'd suspected beneath his T-shirt at the gym. Her palms rode up his firm belly, skating along the delicious playground of satin over sinew as Q dropped to his knees in front of her. He worshiped her right there, with soft brushes of his tongue, teasing her into a frenzy with warm, skillful strokes, pulling her to the very edge of her sanity. Finally, when the elastic band of her arousal had stretched so thin she was about to snap, he touched her—a gentle, barely-there stroke that sucked her breath away and sent her spinning into oblivion.

Tears trickled down Mia's cheeks as her body shook with sweet, miraculous release. Her knees buckled, and Q steadied her and held her upright.

Unable to speak, Mia raised Q by his shoulders, guiding him up her body with grateful kisses. She opened his belt and button-fly, attacking with the precision of a hawk swooping in for its prey. Between their four frantic hands, they worked his jeans and underwear down the firm arcs of his quads and pushed the fabric to where Q was able to kick everything off.

Mia nearly lost her balance once again as their impatient bodies collided. Damp heat gathered between her legs, her freshly awakened desire greedy and demanding. His heavy erection pressed against her hip, and Mia worried she might just swallow him whole.

Instinct took over, which suited Mia fine because all her coherent thoughts were playing hide-and-seek. Q let out a breathy whimper as Mia's hands wrapped around and underneath him and captured what remained of his attention.

He offered no resistance as she shoved him onto the bed and spread him out on his back like a picnic. She feasted on his body, drawing low moans from her willing victim as her mouth glided along bands of muscle and dipped into the delicious hollows in between.

He yelped and hissed as she gnawed on his sensitive nipples, his hands flying into her hair but not pulling her away. In fact, he seemed to relish every single thing she did to him, which only egged her on. She made a game of teasing him, drawing her tongue in wide circles around where he wanted it most, his hips thrusting uselessly into the air.

Q's need was as raw and exciting as her own. She couldn't imagine that the sexual dynamo beneath her had been deprived in any way, but you'd never know it from the way Q was writhing around, begging and moaning and reaching for her.

"Mia, I can't stand it much longer."

Her resolve crumbled. She pressed one last kiss to his lips before taking him in both hands and finally, into her mouth. The noises that man made . . . *holy shit*, he was killing her. With each grunt and flex of his hips, Mia's own desire snowballed. She clenched her thighs together and tried for friction, anything to relieve the tension.

His fingers tightened around her hair and held her exactly where she wanted to be. She consumed him with all five senses. When he tensed, Mia gripped him with renewed enthusiasm. He exploded, and she skimmed the crests of his pleasure right along with him, crashing from one to the next with giddy abandon.

They burrowed under the sheets, taking turns nuzzling and caressing each other. Remarkably, Mia felt him stir again and marveled at her incredibly good fortune in finding such a gifted lover. Q rolled onto his elbows and hovered over Mia, his body stretched taut with desire.

"I need you," he mumbled inside a tender kiss. "Need to be inside you."

"Yes," was all she could manage.

Without being asked, Q produced a condom and made quick work of covering what was easily the finest specimen of manhood Mia had ever seen. She opened for him, and he claimed her. He held the bulk of his weight above her, but Mia—needful of the contact—hooked her hands under his arms and pulled him flush against her body.

Muscles flexed and rolled just beneath the sweaty surface; they rocked together, graceful and efficient. Q only stopped kissing her to tell her, once more, that she was perfect. Their pleasure expanded and multiplied, weaving a spiral of shared ecstasy until finally they lay blissfully exhausted in each other's arms.

Mia pulled her fingers lazily through Q's wavy hair, relishing his soft hum of contentment against her breast. She listened in the quiet afterglow for signs that one of the boys had been awakened by all the noise, and an unspoiled quiet answered. Then, cutting through the dark night, Cupid surprised her yet again.

"I love you, Mia."

20

STATIC

Mia's hand froze, ceasing the hypnotic grazing of fingernails along his scalp. Cupid held still as a statue, but he couldn't stop his heart's wild hammering or the pounding in his ears from the cannon fire of his foolish declaration.

His I-love-you was truer than any words ever uttered, but hadn't Pan warned him about blurting out his feelings? This adjustment was going to take some practice and, apparently, involve pain. How could Cupid be expected to contain this colossal sense of well-being and rightness? How could he not share the news with Mia that she was his destiny?

Her fingers raked through his hair again, and for a moment, he thought it might be okay. Surely, her heart must be on his same frequency, must be vibrating like his—

For the love of Zeus! How could he have forgotten to listen for the echo beat?

Time stopped. Cupid strained against Mia's chest to listen for the almighty buzz. Nothing more extraordinary than the standard *tha-thump, tha-thump.* He shifted, sliding his ear over

Mia's chest in a widening arc around her heartbeat until there was nowhere else to try.

Nothing.

The truth gutted him. Cupid's love, announced or not, had no bearing whatsoever on Mia's heart. Right Love can't grow where it hasn't been planted, any more than a pomegranate can grow from barley seed. Who knew that better than Cupid?

The contents of his stomach tumbled, and he jumped out of bed and raced across the bedroom just in time to spill his dinner into the toilet.

He rested his forehead against the cool, hard seat and sucked in quick gulps of putrid air, nearly bringing on a second bout of vomiting. A terrifying ache rolled in, a bottomless emptiness he'd never known before. As high as his first love had lifted him this morning, he'd plunged that much to the surface and again that far below. His heart felt like five kilos of fresh lamb run through a meat grinder. *So this is a broken heart.*

Releasing his grip on the toilet, he sank to the floor, alone and adrift amid the random sea of black and white tiles. Tartarus had shown itself at last.

"Q? Are you okay? Oh, shit!"

Cupid sensed Mia's warm form behind him, her hands gently lifting his head into her lap, the soft touch of cloth greeting his cheek. Mia had pulled on a shirt, yet another barrier between them.

"Could it be the soup? Maybe you're allergic to soy." She rambled on, blaming herself one ingredient at a time. "I didn't buy organic broth this time. Money's been tight. *Shit.*"

She needed to stop. Her guilt was suffocating them both. "Not . . . the soup."

Mia tensed. Cupid could almost hear his confession replaying in her head. "Oh."

Right.

"I'm sorry," she said, as if that could matter. "You caught me off guard, is all."

While he tried to make sense of her words and formulate a coherent response, a confusing layer of static rolled in around the crushing heartache. He squeezed his eyes shut and listened inward so fiercely he could actually hear the blood whooshing through his body, but it was no use.

"You're a great guy," Mia was saying, "I mean a really, *really* great guy, and there's nothing *not* to love about you." Her apologies were more than he could bear.

Cupid's eyes blinked open to the tortured face of the girl he now knew for certain he could never have. He reached up, tucked a strand of hair behind her ear, and tacked on a brave smile. "Mia."

Her monologue ceased, but the pity in her eyes made his heart ache in a new way. He fumbled out a retraction, aware even as the words left his lips how lame they sounded. "I don't suppose we can pretend I didn't just say that thing I just said?"

Her thighs shifted beneath his neck, and Mia did her best to look anywhere but at Cupid.

Okay, then. Guess not.

Taking a different approach, a *mortal* approach, Cupid dipped his toe into the waters of untruth. "I made a mistake."

Mia's forehead crinkled and tilted. "Oh?"

Cupid could only read curiosity in her response; anything deeper was beyond his reach. "Please don't get me wrong. What just happened was fantastic. Amazing. *Life-affirming.*" Mia giggled. The sound soothed Cupid's frazzled nerves like aloe on a burn.

"Yes, it was lovely," she agreed.

"I think you scrambled my signals."

Mia released a heavy breath, deflating her tensed shoulders. "So, you don't love me?"

Incapable of voicing the words, he simply shook his head. Knee-deep now in his very first lie, Cupid paused to consider why he didn't feel worse about it. The answer was as near as Mia's relief.

She lifted a hand to Cupid's face and traced her fingertip along the edge of his jaw. He became aware of a stirring between his legs that would soon be impossible to conceal.

"For the record, Q, you shorted out my circuits, too."

"Good." His ego answered before his brain had a chance to filter its enthusiasm.

They sat quietly with their thoughts, Mia's nails scritching up and down Cupid's back. "Oh, wow. This tattoo is gorgeous." Her fingers slowed. "Is this Latin?"

"It is." Cupid cringed. Could there have been a worse time to explore Plato's thoughts on love?

"Amor. That's love, right?"

"Yes," he answered, avoiding her eyes and holding his breath. He didn't have the will to make up another half-truth.

Thankfully, she took the hint. "*Anyway*. God, I shouldn't admit this, but it's been so long since I've been with a man, and you were so sweet, and I wouldn't actually mind if we . . ." Her voice trailed off as her gaze drifted down the length of his naked body and halted right *there*.

Now what? This situation had quickly spiraled out of Cupid's control and beyond the boundaries of his understanding. He was capable of pleasuring a woman whose heart didn't vibrate for him. He'd already proven as much with Layla and Rho—and Mia, though he hadn't realized it at the time. The dilemma was whether he *should* have sex with Mia again, knowing his heart was locked onto her coordinates with zero chance for requital.

Through all his pain and confusion, he couldn't find a reasonable scenario where the answer was anything but *no*. No more sleeping with Mia until he understood the parameters of this arrangement and could make sense of this frustrating, indecipherable buzz.

Unfortunately, both his body and the beautiful girl offering herself were flagrantly ignorant of his decision. Feeling suddenly overexposed, Cupid rolled out of Mia's lap and sat cross-legged in front of her, folding his hands with purposeful nonchalance over his midsection.

No sooner had he righted himself than his heartbeat picked up pace. Cupid recognized the mechanics of the terrible motor revving up inside him again, only this time, it was compelling him away from Mia, rather than toward her. "I have to go."

Mia's cheeks colored as Cupid rose and offered her a hand up. "Sure." She acquiesced softly, making Cupid feel even lower. "I get it."

A clipped, humorless chuckle escaped Cupid. Try as she might, Mia couldn't begin to get it. Staring into her warm green eyes, he wanted to explain it all to her—his transgression with Hera, the fall to Earth, Pan, his broken heart—but how could a girl who believed the gods were invented by poets ever appreciate the forces at work here? She'd think his senses had left him, and he might be inclined to agree. His brain raced, but Cupid could not think of a single rational explanation to offer.

I hate you, Mother. The awareness assailed him suddenly, and he gasped aloud.

He'd known the gods to be a vengeful bunch, their judgments sometimes grossly out of proportion to the crime. Neither mortal limitations nor human notions of criminal reform constrained their wrath. But what Cupid couldn't puzzle out was why the Goddess of Love would want to harm Mia. Here was a woman who'd already been brutalized by Love, married to the wrong man and left to raise three boys on her own with limited resources. In fact, Mia seemed to be the exact type of human Aphrodite would champion. Yet Cupid's punishment had ensnared Mia somehow, made her the unwitting victim of divine designs, including feeling rejected now.

The remains of Cupid's heart ripped open, the contents splattering all over the wasted barrel of his chest. He twisted his fingers around Mia's and swept his thumb over her knuckles. "May I call you tomorrow?"

A ray of hope pricked up her eyebrows. "Sure, if you like," she answered.

"Mia," he promised, "I most definitely like."

21

APHRODITE

Aphrodite bolted off her pillow, sodden night-sheath clinging to her skin and pulse pounding against both sides of her skull like twin mallets. Stirred from a deep sleep by the sudden disturbance at his side, Hephaestus forced open a bleary eye.

"Goddess, what is it?"

"The retribution has taken effect." An ancient rocking consumed her. Aphrodite's arms folded over her chest, cradling the baby far outside her reach in space and time.

Her husband wiped the sleep from his eyes and rolled onto his side. "What can I do for you, my beloved?"

"Bring me my gaiascope?" She knew better than to spy, knew her heart wasn't landscaped for punishing her son—that would be his father's area of expertise—but she couldn't override the maternal instinct to watch over Cupid in his time of suffering.

The mattress beside her groaned as Hephaestus pushed himself up with a heavy sigh. Three thousand years of marriage had worn the necessary grooves into his neural pathways; he'd sooner attempt to drag the moon from the night sky than try to dissuade his wife once she'd made up her mind. She barely registered his ungainly body as he limped across their bedroom and retrieved the looking glass from its mahogany stand on her desk. Hephaestus's eyes were soft and resigned as he set the instrument into her outstretched hands and gave her shoulder a gentle squeeze before falling back into bed.

Her fingers molded to the customized indentations in the oil-rubbed bronze handles on either side, lovingly crafted by Hephaestus and presented to her on their eighth wedding anniversary. He'd forged other gaiascopes since—what divine being wouldn't pay a god's ransom for a customized window into the affairs of mortals?—but only Aphrodite's bore the inscription between the thumb rests: *For My Divine Prize*. The endearment seemed as deeply engraved onto her husband's heart as into the metal, as evidenced by his re-etching of the lovely script on the eighth year of every new century.

Like an addict reaching for the opium pipe, Aphrodite set her gaze upon the scope between her white-knuckled fists. An anguished sob sprang from the depths of her long–expired womb, and the rocking began anew. Hephaestus snuggled closer and wrapped his thick hand around her waist.

She wilted into the security of his massive body. "He's hurting, Heph. All these years, I've protected him, but now, my baby knows the pain his arrows can inflict." She shook her head as she wept. "This can never be undone."

"I'm sorry, love." He dropped a tender kiss into the crook of her neck, then cautiously ventured, "That is the point though, is it not?"

Though not handsome by any standards, her husband's auburn-framed, pitted face had done its share of growing on Aphrodite over the years—and foisted as he was upon the beautiful goddess through an arranged marriage, he'd had a great deal of growing on her to do. In the early years of their marriage, Hephaestus had charmed his wife by fully accepting her mischievous son, the offspring of Aphrodite's affair with Ares, none other than his own brother.

Aphrodite had always admired her husband's capacity for forgiveness. Not at first, of course, when he'd forged the chain-link net to catch the naked lovers together for all the pantheon to witness. But once they'd all moved on from the whole debacle, Hephaestus had embraced his role of stepdad with gusto, raising Cupid as his own and nurturing the boy's aptitude for archery. In fact, it was Hephaestus who'd crafted Cupid's first bow and arrows and who had continued to supply him with the unique love-tipped shafts right up to the day of Cupid's unfortunate prank. They'd built enough history by now for Aphrodite to believe her husband was not being cavalier about the boy's discipline.

Aphrodite returned her attention to the ever-compelling one-way window to Earth, its destination directed by her desires and thus delivering her to the open front door of the object of Cupid's adoration.

"Thanks again, Mia, for everything."

Despite Cupid's relaxed grip of Mia's wrists, the anguished ridges at the bridge of his nose were a dead giveaway to the mother who knew him so well. Cupid was anything but relaxed. Tight coils of tension radiating off Cupid's body permeated the thick layer of glass between the two worlds and wrapped their ruthless vines around Aphrodite's heart. As Cupid leaned forward to press his lips to Mia's temple, his eyelids pinched closed. When he pulled back, his lashes glistened with unshed tears.

Aphrodite tossed the scope to the end of the bed. "Cursed be Ares for talking me into this dreadful punishment."

The reassuring arm slinked from her waist. "Yes, well . . ."

Aphrodite fixed Hephaestus with a glower. "I'm really not in the mood, dear husband."

Immediately, his two hands shot up toward the fresco above their bed. "I didn't say it."

"As if words are necessary after all this time."

"Okay, okay." He surrendered, patting an invisible wall in the air between them. "You know you had no choice. Why torture yourself?"

Aphrodite's focus darted toward the gaiascope at her feet. "Cupid is so fragile," she said. Biting back a quivering lip, she asked the unimaginable. "What if he can't take it?"

"You're not giving the boy enough credit."

In the kindest way possible, Hephaestus had uncloaked the goddess's maternal insecurities. Her bravado collapsed in a deluge of tears.

"I know what Ares thinks, that the humiliating caricature of my son as a diapered cherub is all my doing, that I've coddled him and turned him into a mama's boy."

Hephaestus offered her a gentle smile. "To be fair, the boy has willingly assumed the role. Perhaps it's time to snip the umbilical cord and free both mother and son from the cycle of co-dependency?"

"Oh, Heph. Have you been reading *Cosmo* again?"

A hearty laugh escaped him. "The articles are highly instructive."

Aphrodite rolled her eyes. Her husband was a reasonable man, even if inflamed by the occasional blaze of jealousy. His counsel almost always steered her onto the right path, and she suspected his read on this situation was accurate as well.

"My son's punishment is going to be a monumental trial—for all of us."

"Yes, dear, I'm afraid so." Hephaestus gathered Aphrodite

into his brawny arms. While she succumbed to a long-overdue cry, he soothed her with whispered words and loving caresses. When her tears were spent, Hephaestus placed himself between Aphrodite and her troubles as he had time and time again. "Why don't you let me keep watch for now?"

Pulling back from his loosened embrace, she nodded most gratefully. Hephaestus reached across his wife, and while he was stretched over her lap, Aphrodite stroked her fingertips down his furry back. He smiled at her tender gesture as he drew the delicate instrument into his lap. "No peeking, wife," he said, shaking a meaty finger.

Aphrodite circled her arms around her knees, tightly grasping both elbows to ward off temptation. "Ready."

Hephaestus peered through the glass, his pale face darkening with the reflection of Earth's night sky. "Huh."

Was he actively trying to get on her nerves? "*What?*"

"Cupid is driving a car."

"Pan must've taught him."

"Of course." Hephaestus turned to regard his wife. "That must've been quite the reunion."

She hardly needed his reminder of her greatest deceit. She'd squandered two thousand years' worth of opportunities to come clean with her son. Maybe he would have asked to join Pan, maybe not. Perhaps the decision should have been Cupid's to make. It was too late now.

"What was I to do, dear husband? How could I have denied my son if he'd begged to leave, and how could I manage a single day up here without him?"

Hephaestus set his battle-weary frown upon her. "I suppose we're about to find out."

"Pan has probably told him everything by now. My son must hate me." Tears stung her eyes again.

"Cupid will do what needs to be done and find his way back to you."

Aphrodite wanted desperately to share in her husband's optimism, but with the mother-son bond shaken to its foundation, no one could predict how this would end. In addition to reuniting Cupid with his best friend, the planet below offered the potent lures of freedom and novelty, not to mention the double-edged sword called Love.

"I haven't always been the best wife, but I always thought I was a good mother." The crushing burden of all of Aphrodite's parental mistakes and marital infidelities threatened to grind her heart to a fine powder. "What have I taught my son about Love?"

Hephaestus set the gaiascope down and angled his body toward her. "That's what the Worthies are for."

"Yes, but how many must he—?"

"Hush now, my goddess. You know that's entirely up to the boy."

Yes, of course she knew. The whole operation depended on how quickly and thoroughly Cupid learned his lesson.

Hephaestus lifted his hand to cup Aphrodite's chin. "There's only one question for you at this juncture: are you sure about this Mia?"

"Yes," she answered without hesitation. In the matter of Worthies, Aphrodite's confidence did not waver. Cupid would deliver Mia into the arms of her intended and grant her the Right Love she'd missed the first time around. Aphrodite hoped, for all their sakes, Cupid would swiftly realize brooding over the girl would simply waste precious time. The faster he accomplished his mission, the sooner he'd be reinstated on Mount Olympus.

Assuming he didn't pursue a Permanent Descent.

"Aph," Hephaestus said firmly, tipping Aphrodite's chin so she had no choice but to hear him, "how about we let Cupid do what Cupid needs to do, and save our worries until they're necessary?"

Aphrodite swallowed over the lump in her throat and nodded bravely.

PANIC

Step, *clack*. Step, *clack*. Step, *clack*. Pivot.

The trendy flip-flops had grown on Pan over time, though the leather thong between his toes had never quite stopped feeling like a twig lodged in his hoof. He found the lift-and-slap a comforting rhythm for his manic pacing up and down the driveway.

Step, *clack*. Step, *clack*. Check time.

Eighty-four minutes had dragged by since Cupid's distress call, and Mia only lived eight miles away, twenty-two minutes *tops* allowing for traffic, not a factor at 11:41 p.m.—*shit*, 11:43. With a frustrated grunt, Pan chucked his phone from one hand to the other.

Step, *clack*, toss. Step, *clack*, toss.

Pan lifted his eyes to the constellations, hungry for answers the characters in the northern sky wouldn't give up, certainly not the magnificent Cygnus. All summer long blinked the dazzling swan disguise of Zeus, a haunting nightly reminder that even the Queen of Sparta was not off limits if the God of Gods set His mind on seducing her.

The soft purr of the Prius was nearly indistinguishable beneath the roar of night critters, but Pan sniffed out Cupid's scent long before the car rolled into sight. Relief shot through him at seeing his friend intact—at least physically—but Pan's worry had fermented into a terrible brew.

Step, *clack*. Step, *clack*, plant large body in the middle of the driveway, place hands on hips, quell the urge to put fist through friend's face.

The Prius coasted to a stop just inches from Pan's knees. Cupid pushed the button to shut down the engine and collapsed against the seatback, staring straight ahead with vacant eyes.

For fuck's sake! Pan couldn't decide whether he was more pissed at Cupid's radio silence or the fact that he was too god-damn pathetic for Pan to stay pissed at. Either way, it made sense to yank the door open so hard the hinges creaked. The interior light flipped on and momentarily blinded them both.

"Why didn't you answer my calls?"

"I was busy."

Adrenaline pumped hard and fast through Pan's system; his body itched for the fight. Cupid wasn't the first of his gods to go off-grid, but he was easily the most important. Though Pan resisted copping to the sentiment, Cupid was more than one of his wards, even more than his best friend. Take away the novel physical attraction, and Cupid was a brother. Nobody gets a guy's goat like a reckless kid brother.

Pan reached into the car and grabbed two fistfuls of Cupid's shirt. "Ignoring my calls is not an option."

Cupid's head snapped up, the mesmerizing irises almost completely engulfed by rapidly dilating pupils. *Raw animal fear.*

Pan smirked with cruel satisfaction, his protective instincts offering only the narrowest mastery over his baser reflexes. "Good. I finally have your attention."

Cupid regarded him warily, wisely keeping his yap shut.

Pan breathed in and out so hard, he moved the hairs on top of Cupid's head—and what the hell was that rat's nest? "Did Mia do that to you?" Clearly, Pan hadn't given the girl enough credit.

"What?" Cupid asked, thrown off guard by the sudden shift in Pan's tone.

"Why does it look like the Harpies had a rave on your head?"

Cupid's hand flew to his hair, and he poked at the tangled mess with little success. "What's a rave?" he asked, checking himself in the rearview mirror.

Pan huffed out one final, frustrated sigh and unfisted Cupid's shirt. "A rave is an all-night dance party where people go nuts with all kinds of mind-altering substances, and you wake up the next morning with a big smile on your face, but you can't remember why."

"None of that happened," Cupid said with great certainty, climbing out of the car and using the reflection in the window to flatten his hair.

Cupid's innocence struck a chord with Pan; the beast in him receded. As Cupid's reflection kept careful watch, Pan scrubbed his hand through Cupid's hair. "Let's go inside." He led Cupid through the garage and into the mudroom, spinning around at Cupid's groan. "What's wrong?"

"Smells good in here." Cupid's hand had moved to his belly, forming tight circles over his shirt.

"You hungry?"

"Starved." Cupid followed Pan into the kitchen and sat at the counter. "Mia's dinner tasted good, but I think it was mostly water."

Pan chuckled. "I'm not surprised."

"Plus, I lost most of it."

"You yacked on your first date?"

"If that means getting sick, yes," Cupid answered with a frown.

No wonder the dude looked like roadkill. "Man, that's rough. I grilled lamb. Want some?"

"Yes."

"You know," Pan teased, while pulling containers of leftovers out of the refrigerator, "if you'd set your heart on me instead of the skinny yoga instructor, you wouldn't be walking around with an empty stomach right now."

When Cupid didn't respond, Pan glanced across the room at his friend, whose hand had glided upward from his belly and threatened to rub a hole in his shirt right over his left nipple. *Shit.* Not that either of them needed the reminder, but Cupid hadn't set his heart on anyone. Those strings were being jerked around from high above.

Working quickly, Pan pulled a plate from the cupboard and loaded it up with lamb and rice before shoving it into the microwave. "What the hell happened tonight, Q?"

The defeated expression returned to Cupid's face.

Pan leaned forward, elbows propped on the counter. "We'll figure this out. Tell me what you remember."

Cupid's eyes glazed over in a faraway stare. "Things were going so well at first. I drove there, no problem. I gave her the flowers and the wine. I kissed her—"

"Whoa. Details, man. What kind of kiss?"

The trance broken, Cupid hit Pan full-on with his lovestruck baby blues. "The kind worth waiting three thousand years for."

Well, fuck. Pan had been thinking more along the lines of tongue or no tongue. "Okay, you kissed . . ."

"Yes," he said, finding his place in the story once again, "and then Jonah interrupted us."

"Hold up. Who the hell is Jonah?"

"He's her son."

"Mia has a *son?*"

"She has three, but the other two were asleep, so I didn't get to meet them."

"Oh-kay." Not one but *three* kids Mia conveniently failed to mention, and from the way Cupid was skipping over the details, this wasn't even what had ruined his date. "*Then* what?"

"Then we ate dinner and dessert and went into Mia's room, and everything was going really well"—Pan pulled his top lip between his teeth and bit down hard. *Wait for it*—"until I told her I loved her." Cupid's entire expression was transfixed by what could only be described as grace.

Just then, the microwave beeped. Pan swallowed his *I told you so* and the accompanying curses and took advantage of having his back to Cupid while collecting the leftovers and silverware and a napkin. Neither of them needed another emotional display from Pan right now.

"I know, I know," Cupid said. "That was a mistake, but I haven't even gotten to the horrible part."

"Eat," Pan said with admirable cool.

Cupid sliced off a corner of the lamb and brought it to his mouth. "Praise Artemis, this is delicious."

"Artemis. Right." It had been a long damn time since Pan had invoked the goddess of the hunt. "So, the horrible part, you mean the barfing?"

"No." Cupid stopped chewing and frowned at whatever he was remembering. "She wasn't vibrating for me."

Well, *there* was an interesting development. "You didn't please her?"

Cupid rolled his eyes. "Of *course* I pleased her. More than once," he added. "What do you think I am, an animal?"

Pan ignored the cutting reference to his old body. "Then what did you mean by 'vibrating'?"

Cupid set down his utensils and fixed his stare on Pan. "Her heart. There was no return signal."

"Wait, what? I thought you were hers and she was yours and all that happy hooey. Isn't that the whole point of your satellite system?"

"That's just it, Pan. I don't know the point."

Pan had to admit to feeling more than a little confused. Physical labors he understood. *Hold the sky. Muck the stables.* This esoteric mumbo jumbo about heartbeats and vibrations was above Pan's pay grade.

"Is your heart still pulling you around like at the gym?"

"Not right now," Cupid answered.

"Then, why do you keep rubbing your chest?"

"Because it feels like a python is coiled around my heart and choking the life out of me."

"Oh." *Oh, fuck* would have been more appropriate. Pan recognized that ache though it had been several years since love had so thoroughly fucked him over. "When did this new problem start?"

"The moment I realized Mia could never be mine."

Pan had to hand it to the gods; they'd really done it this time. Of all the tortures Pan had witnessed through the centuries, unrequited love remained their most diabolical.

What really chilled Pan to the bone was that Cupid still walked the earth. Punishment dealt, why hadn't Cupid ascended to the Mount to languish forevermore over his never-to-be love? That he was still here could not be good for any of them.

"Hang on." Pan paced along the wood floor behind the kitchen counter. "Mia didn't vibrate tonight, but sometimes it takes a while for love to grow, right?"

"Wrong. It might take a while for love to blossom, but if it's Right Love, the echo beats are present from the beginning." Cupid sighed heavily and set down the bone he'd been gnawing.

"From the beginning? Like, the very, very beginning?" Pan was catching on now, a giant boulder rolling downhill and gaining momentum. "So, at the gym, when you were talking to her before class . . .?"

Cupid's hand balled into a tight fist and banged hard against his chest. "Yes, if I hadn't been so thoroughly distracted, I might have noticed before class"—another bang—"after class"—and a third—"and after dinner, before we . . ." He crumpled to the counter with a moan, dropping his forehead into the cradle of his folded arms.

"That's when you called me, after you realized you couldn't have her?"

"Yes," Cupid answered. "Is there dessert?"

Pan slid a tin of brownies along the counter. "So you fucked her, your heart broke, you barfed, and then you drove back here?"

Cupid lifted his head and leveled Pan with a glare. "You might want to work on your empathy."

It wasn't the first time Pan had been accused of skipping the niceties. Pretty words and validations only wasted valuable time. Pan had a job to do.

"There must be something you haven't told me."

"Yes," Cupid answered, transferring three brownies to his plate and licking the crumbs off his fingers. "The part where I turned my car around four separate times and drove back to her street because even though that GPS inside me wanted to drag me here, my heart nearly ripped from my chest when I tried to drive away from Mia." Cupid shoved a brownie into his mouth, chewed for several seconds without registering an ounce of pleasure, and swallowed. "The part where I sat in front of Mia's house and begged my mother to release me from this torture."

"You did make it back here in one piece," Pan observed. "Maybe Aphrodite answered your plea."

"She didn't."

Pan snagged the metal tin with his pinkie, wrenched free a large brownie, and chewed thoughtfully. "Come on," he said. "Let's work this out."

Cupid followed Pan to the great room and sank into the couch with a loud sigh. Pan plunked down in the recliner across from him and slammed his back against the seat to pop out the footrest. "All right. Aphrodite told you to follow your heart, which led you straight to Mia. You're in love with her, but she's not in love with you, and that's not going to change."

"Apparently not," Cupid responded, narrowing his eyes at Pan.

"And now, this compulsion has driven you back to me but this time with a broken heart."

"Right again," Cupid said, his voice laced with sarcasm. "I thought you were good at this."

"I am. Yours is a puzzling case. Let me think." Pan's hand brushed along his beard. "Hmm. You love Mia, but she doesn't love you."

"Seriously, Pan, if you say that one more time, I swear I'm going to—"

"Hang on; I think I'm onto something. It doesn't seem to be *your* heart's desire that matters."

"Obviously."

"So maybe you are meant to make things right for Mia." Pan delivered his insight with a surge of enthusiasm Cupid did not share.

"I'm meant to help Mia find love—with someone else?"

Pan shrugged. "Got a better idea?"

"I have a million better ideas."

Pan waited silently while Cupid swallowed the bitter pill of his true punishment.

"Well, I guess this is good news for Mia, at least. Mother has chosen her to be a Worthy." Despite his devastation, Cupid managed a genuine smile for Mia. *Poor fucker.*

"Q?"

Cupid's attention snapped back to Pan. "Yeah?"

"You okay?"

"What if I say no?"

This situation was likely to get a whole lot worse before it started getting better, though "better" might well be the last emotion Cupid would feel once he finished the job. Pan shrugged, his frown providing the whole, sorry answer.

"Yeah, that's what I thought," Cupid said sadly.

"Hey," Pan said, "at least we're in this together." Easy enough to say when it was Cupid's heart getting ripped apart.

Cupid took a long, hard look at Pan, then sighed again. "Well, it's not as if I don't know how to do this. How many hundreds of thousands of times have I brought two intendeds together? All I have to do is find Mia's Right Love and pierce his heart with one of my—" Cupid reached over his shoulder and stopped cold. "*Right.*"

"Easy, buddy," Pan said, shoving the footrest against the chair and scooting forward in his seat. Cupid wasn't looking so good. "You gonna hurl again?"

Cupid sucked in a deep breath. "I can do this," he mumbled. "I am the God of Love. I can do this."

Pan gave him an encouraging nod. "There ya go."

"I'll talk to her."

"Good," said Pan, relieved to see Cupid gaining back his confidence and some of the color in his cheeks.

"I'll just tell the girl who believes our world was invented by poets to trust *me*, the self-proclaimed God of Love, to find her Right Love." His voice died on a strangled whimper.

Oh. Not good, then.

Cupid turned and met Pan's gaze with an anguished expression that sent a chill down his spine. Pan couldn't remember the last time he'd seen anyone, man or god, look so utterly lost.

"Pan?"

"Yeah, buddy?"

"How in the cosmos am I going to do this?"

23

MELONS

Cupid woke to an urgent beating in his chest. The gods were not going to sit around and wait. The pulsating only subsided when Pan convinced him to catch Mia's first class of the day.

"In the meantime," Pan said, "you and I are going grocery shopping, so put these baggy shorts on over those ass huggers, or I'll never get you through the market in one piece."

"I'm *really* not looking for that kind of companionship right now." Cupid's response drew a dark chuckle from Pan.

"*Pfft.* As if anyone will care."

"Seriously, Pan? We're going food shopping. How sexy can that be?"

Pan clapped a hand on Cupid's back and led him to the garage. "I can't explain it, but women go nuts when they see a man in the grocery store. The more helpless you are, the crazier it makes them."

"I really do have a lot to learn about Earth girls."

Pan let out a snort as he folded his body into the driver's seat. "For a guy who has no clue, I'd say you're doing fine."

"Not with the one who really matters." Cupid gave his chest a firm rub that did nothing to ease his desolation.

"To be fair, it's not that Mia didn't *want* you, right?"

The memory of their heated, joined bodies assaulted Cupid, topped off by Mia's half-embarrassed offer for another round. "She definitely wanted me."

"Well, there ya go," Pan said. "Your record is untarnished. I mean, you can't help it if the gods are playing hot potato with your heart. At least you don't have to worry you've lost your touch."

"Ha! Anything but."

Pan shook his head. "You're making me want to bash your teeth in again."

"Is it my fault this equipment they gave me is epic?"

"Dude, I do not want to hear about your pecker. That is seriously not cool."

"Then I won't tell you my recovery time is practically zero."

"You're lucky I'm driving right now, you little shit. I might still deck you when we get to the store." Pan appeared to be deep in thought over the issue.

Cupid wasn't trying to irritate him; it just happened. He folded his arms over his chest, shifted his body toward the door, and absently watched the scenery pass by. Their truck veered sharply to the left and careened into a parking space near the store entrance.

Pan stuffed the key into his pocket. "If we're done discussing your dick now, perhaps we can go inside?" He didn't wait for an answer.

Cupid scrambled out of the truck and followed him through a door that opened on its own into the brightly lit market. "Great Zeus!" Cupid exclaimed, stopping dead in his tracks as his gaze skittered across colorful pyramids of ripe fruits overflowing their display tables. "Where are the orchards that produce all these crops?"

Pan appeared by his side with a large metal cart on wheels. "Come on," Pan said, nudging Cupid forward with his elbow. "I'll explain as we go. Otherwise, you're never going to make it to Mia's class. You still like pomegranates?"

"Yes, I do." Cupid turned just in time to catch the red globe flying toward his head. On the other end of the toss stood the playful Pan of Cupid's childhood, a wide grin on his face. He never could stay angry with Cupid for long.

Much relieved, Cupid palmed the nearest object—a ropy, greenish-white ball that barely fit in his hand—and picked up the name from the nearby sign. "How about you? Are you a fan of the cantaloupe?" With a powerful thrust that surprised both of them, Cupid hurled the heavy fruit at his friend's belly.

"Whoa there." Pan chuckled, easily catching the melon. "You're gonna get our asses thrown out of here."

"Yes, they tend to frown upon food fights in the produce department."

Cupid turned to find a woman dressed in a very short, white skirt swishing across her bottom as she pushed her cart along past him. *Want* was a reflex he couldn't control, but there was nothing to it beyond the physical urge.

"What a shame," Cupid replied. "So many colorful globes just waiting to be flung." He waited a tick for the woman to realize she was smitten, not that he planned to do anything about it.

Without so much as a glance in Cupid's direction, the woman wheeled her basket straight toward Pan and gave him a bright smile. "Nice catch."

"Huh?" Pan held his pose, melon raised in one hand and confusion etched into his forehead. He glanced at Cupid, who could only shrug his shoulders.

The girl giggled too high and too loud. "I said, 'Nice catch.' You have great hands."

Pan's nose twitched. He too had caught the scent. "Uh . . . thanks."

"You look like you could use some help with the melons," she said, throwing back her shoulders so her bosoms filled Pan's view.

Pan's gaze locked on the offerings for longer than Cupid felt was appropriate, but the woman seemed more hopeful than put off. When Pan finally snapped out of his bosom stupor, he cleared his throat and dropped the cantaloupe into his cart. "My *friend* and I are doing fine, but thank you." Pan gestured to Cupid, but the girl's attention could not be coaxed away.

Unused to being ignored since his fall to Earth, Cupid concluded she must be playing that hard-to-get game. Testing his theory, Cupid scurried to Pan's side. "Actually, I was curious how you know which fruits are ripe."

The woman smiled and sidled even nearer to Pan, whose eyes closed for a split second while he drew in a deep whiff of her. "It's easy," she answered, flapping her eyelids at Pan as if he'd posed the question. "You just need to know where to squeeze."

Pan gave Cupid a what's-a-guy-to-do smirk before closing his hand around the girl's bare upper arm. His voice sounded gooey and weird. "That's never really been a problem for me."

"I can believe that." A sigh fluttered out of her pretty mouth. *She's not faking. It's Pan she wants.*

Exactly why she'd chosen Pan over Cupid was a question for another time. Right now, the only question was what Pan intended to do about it. Cupid didn't need to check Pan's shorts to know his friend had hoisted an erection to rival his own; their musk settled over the fruits and vegetables like a shearling blanket. The least Cupid could do was make himself scarce.

"If you two will excuse me," Cupid said, grabbing the handle of the metal cart and spinning away from the two of them.

"Hang on." Pan yanked him back by his collar and pinned him in place with a fierce glower. Cupid slipped a finger inside his neckline, glaring at Pan until he released his powerful grip. The two men traded scowls until Pan muttered, "Gimme a damn second, will you?" under his breath.

Gooey Pan resurfaced, setting his hands on the girl's shoulders. "I'm afraid we're in a bit of a hurry this morning, or I would absolutely take you up on the melon-squeezing lessons."

"Oh." Rejection jarred her out of her trance. "Maybe another time, then? I'm here just about every day after tennis."

"Sure," Pan answered, and Cupid read the longing all over Pan's face as the woman slipped through his fingers.

The two friends gawked at the pleated skirt swinging against the back of the muscular thighs. *Swish, swish, swish, swish.* Pan snapped out of it first, slapping Cupid on the back and pushing their cart toward a row of green vegetables. "Look at all the damn lettuce choices they have down here. Is it not ridiculous?" Pan plucked a bag of lettuce off the shelf.

"Pan, what just happened?"

"You don't want kale? I'm flexible. How do you feel about arugula?"

Cupid grabbed Pan's wrist. "That woman completely ignored me."

"Yeah," said Pan with a weary sigh, "sure seemed that way."

"What do you make of it?"

"A sample of one doesn't necessarily prove anything."

"Is it just one?" Cupid had raised their least favorite topic again, but he had to know if Pan still wanted him.

Pan's forehead squinched as he worked out what Cupid was asking. "Come to think of it, the urge to jump your bones is more of a pleasant buzz than a burning need."

"Oh." The sample size had just doubled.

"Maybe I'm just getting acclimated." Pan offered a hopeful but unconvincing shrug.

"Maybe."

"Hey, with or without erotic superpowers, you are easily the hottest guy walking this planet." Pan squeezed Cupid's shoulder and gave him a reassuring smile. "I'd still do you in a heartbeat."

Cupid half-smiled back. It was something, at least.

"But," Pan continued, "it doesn't seem like you'll be having any more of those little morsels you've been feasting on since you got here."

He'd suspected as much, but hearing Pan confirm his suspicions still set Cupid's teeth on edge. "Forever?" Maybe he didn't hunger for anyone besides Mia right now, but if he couldn't have her, and nobody else would ever want him, the idea of eternity stretched ahead of him like a cold, dark tunnel leading straight back to his miserable past—with the notable difference being he now knew what he was missing.

"Whoa. We don't know that yet," Pan said. "Let's not get ahead of ourselves here."

While not exactly reassured, Cupid at least appreciated the solidarity. Pan "had his back," as they were fond of saying down here, though Pan's gaze had drifted down Cupid's front and caught on the conspicuous hump punching through his baggy shorts like a large fist forced into a small mitten.

"You seem to have a situation there."

"I'm really not in the mood, Pan."

"Your heart might not be in the mood, but your dick sure as hell is."

"It'll go away."

Pan's eyebrows shot up. "Need I remind you, you're about to show up for Mia's class, wearing nothing but a pair of skimpy shorts over that thing?"

"What would you suggest I do about it?"

"I suggest you take care of it."

"*Myself?*"

"Sorry, I didn't realize you needed detailed instructions." Grabbing a zucchini from the display to his right, Pan stepped in close to Cupid. "Observe." Pan curled his hand around the zucchini and pumped his fist up and down along the poor vegetable, waggling his eyebrows at Cupid all the while.

"Thanks, but I don't think I'll ever forget how to do that."

"I should certainly hope not. Now, go on and make it quick."

Taking himself in hand in the grocery store washroom was about the most unromantic encounter Cupid could have imagined, but he couldn't argue with the economy. Fifteen minutes later, however, a massively frustrated Cupid scuffled out of the bathroom to find Pan pacing by the exit, plastic bags hanging off his arms.

"'Bout time!" Pan huffed his way through the automatic door. "You sure picked a shit time to draw it out."

"I didn't draw it out, Pan. I couldn't . . ."

Pan spun around so quickly, the bags crashed together against his side. "*What?*"

Cupid held his hands up so Pan could see the problem. And there it was—still.

"Motherfucker," said Pan.

SHOWING UP

Q didn't simply enter the studio; he redefined the space. Mia's godlike lover with the iridescent eyes and sweet, guileless smile was *here* in the glorious flesh, and no, her memory hadn't embellished a single detail. Mia's cheeks heated as snippets from last night replayed like a porno across her mind. If not for the premature release of those three little words and his awkward retraction, it would've been the perfect date.

Damn him, a little bit, for putting the cart a mile before the horse. Mia was nowhere near ready to ask herself those questions about someone she'd just met, but that didn't mean she had to push this guy away over a postorgasmic blurt, did it?

"Hey. I thought showing up might be better than calling. I know I'm a little early for class. Is this okay?" Showing up was already light years ahead of the last guy who looked at her like that. This one seemed almost too good to be true—childlike, yet somehow trustworthy.

"Sure. You ready to work?" Mia felt her lower lip slide behind her teeth and knew she was flirting but couldn't resist the pull.

He let go of a shaky breath and nodded. "Yep, and I brought water this time."

"Quick learner," she answered. "Did you bring your friend?"

Q's easy smile flattened into a straight line. "Don't tell me *you* want Pan too?"

"Want?" Mia shrugged. "Just to say hello."

"Oh." He sighed again and seemed to be working something out in his head. Q took a tentative step forward, and Mia's body answered with an all-over tingle that defied the heat and raised goose bumps all across her flesh. "No, Pan's not here. You're stuck with me, I guess."

Those crazy-sexy eyes of his flashed at the husky gasp that escaped her. Lucky for Mia, Q couldn't see the twinge between her legs. "Eh. I suppose I'll deal."

Q grinned full-on, and Mia's cheeks filled with her smile. That dizzy, weak-kneed, swoony thing was happening again.

"Is it okay if I kiss you?" His question was more foreplay than request; his lips were already moving closer even as his whisper caressed her.

Mia nodded, wondering if she needed to add, *Yes, but you better hold me upright while you do.*

Q's pretty mouth closed over hers, blotting out such mundane considerations as gravity and balance; luckily his arm tightened around her waist just in time. Mia jumped when the cold bottle hit the small of her back. They broke apart with laughter and apologies.

"Sorry, I forgot I was holding that," he said.

"*I'm* sorry. I think I bit your tongue."

"Don't worry about it." Q rolled the injury around in his mouth, still breathing heavily while he assessed the damage. "I'm a quick healer," he added.

"I certainly hope so. You might be needing your tongue again soon."

Q's eyes popped open wide.

Whoops. Forward much, Mia? "Lunch. It's nearly lunchtime."

"Ahh, so *that's* the hunger growing inside me?"

Do not look down. Do not look down. Okay, no lower than his belly. Oh, holy hell, there it is. Her gaze locked so very inappropriately on his tightly contained erection, but she was powerless to stop herself. *What the hell is it about this guy?*

The studio door opened with a whoosh, and one of her regulars skated inside. "Morning, Darren," she called out.

"Hey, hot stuff."

Q's eyebrows banged together with a serious *back-off* glare aimed at Darren. Mia had to admit, the possessive flare-up felt kind of nice, even if Darren's endearment was completely innocent.

She pushed her fingers into the spaces between Q's and squeezed his hand. "Maybe we should continue this conversation later?"

"Sure. Can I take you to lunch after class? I know this deli with a great pastrami sandwich. Come to think of it, that might not be the best idea—"

"Thanks for the offer, but I have a hot date with my three guys."

"*Three?*" Unibrow was back.

"Easy there, killer. You're welcome to join us if you'd like," she added. "My sons are in the day care. I have a picnic blanket and PB&J in my car. I'm gonna be sweaty and gross. You game?" Truth be told, Jonah had already asked when he could see Q again.

"Sounds perfect."

Mia searched his face for signs of sarcasm but found only the eager frankness she'd come to expect. "Better stick close to me again—so I can keep my eye on your form."

He played along with a solemn nod. "For safety's sake."

"Oh, absolutely. Go get a mat," she said, tipping her chin toward the closet.

Q's gaze fell to their joined hands. He brushed his thumb across her knuckles and back again, sighed heavily, and released her fingers as if it were the hardest work he'd done in years.

Mia considered herself a pro—the locals had voted her a "Best of Tarra" three years running—but the next ninety minutes, she struggled to remember the other twenty-four people in the studio. Q had a way of muting everything and everyone else in his presence. Mia slid her limbs and torso effortlessly from one pose into the next, loosened by the heat and inspired by Q's vigilant watch, which he made no effort whatsoever to hide.

Only his sun-and-moon pose gave her true cause to lay hands on him, but Mia invented enough reasons to remind herself exactly how tight and flexible that body of his was. Mia's final meditation was alarmingly unpure, and the blush accompanying her "Namaste" surely gave everything away, not that Q's hooded gaze was any more chaste.

He waited for her near the door, chugging down the rest of his water while Mia closed up shop. "Ready?" he asked.

"Yeah, I'm just gonna freshen up. Meet you back here in a few?"

"Freshen up? You promised me sweaty and gross and something called PB&J."

"You've never had a peanut butter and jelly sandwich?" Where on earth had this guy spent his childhood?

"Nope, but I can't wait to try it—if you have enough. I wouldn't want to take food out of your kids' mouths."

"Tell you what," she answered, "I'll split mine with you, and we'll make up the difference at dinner." *Yeah, you just did that, and without a sitter again.* Another date with Q at home with the kids . . . and her bed.

"Dinner?" A smile teased his cheeks but couldn't quite make itself at home.

Might he have been mulling over the whole single mom situation? *Fantastic.* Now, Mia had scared the guy away from a simple lunch by hitching a trailer to the picnic blanket.

"Hey, never mind about—"

"You have yourself a deal, Mia."

25

THREESOME

"Q!" Jonah dodged his mother's outstretched arms, his entire being bursting from captivity like confetti shot from a cannon. Cupid barely had time to shield his crotch before the boy crashed into his knees and wrapped his arms tight around Cupid's sweaty thighs.

"Hey, buddy. Good to see you too," Cupid said, bubbling over with laughter and ruffling the boy's hair.

"Mommy said we might not see you again, but here you are."

Cupid's mirth died under the crushing weight of his predicament. Searching frantically for the proper response, he located Mia across the room as she bent to hoist the toddler into her arms.

Dropping to his knees, Cupid wrapped his arms around Jonah. "Of course I am. I couldn't stay away from you guys." If Jonah only knew how much truth that statement held. "Are you taking good care of your invisible arrow?"

"Mmhmm," Jonah hummed against Cupid's chest. "Will you tuck me in tonight?"

"That's up to your mother."

"What's up to me?" The baby's stroller rolled to a halt.

Cupid cleared the frog from his throat and peeled Jonah off his sweaty chest. "Uh, Jonah was just asking if I could tuck him in tonight."

Mia set her hand on her oldest son's shoulder, sandwiching the boy between Cupid and herself. "We'll see," she answered.

Jonah's face lit up again, and he leaned in and cupped his tiny hands around Cupid's ear. "That means yes." Jonah's too-loud whisper spilled warm, moist air all over the shell of Cupid's ear, and Cupid couldn't help but giggle.

Scooping up Jonah, Cupid stood to meet Mia's eye roll head on. The toddler in Mia's arms glared at Cupid. "Well, hello there, little guy. You've got your mother's pretty green eyes."

The boy whipped his head around and buried his face in Mia's bosom.

"And this would be Eli," Mia said with a smirk.

"He's only shy at first," Jonah said.

"Oh yeah?" Cupid and Mia shared a grin. "How about Lucas? Is he shy too?"

"Lukie doesn't talk. He's just a baby."

"Ahhh, *right*." Damn, Cupid was falling for sweet, earnest Jonah, so very eager to please.

"Let's go, J-man. Mommy's got your favorite, PB&J."

"Can Q come too, Mommy?" Jonah asked, digging his fingers into Cupid's shoulder.

"Of course I'm coming," Cupid answered, taking off toward the exit with a sudden sprint that left Jonah clutching him even tighter and trailing his breathless, deep-throated trill all the way to the patch of grass where he'd helped Mia set up their picnic. Greedy for more of Jonah's giggles, Cupid grabbed the boy's hands and twirled him around in tight circles until Jonah's body stretched out from Cupid's extended arms like a wood plank slicing a neat disc through the sky. Mia and the little ones caught up just as Cupid and Jonah collapsed onto the blanket in a pile of dizzy laughter and weary limbs.

"I flied, Mommy! Didn't I, Q?"

After a knee-jerk moment of grief over his own lost wings, Cupid nodded. "You sure did, Jonah."

With Eli still clutching Mia for all he was worth, she sank down next to them, shaking her head and grinning. "Honestly, I don't know which of you is the bigger kid."

Cupid popped up onto his elbows. "That would be me, or have you forgotten my size already?" He waggled his eyebrows, drawing, "Oh brother," and a deep blush from Mia.

Whatever strange force had overtaken the woman at the food market earlier, Mia's desire for Cupid had clearly not diminished. Nor had his, er, situation, which had progressed well past irritating and into downright painful. Even the heat and exertion of yoga had not stemmed the tide of Cupid's unrelenting arousal. While the prospect of infinite staying power intrigued him somewhat, he couldn't bear to imagine how long he might be afflicted with this new torture. For the first time, Cupid genuinely empathized with Priapus, whose permanent, colossal yet useless erection served as a living reminder that no body part is exempt from divine "justice." Poor Priapus had simply been the wrong fetus of the wrong seed in the wrong womb, although in typical Olympian fashion, it was unclear whose womb and whose seed, only that Hera had inflicted the curse because Aphrodite's beauty eclipsed her own.

"Joe, why don't you show Q how you help Mommy with Eli so I can feed the baby?"

"Okay." Jonah walked on his knees across the blanket to the picnic basket. "Here's what you do, Q. First, you take off this straw." He demonstrated pushing the sharp end of the straw through the wrapper. "Now poke it through here," Jonah said, puncturing the silver circle in the juice box, "and then you hand it to Eli."

Eli snatched the juice box out of Jonah's hands and shot Cupid a suspicious glare while gnawing on the tip of the straw.

"And then, you find his *samwedge*"— Jonah dug deeper into the basket and pulled out a plastic bag containing bite-size piec- es—"and you open it up."

"Can I do that for him, Jonah?" Cupid asked, figuring the surest way to win Eli's heart was by filling his belly. It usually worked on Cupid anyway.

"Sure." Jonah handed Cupid the bag.

Eli's eyes narrowed. He flung out his hand and yelled, "Me!"

"Here you go, buddy," Cupid soothed. "I'm opening it for you."

"*Nnnn.*" Eli kicked the bag out of Cupid's hand.

Mia cupped Eli's chin in her hand and swept her thumb across the tiny dimple. "Eli! Is that any way to treat our new friend?"

Cupid backed away from the toddler. "It's okay, Mia." *Give the boy time,* he wanted to say, but Cupid had no idea whether winning over the boy was included in the gods' plan, and the last thing Cupid wanted to do was give anyone, including him- self, false hope.

"Here you go, Mommy. For Lukie." Jonah handed his mother two plastic boxes and a spoon with a soft white tip.

"Thank you, sweetie." She unstrapped the baby from his stroller and pulled him into her lap. "You hungry, Lukie? Mom- my's got some nice, mashed carrots for you. Num, num, num." The adoring expressions shared by mother and son mesmerized Cupid as Mia dipped the spoon into the bright orange mush and delivered it to the baby's mouth. "'Zat good? Mmhmm."

"Uh-oh." Jonah had dug through the basket once again, pulled out the two remaining sandwiches, and worked out the math.

"It's okay, bug. You take one and give the other to Q. I'll just have some grapes when I'm done feeding Lucas."

Cupid took the sandwich and thanked Jonah. "We're splitting, remember? We both need our energy for your next class." Pinching the soft bread in the middle, Cupid tore the sandwich in half and stretched his tongue to catch the filling before it oozed out onto the blanket. "Mmm, sweet and salty. I'll have to tell Pan about this."

Mia's gaze flitted over to Cupid. "We *both* need our energy?"

"Yes," he answered, trying but failing to keep the smug grin off his face, "you're not getting rid of me so easily this time."

No, the gods will take care of that when the time comes.

Mia went on about the business of feeding the baby, but Cupid saw a smile creep into the corners of her mouth and knew he had pleased her. He scooted around Mia's out-stretched legs, inching close enough to extend the sandwich to her lips. Mia bit off a small piece, turning a lust-filled gaze on Cupid as she licked the dollop of peanut butter off the side of her smile.

Cupid nearly forgot himself and the gods surely watching from above, nearly forgot Jonah and Eli and Lucas, not to mention all the passersby on their way in and out of the gym. He wanted so desperately to kiss her, to taste the nut-and-fruit mixture on her tongue, to trace a trail down her throat with his lips, to fill his hands with her flesh, and to use this awful curse set upon his manhood to bring Mia pleasure.

If only his longing ended right there, but it didn't. Cupid couldn't escape the thick, woody vines of a new, even more impossible desire wrapping its tendrils around his beleaguered heart: the yearning to be a part of this perfect scene of domestic bliss with Mia and her little family. How quickly his love for Mia had spread to encompass all four of them. Worse, he had every indication she was feeling exactly the same, minus the all-important beat.

A cool, wet sensation met Cupid's thigh and seeped inside his shorts.

"Eli, naughty! Mommy, Eli spilled."

Their two heads swiveled around to find Eli unapologetically squeezing out the contents of his juice box all over Cupid's lap. In the chaos that followed—the mad rush for napkins, the extraction of the juice box from Eli's grasp, the cries of the hungry baby demanding the rest of his lunch, the scolding, and the tears—Cupid could only imagine how bereft he would be when Mia's Right Love stole his spot in the family circle.

26

WILD THING

Though experience had taught Pan that the gods' little surprises were rarely pleasant, he did enjoy the occasional windfall as a reward for extraordinary services rendered: VIP tickets to Springsteen, a well-timed tip on Apple stock, a bottle of wine from Dionysus's cellar. No bonus he'd earned in the past, however, could compare to the embarrassment of riches Pan was enjoying since Cupid's fall. By far the best of these gifts was the transfer of Cupid's supernatural sex appeal. Smart enough to recognize a sweet deal when it kissed him in the groin, Pan intended to do everything in his power to stay in the Divine Council's favor.

Job number one: concierging.

With only one fallen to keep track of at the moment and Cupid presumably where he was supposed to be, there wasn't anything for Pan to do but keep himself entertained until needed again, not even a mild challenge for an irresistible demigod with a boundless sex drive.

Job number two: flying under the radar. Unflaunted benevolence had a better chance of lingering.

The gods who'd raised Pan were hardly paradigms of discretion. True to his heritage, in his earliest years on earth, Pan had eagerly hopped from bed to bed—with many a floor and back alley in between—enjoying every possible permutation of pleasure afforded by his human form. He hadn't bothered discriminating between genders or even the shades of gray coloring the range from male to female. If he felt an urge, he went after it, and with his confidence and otherworldly gifts, he usually enjoyed success.

Generally speaking, humans practiced a bit more restraint. Yes, pregnancy and diseases were powerful deterrents, but Pan had come to believe that the bigger motivator was morality, an inner voice either absent or ignored by the gods. Olympian family trees were messy organisms with branches extending every possible direction. Like a jagged stone tossed into a mighty ocean, Pan had softened around the edges, gradually taking on the luster of the other stones around him. His frantic pace eased. He applied a more discriminating, more human standard to choosing his partners. The gods watching from above lost interest, and that suited Pan just fine.

Surely, he was under close scrutiny now. This was no time for pushing boundaries. Better to stick with a known quantity.

He fired off a text to Cheri: *Up for a walk on the wild side?*

Fairly confident of her response, Pan stepped into the shower and took extra care with the trimmer, anticipation for the night ahead blooming into a throbbing he had no reason to ignore. Pan closed his eyes and slid his palm down his chest. As he wrapped a slick hand around his erection, he grinned at the memory of the zucchini demo. Truth be told, Pan had been semihard ever since—not from the melon lady, but from the thought of his friend jerking off in the men's room. *Poor Cupid,* Pan lamented, but his cock twitched without conscience.

Refocus.

Grocery store blondie. Thighs, tits. Cheri. Cupid. Blondie. Tits. Cheri. Cupid. The merry-go-round of desire spun out of control, and Pan exploded with a bright burst that left him panting against the tile wall. Reaching for his towel, Pan shook his head and chuckled to himself. *Yeah, I should probably sort that out at some point.*

Then again, Cupid would accomplish his task soon, return to Mount O, and put Pan out of his misery. Problem was, that eventuality grew more depressing as time passed. This unexpected reunion with his old bestie and the chance to clear his conscience of the ancient lie were the best gifts Pan had received in centuries. He couldn't even think about losing Cupid a second time.

Pan stepped in front of the sink and reached for his aftershave but thought better of it. The gods had blessed him with erotic omnipotence; who was he to tinker with body chemistry?

Scrolling through his messages, Pan smiled at Cheri's reply: *Rawr! All yours after work.* She'd have to finish her shift, but Pan's work was done, and he wasn't a devotee of delayed gratification. He hopped into his truck and headed to The Stagecoach.

The air around him buzzed with erotic energy as the restaurant patrons took note of his entrance. Bodies moved closer; eyes locked on the target. Unspoken offers filled the air.

Bless you for these gifts, gods of the Mount, however mysterious and fleeting they may be.

From her post behind the bar, Cheri turned toward Pan's approach. He advanced with the slow, confident swagger of a man who knew he could have any woman in the restaurant and most definitely the one he'd reserved in advance. The scent wafting up Pan's nose told him many of the men were interested too, including several who were very likely mystified right now at their attraction.

The memory of Pan's last time with a man still resonated vividly, though his affair with Pablo had ended long before leaving New York—wow, was it twelve years ago? *Ahhh, Pablo.* An exotic delicacy, that one, with his chiseled cheekbones and eyes the color of a forest bed after a long rain. Graceful and intense, Pablo had moved like a panther on the prowl, and Pan had never quite known when he might leap. At first, the not-knowing was exhilarating, but eventually, Pan found it all exhausting. Pablo was a jealous lover, and Pan enjoyed a varied palate; the end wasn't pretty. Pan hadn't dwelled on it, but he hadn't pursued an attraction to another man since. It's not that men failed to whet Pan's appetite; he simply limited his diet to what was easier for his system to digest.

Hard and wanting from the desire flying at him from all sides, Pan only had eyes for one girl. The god of the wild was by no means a slouch, especially now that the lumbersexual vibe was all the rage, but Pan knew his limitations. Sooner or later, when the gods were done toying with him, his newfound animal magnetism would be returned to Cupid or revoked altogether. When the dust cleared, Cheri would be the girl topping off his mug, and Pan was not about to mess that up.

Pan settled onto a stool at the bar, and Cheri rushed over to take his order. A simple scotch, neat, would've satisfied him, but Pan ordered a sidecar for the sole pleasure of watching Cheri squeeze the lemon and strain the drink. She was agitated. Their careful equilibrium had tipped, and now Cheri was trying too hard, sticking too close to Pan's little slice of the bar. Pan leaned forward, trapping her hands beneath his and murmuring toward her ear, "Relax, babe. I came for you, and I'm leaving with you."

Cheri nodded and took him at his word. After that, the evening went easier for both of them. Pan tucked into a veal chop and a few more drinks, absorbing the sexual energy like a giant, contented sponge, and Cheri served her customers with impressive accuracy. At the end of her shift, Cheri claimed her prize, strolling out of the restaurant under Pan's arm to the audible disappointment of the envious crowd.

They barely made it to the front seat of the truck before Cheri's head landed in Pan's lap. Running his fingers through her shoulder-length brown hair, he chuckled at her contented purr. "Gimme a second, tiger. Let me get you away from your place of employment."

Pan maneuvered out of the parking space and onto the main road with Cheri's cheek bouncing on his thigh. The moment the truck shifted into cruising gear, he unbuttoned her shirt. Her flesh pebbled with goose bumps as he pushed his hand inside her bra, and she answered with a lusty moan. He shifted and squirmed and shoved the seat belt lower in his lap. If he got any harder, his dick would be steering the truck.

Cheri rolled onto her belly, unzipped Pan's jeans, and inched his boxers down. "I've been wanting to do this since you walked into the restaurant tonight," she confessed. He liked her idea very much. In fact, Pan may have had the very same idea, but he'd learned when to keep his mouth shut.

Pan tightened his grasp on the back of Cheri's head. Keeping the truck between the lines offered enough of a challenge without his lover's head banging against the wheel. His thigh quivered with the effort of keeping even pressure on the gas pedal. The tension in his groin consumed him, his whole world reduced to the dimensions of her mouth.

He held his breath as the orgasm tore through his body like a tornado destroying everything in its path. Amid the mad swirl clouding his concentration, Pan made a note to himself: *warn Q about hazards of road head.*

Grateful to have arrived home in one piece, Pan tugged open the passenger door and dragged Cheri out with a bit less elegance than he'd intended. She giggled as he swept her into his arms, rushed her through the house, and dumped her onto his bed.

"Need anything?" he asked, kicking off his jeans and mounting the bed one knee at a time.

Busy ripping her own clothes off, Cheri dropped her gaze between his legs and gave him a coy nod. "Mmhmm."

He covered her with his warm body and gave her exactly what she wanted, then flipped her onto her stomach and did it once more. Though he sported an erection again almost immediately, they both needed a break.

Pan dozed briefly, his dreams dancing with juicy nymphs no longer out of his reach. His miraculous erection woke them both, pressing against Cheri's thigh until it could not be ignored. *Four in one night, a personal best.* Good thing the lights were off, and Cheri couldn't see his smug smile when he rolled on top of her.

Cheri yawned and ran her hand up Pan's arm. "Again?"

"Can I help it if you're irresistible?" He dipped his chin and tickled her ear with the tip of his nose.

Sleepy but game, Cheri flopped onto her side and giggled. "Do what you want. I'm going back to sleep." He disturbed her slumber only at the very end, with a long, shuddering orgasm that drew out every last molecule of want from Pan's physical being and left him too exhausted to even care he was hard again not three minutes later.

27

WAR ROOM

Hephaestus loved his lamb. Back in the good old ancient days, when mortals sacrificed the finest of their flock to the gods, the storerooms of the palace overflowed with tender meat. Now procurement involved wheedling with merchants in the city square, a crass task left to the servants who were clever enough to supply the god of the forge with his favorite delicacy without driving prices through the roof.

It wasn't so much the cost of her husband's addiction that rankled Aphrodite; it was the way he attacked his dinner as though he were hunting down the poor animal all over again. She'd tried to instill manners, even commissioning Hephaestus himself to forge the sharpest set of knives with which to carve the meat, yet he'd laughed in her face when she suggested he make use of the utensil himself. "Lovely wife, what need have I for such tools when I can rip the bones apart barehanded?"

A half century ago, perusing the holiday issue of her favorite cooking magazine, Aphrodite had spied a rack of lamb with each rib topped off by a frilly, pink paper crown. She'd sent trusty Mercury to purchase the crowns, then held her breath that night as the servant on dinner duty placed the adorned dish before Hephaestus.

His eyes had opened wide, and Aphrodite had dared hope for a sweet second he might adopt a more genteel approach. "Oh, look. My dinner is dressed in little festive hats tonight," he'd said, shooting an amused smile in Aphrodite's direction while flicking a forefinger at the first of the crowns.

As casually as possible, she'd responded. "I thought they'd add an air of elegance to the room."

"Hmm," he'd answered, nodding thoughtfully, "I see your point." Before Aphrodite had had a chance to celebrate her victory, Hephaestus swiped his giant hand across the rack, captured all eight caps at once, and flung them across the room. In a voice booming with laughter, he'd said, "Yes, you're right, sweetheart. Look how beautifully they adorn the floorboards." The horrified servant had flown to the crumpled mess as Hephaestus lifted the entire rack to his face and twisted until the spine split in half, gushing lamb marrow into his waiting mouth.

Since that night, Aphrodite hadn't tried again to reform Hephaestus—not his eating habits anyway. Still, she'd never quite mastered the rise of bile brought on by the grease, first saturating the jungle of his beard, then overflowing onto his cheeks until his whole face glistened from ear to ear. When her delicate eyes needed reviving, she'd avert her gaze to the colorful frescos, cheery scenes from happier, god-fearing times. As for the loud slurping of marrow from the depths of the bones, that's why lutes and lyres were invented. Aphrodite's musicians were specifically chosen for their ability to pluck their instruments with enough force to drown out the grunting and sloshing at the other end of the table.

So loudly were they plucking on this night, Mercury's entrance went completely unnoticed until he skidded to a halt at his half brother's side. "Greetings."

With the rib bone lodged between his teeth, Hephaestus bellowed, "What'cher bishnish here?"

"Pardon the interruption; I bring an urgent message from Ares."

Hephaestus shot him a murderous glare, sending Mercury gliding on winged feet toward Aphrodite's end of the table. The goddess dropped her fork into the salad bowl with a clatter. "It's about Cupid, isn't it?"

"You are both summoned to the War Room."

Aphrodite leapt from her chair. Unmoved, her husband defiantly twisted off the next rib and opened his mouth wide to receive it.

"Heph!"

"I'm supping. The mighty Ares can wait."

"He said it was urgent." Aphrodite punctuated her statement by tossing her linen napkin onto the rich walnut table. Her fingers curled into a fist by her side, but Hephaestus didn't budge. Vibrating with fury, she played her trump card. "Shall I go without you?"

Mercury drew in a sharp breath and held still enough to be confused with Giambologna's bronze likeness. Hephaestus stopped mawing, the bone aloft in his fat hand. Aphrodite could have sworn she saw actual flames in her husband's eyes as he debated whether to call her bluff. Family history being what it was, he didn't deliberate long.

Dropping the bone onto the massacred carcass, Hephaestus made a great show of meticulously wiping each finger with his napkin and running the cloth over his greasy face before rising. "I'm finished."

The horses were hitched to Hephaestus's chariot and waiting when the couple arrived in the forecourt. They journeyed but a short distance, but Aphrodite's nerves had bundled into a tight knot by the time they reached the God of War's compound.

With his attention focused at the gaiascopic wall Hephaestus had installed during the Peloponnesian War, Ares did not acknowledge their arrival. Where Hephaestus was broad but fleshy, Ares was a finely honed weapon whose self-discipline outstripped his desires, though his legendary craving for companionship was not an urge he felt the need to curtail. The god's wavy locks offered the only hint of softness on an otherwise unyielding exterior. Aphrodite wondered if he recognized the father-son resemblance in Cupid's Earthly form. The tense set of his shoulders, exaggerated by the crisp folds of his crimson himation, did nothing to ease Aphrodite's anxiety. The God of War was not happy.

"A-hem," Hephaestus rumbled, earning an elbow in his side and an angry glare from his wife.

"This is some punishment." Ares sneered, his gaze not wavering from the giant floor-to-ceiling window. "I should think I'd like to earn a measure of this justice for myself."

When Aphrodite had last checked the gaiascope, Cupid was a gnarled ball of hurt, hardly someone to be envied. Aphrodite rushed to the window, slapping a hand over her gasp as blurry mounds of naked flesh sharpened into focus—along with the horrible realization her son had just climaxed inside the strictly forbidden girl. Small consolation to the mother that the girl moaned out an emphatic orgasm of her own only seconds later, though Ares—and Hephaestus, who'd peeked over his wife's shoulder—seemed to enjoy that part immensely.

The three continued to watch, transfixed by the scene they couldn't quite believe was unfolding: Cupid rolled onto his side, a sated grin stretched ear to ear. "You have no idea how great that felt," he mumbled into her neck.

Ares pivoted abruptly, his deep, commanding voice rattling Aphrodite's bones. "Why should that feel *great?*" His arms worked into a wall over his chest as he interrogated Aphrodite. "The girl is not his, and Cupid knows this. Am I correct?"

Aphrodite lifted her chin with a bravado she did not possess. "Yes, he knows. He left her house last night once he realized there was no echo beat."

"Yet he finds his pleasure between the girl's legs not twenty-four hours later? And how many others has he taken in between?"

"None," Aphrodite answered swiftly. Of this, at least, she was certain. "His gift has been temporarily transferred to Pan."

"Oh?" Ares lifted his eyebrows in amusement. Had Aphrodite finally impressed him with her handling of the situation? She had to admit, this co-parenting stint had its advantages. Maybe next time, she and Ares could sit down and discuss their son's predicament without a chaperone.

"Until Cupid connects the Worthy with her Right Love, there isn't a being on Earth who can relieve our son of his"—a blush heated her cheeks—"his *need*," she asserted with an irritated harrumph. "Even himself."

"Huh." Returning his gaze to the gaia wall, Ares asked, "If that is so, why does the boy appear well and satisfied? What am I missing?"

Aphrodite swallowed the lump in her throat. Standing here between former lover and cuckolded husband, Aphrodite wouldn't have chosen the rise and fall of her son's phallus as the topic of conversation. How could she avoid it, though, with the brilliant dagger eyes of the God of War bearing down on her? Damn if his cruelty didn't still stir her passion.

"I decided—"

"*We* decided," Hephaestus cut in, overriding Aphrodite with uncharacteristic macho posturing clearly meant to impress Ares, "the boy deserved a chance to prove himself."

Aphrodite sighed. "Clearly, we gave him more credit than he deserved." A single tear rolled from her eye, and Hephaestus scooped her chin into the palm of his chubby hand and swept away the moisture with the pad of his thumb.

"Sweetheart," he began tenderly, "Cupid is but a foal. Give the boy a chance to get his legs under him without his mother to catch him when he stumbles."

Ares exploded into a low, rolling laugh. "Oh, this is rich. You two fixed it so the one girl he can't have is the only one who can relieve him?"

"Yes," they answered together.

"Devious. I like it." Ares turned his wicked sneer toward Hephaestus. "I have to say, brother, I didn't think you had it in you."

Hephaestus slid an arm around his wife. "It wouldn't have been much of a test if the girl didn't welcome his advances—or offer the boy release."

"Indeed," Ares agreed. "She certainly is a hot, needy creature, one who would be a challenge to resist"—*oh, to be wanted by Ares,* thought Aphrodite—"especially since the boy's heart is tethered to hers until he conquers the task set before him."

Aphrodite snuck a peek through the glass as the postcoital couple succumbed to the pull of Hypnos. Grateful for her son's physical reprieve, she still couldn't help feeling disappointed by his selfish choice. "Perhaps he believes he's doing right by her. She does look happy." Even as the words left her mouth, Aphrodite recognized she'd crossed the fine line between mothering and enabling.

Ares was quick to jump. "Oh *please*, Aph. Let's not turn consorting into some act of heroism, shall we? Next, you'll suggest a parade through the streets of Tarra for the boy's cock." Ares's sarcasm had always been the weapon Aphrodite dreaded most, and it seemed his zeal for inflicting pain had only multiplied with time.

Hephaestus stroked his thumb along the nape of Aphrodite's neck. "I suppose we could make Mia reject him as well. He'd be forced to act with haste."

"That feels like cheating somehow," Aphrodite said. "Shouldn't he choose the right path despite more attractive options?" If a boy's mother didn't hold the bar high, who would?

"Yes," Hephaestus agreed, "and if Pan were doing *his* job properly, Cupid would understand that."

Ares snorted. "Did you not just tell me that your nephew is the beneficiary of all that redirected carnal energy? What force would motivate him to encourage Cupid to resolve the situation?"

Hephaestus stiffened beside Aphrodite. "Integrity. And Pan is *your* nephew too."

Ares dismissed the relationship with a flick of his hand, then stared hard through the glass. Aphrodite clutched her heart. She knew that look, the brilliant military strategist calculating his victory at any cost. There was no telling what evil the God of War might loose.

His lips curled into a sneer as the idea took hold. "Perhaps it's time to provide the satyr with some performance incentive."

Hephaestus gasped. "You wouldn't."

Ares gestured toward the window. "Care to have a look?"

2 8

HOUSE CALL

Morning wood was a certainty. Helios drove the sun across the sky, and Pan rose with the flaming orb. But now, as daylight burst through the pinholes of the vertical blinds, Pan's flaccid flesh ignored the pull, even with Cheri's enticing bottom for inspiration. No stranger to the whims of the divine, Pan understood better than anyone: the gods hath taken away.

Cheri grunted into her pillow and wiggled her ass. She was a trouper; he'd give her that.

"Sorry, I have an early meeting today," Pan said, swatting her playfully and stealing one last lick of the soft skin behind her ear.

Cheri rocked back, eyeing him over her right shoulder. "You're seriously leaving me all hot and bothered? Hmph!"

He gave his disappointing dick one last glance. *Nada.*

The paradigms were shifting so rapidly, Pan strained to make sense of it. Sadly, he couldn't get it up, but clearly, Cheri still wanted him. *Interesting.* Was that the Cupid Effect or just a Cheri thing?

The girl deserved a decent send-off, but Pan knew better

than to ignore the divine whistle blow. He shuddered to think
what functions an angered panel of gods might remove from his
mouth or fingers, should any substitute body parts be so bold as
to accommodate Cheri's needs.

"Sorry, babe, I have to close up shop here. Text me?"

With a dissatisfied grunt, she forced out, "Fine."

Pan chuckled. "You're not gonna forget me now, are you?"

"Fat chance. I won't be walking straight for a week, thank
you very much."

He bent over and cupped her pouty chin in the palm of
his hand. "No, Cheri, thank *you*." Sucking the breath out of
her lungs and into a vigorous kiss, Pan left her barely breathing
between his sheets.

Cheri was gone by the time Pan emerged from his shower,
all evidence of their sexual gymnastics tactfully folded inside
the neatly made bed. Pan's droopy member settled into his boxers while his loud sigh filled the empty bedroom. He held no
illusions about his predicament; any hope of straightening his
cock again depended on sorting out Cupid.

Pan unplugged his phone from the charger and speed-di-
aled Cupid, each unanswered ring sending Pan another note
higher on the *oh shit* scale. Phone glued to his ear, Pan stomped
to the garage, yanked open the truck door, and heaved his body
into the driver's seat. He muttered and huffed while he waited
for the voicemail beep.

*Hello, this is Quentin. I'm not available to take your call right
now . . .*

"Goddammit, Q! I gave you one rule. ONE RULE: Answer
your fucking phone. Call me back. NOW!"

At the bottom of the driveway, Pan kicked the truck into
drive and hurled his phone against the passenger door.

What does he think he's playing at? Ungrateful bastard.

Crap. What if he's lying in a ditch somewhere—or worse?

How many times have I told him to answer his fucking phone?

"I am gonna rip that prick a new one."

Pan's tirade was cut short by the memory of Cupid's admission at the grocery store yesterday. *"I couldn't."* Pan could relate only too well, unable to get a rise of his own useless cock this morning, even with his favorite menthol body wash.

His emotions lurched back and forth the whole ride to Mia's, unable to settle on which of their dicks deserved more pity—the one that couldn't rise or the one that wouldn't fall—but he was wise enough to understand their genitals weren't the problem. Cupid was in a heap of trouble, and Pan was doing a shit job so far. Poor Q's balls had to be bluer than his eyes by now, and his chest must feel like a bomb went off.

By the time he parked his truck behind Cupid's Prius, Pan had mustered enough sympathy to trust himself to ring Mia's doorbell. A baby's wail penetrated the walls of the house, and a stampede of footsteps grew louder until the door swung open. Pan gawped at the half-dressed, wild-haired man before him. With one boy wrapped around his neck and another hiding behind his ankles, Cupid was barely recognizable.

"Pan? What are you doing here?"

"Who's that, Q?" asked the kid on Cupid's back.

Cupid wrapped both arms under the boy's bottom and hitched the little body toward his shoulders. "This is my friend Pan. Pan, say hi to Jonah."

"Pan, like *pancakes?*" the boy asked, his eyes opening wide.

Pan nodded at the little boy. "Something like that. Nice to meet you, Jonah."

Cupid gave Pan a wary frown. "Coming in?"

Nodding again, Pan stepped inside. Cupid spun to lead him, nearly tripping over the toddler tugging on his jeans.

"Ee-wyy." Pan's gaze dropped to the rug rat clinging to Cupid's leg. "Eeee-wy," the boy repeated.

Cupid shook his head, chuckling. "And this is Eli."

Pan crouched down and held out his palm. "Hello there, Eli. I'm Pan." Eli slapped him five with a throaty giggle.

"Eli likes you," Jonah said.

"Yeah, what's up with that?" Cupid muttered.

"Twuck!" Eli grasped Pan's fingers and tugged him toward the construction vehicles littering the floor near the TV.

"Okay, sure, buddy," Pan answered, adding a stern, "We need to talk," as Eli pulled him past Cupid.

Cupid squatted down to slide Jonah off his back. "Hey, Joe, can you do me a favor? Can you tell your mommy my friend Pan is here?" Jonah took off toward the kitchen, and Cupid plopped down next to Pan on the floor. "What's going on?"

The little ball of energy running a backhoe up Pan's leg nearly made him forget why he was so angry. "How should I know? Maybe if you'd answer your phone, I wouldn't have to hunt you down to find out."

Cupid reached around and patted his back pocket. "Oh, fudge. I'm sorry. It must've fallen out last night when I got undressed." The apology on his face quickly turned to swagger. "We were in a bit of a hurry."

"Jzhhhh, jzhhhhh." Eli pushed the backhoe over Pan's knee. "Puh-ch!"

"Did you say 'fudge'?"

"Oh, yeah. That's what Mia says. The kids . . ."

"Never mind. You two . . .?" Pan cut himself off, dropping his gaze to Cupid's crotch to check for himself. Sure enough, the telltale lump had shrunk. "You're cured?" Pan didn't know whether to be angry or just continue being confused. He couldn't keep track of the ups and downs.

Cupid leaned in, speaking softly into Pan's ear. "Mia has the magic touch."

Pan jerked his body so violently, Eli fell over. "Sorry, kiddo," Pan murmured, righting the little guy before whisper-yelling at Cupid. "What were you thinking? That's a terrible idea."

Cupid shrugged. "What's the big deal?"

If Cupid had been wearing a shirt, Pan would've grabbed a fistful and yanked Cupid to his chest. He settled for clenching his jaw as hard as he could while spitting out the answer between his teeth. "The big deal is, that's a no-no, and the gods are displeased."

The smile fell away from Cupid's face. "How do *you* know?"

"Jzhhhhh zoooom zoooom!" The plastic tires rolled up Pan's inner thigh, and he threw his palm up just before the front wheels reached the critical juncture. Scooping up Eli and the truck in one hand, Pan flipped the boy around and sent him in the opposite direction with a pat on his bottom.

"Trust me; I know." Pan glanced over at Cupid, debating how much to share. "It's my job to know."

"I don't get it. I thought I was supposed to make Mia happy. She sure seems happy. I know *I'm* happy. How is this wrong?"

"You told me yourself," Pan said, reining in his growing frustration, "you're not her Right Love. Has that changed?"

Cupid's chest deflated. He sank back onto his palms. "There's no echo beat, but I don't get why it only . . . *works* with Mia now. That has to mean something."

Pan chose his words carefully, ever mindful of the audience they couldn't see. "It's a test, Q. They like to throw in curveballs, make the wrong answer seem like the only right answer. It's up to you to do what you were sent here to do, and that does not include what you've obviously been doing all night."

"And twice this morning," Cupid added miserably.

"Ugh." Pan had gorged on erotic delights last night as well, but now there was no telling when or if he'd have another chance.

A giant question mark drew itself across Cupid's forehead. "What's your deal, Pan? Every girl in town was sniffing between your legs yesterday. Why are you giving me the face?"

"What face?"

"That face I used to see all the time, back when you had hooves and horns. Did you not get your fill?"

"Dammit, Q, this is not about me."

Eli froze, took in Pan's angry expression, burst into tears, and hopped off Pan's legs. The truck clattered to the floor as Eli toddled into the kitchen to the comfort of Mia's arms. "Mommeeeee!"

"Shit, sorry," Pan said, pushing himself off the floor and offering Cupid a hand up. "Look, Q, you gotta fix this now. You hear me? This little game of house you're playing here is not meant to be, and I don't care how you do it, but you need to tell Mia."

Cupid gazed over Pan's shoulders, blinked a few times, and swallowed hard before answering. "I think you just did."

29

TELLING MIA

"Hello, Pan." There was not a trace of *Namaste* in Mia's greeting. A shiver ran down Cupid's spine.

Pan whipped around to face her. He cleared his throat, but when he answered, his voice sounded more sheep than goat. "Morning."

The unmistakable ire Mia directed at Cupid twisted his gut. "Well, Pan, it seems you've dropped into our little 'game of house' just in time to play 'let's eat breakfast.' Can I interest you in some whole wheat pancakes while your friend explains why we're not meant to be?"

"Oh, I, uh . . ."

Cupid slapped Pan on the back and gave his shoulder a squeeze. "Stay."

Pan's head swiveled enough to take in Cupid's *Don't leave me alone to deal with this mess* expression.

"Hey, Jonah," Cupid said, "how about setting another place for Pan?" Before Pan had a chance to retreat, Jonah skidded into the kitchen, clattering plates and rattling silverware to make room at the table. "Pan, meet my friend Lucas."

Mia glared hard at both men before turning the baby in her arms to face Pan, who offered his finger to Lucas and a wary glance toward his mother.

"Don't worry," she said with a smirk. "He won't bite it off."

Pan shot her a winning grin. "It wasn't the baby I was worried about."

Lucas latched onto Pan's finger and let out a squeaky whimper into Mia's bosom.

"Right. Someone needs a diaper change. Think you two can hold down the fort?"

Cupid had a pretty solid feeling his blissful little arrangement was about to be irrevocably shattered. He gave Mia a brave, "Sure," and a hopeful peck on the cheek. Mia sighed as she set off toward the boys' room.

"Sorry, man," Pan mumbled.

"Not your fault. It just stinks, you know?" Misery seeped out of Cupid's every pore, but there were mouths to feed. "C'mon, guys. Pancake time!"

"I'll pour the milk." Jonah ran over to the counter, and Pan dove in and grabbed the carton just before the whole thing splattered all over the floor.

"Whoa there, big guy, let me help you with that."

Cupid had never really thought of his gruff, wild friend as father material before, but it shouldn't have surprised him that Pan was good with the boys. After all, had Pan not exhibited that same paternal instinct while carrying out his protective duties with Cupid?

"Up-py!"

"Oh, you want *me* now, do you?" Cupid chuckled and bent to pick up Eli. Strapping the toddler into his booster seat, Cupid said, "I'm the lesser of two evils, I guess."

Pan guffawed. "Depends who you ask."

"I think the people who live in this house would choose me—
hey, speaking of which, have you noticed a certain lack of *melon
choosing* going on here this morning?"

"Q!" Pan's glare stopped Cupid cold.

Right. Don't give the gods any bright ideas. Cupid couldn't have
stomached Mia going all gooey over Pan under any circumstances.

Eli brought his fists down on the table. "Cake! Cake!"

"Eli wants his pancakes," Jonah chimed in.

"I'm on it," Cupid answered. "How about cutting up that
banana, Pan?"

"Yeah, sure. Why not? That's just what I came to do," Pan said.

Leaving Jonah to supervise Pan's banana-slicing technique,
Cupid whirled toward the stove and smacked right into Mia.
"Sorry," he said, bracing the baby in her arms before Mia's glower
forced Cupid to take a step backward.

Plowing right through him, Mia strode to the highchair,
strapped Lucas in, and checked the security of Eli's belt. "Exactly
what *did* you come to do, Pan?"

Pan glanced up from the banana, registered Mia's agitation,
and calmly divided the cut-up fruit between the two boys. "Hey,
I'm just the messenger."

Mia's scowl moved from Pan to Cupid. "You. Bedroom. Now."

Pan blinked at Cupid, sympathetic but useless. "Go ahead,
Q. We got this, right, Jonah?"

Without waiting for Jonah's response, Mia hooked her finger through one of Cupid's belt loops—yet another reason for
Cupid to hate the cursed things—and dragged him down the
hall. He barely made it inside the room ahead of the door slamming behind him. Mia spun on him, hands balled into fists on
her slim hips.

"Who the hell does he think he is, barging in on our morning
to deliver his pronouncement of doom, and what's so wrong with

playing house?" The fire in her eyes shifted, replaced by something more vulnerable, which just about broke Cupid's heart in two. "And since when is he the authority on our relationship?"

Cupid closed the distance between them and pulled her hands into his. "Mia."

"Darn it, Q. You said you loved me. But we're all too much responsibility, the four of us, aren't we? I get it. Run from the scary single mom while you still can," she said in a voice rising with hysteria. "You're too young and hot to get trapped. Don't waste your prime on someone else's mess. Hell, sometimes *I'd* run if I could." Her shoulders slumped in defeat; even Mia's impeccable posture couldn't stand up to the desperation of their situation.

"Whoa. Whoa. Slow down." Cupid pulled Mia into his chest and wrapped his arms tight around her back. "You've got it all wrong, Mia. Nobody feels trapped. Those boys are fantastic, and I do love you even though I know it seems impossible in such a short time."

Her tears slid down Cupid's bare chest. "You shouldn't throw that word around like it doesn't matter."

"I would *never*, Mia. I mean that."

She shook free of his grasp. "Is it because I can't say it back?"

"No. It's not about that at all."

She crossed her arms and tried to round up more fierce indignation, but the hurt and betrayal had sucked the fight right out of her. "I don't get it. Can you help me understand, *please?*"

Explaining that Aphrodite had chosen Mia for a Right Love match probably wouldn't be all that comforting, he guessed, so with no other good options, Cupid tried a different version of the truth. "I'm not right for you."

Indignation came roaring back. "Were you right for me while we were screwing?"

He shook his head and let out a sad sigh. "Don't, Mia. It's not that we're not great together. That's why this is so damn painful."

"You're breaking up with me because we're great together? Does this even count as breaking up? Were we even together?" Mia tipped her face toward the sun shining in through the window, as if trying to regain the warmth Cupid was stripping away. "So, what was all that crap about me being the one?"

"You *are* the one for me; I'm just not the one for you." Lying would have been so much easier.

"Wow. Somehow, I expected you to be more original than it's-not-you-it's-me. I guess I was wrong about that too." She nailed him with eyes brimming with tears. "God, I am so weak. I should be furious with you, and instead . . .? Ugh, listen to me, trying to talk you out of dumping me. This is so humiliating."

Cupid brought a hand to his chest and tried in vain to tamp down the fire inside. Standing here discussing this like any of it made sense was the worst kind of agony, but Cupid had no choice but to keep her close. Whatever he was meant to do, he needed Mia to trust him. If she banished Cupid from her life, he would wallow in heartache for the rest of his days. Even worse, Mia might never find her Right Love.

"Your instincts aren't wrong, Mia. We have a connection, and I don't want to break it."

"Now you're confusing me. Are you dumping me or not?"

Cupid frowned. "I wish you would stop using that word. We need to end the physical part of this, but—"

"Oh, nuh-nuh-nuh-nuh-no." Mia's hand shot up. "Please, whatever other clichés you inflict on me, don't insult me with the let's-stay-friends speech."

How could he possibly explain? "Not friends exactly."

"Not friends, not physical. Oh my god. Are you *gay?*"

"Gay?"

"Are you and Pan . . .?"

Well, there was a surprise. "After that marathon . . . *fudging* session, do I *seem* gay to you?"

Her lips twitched with amusement. "Not particularly, but I'm stumped. Where are you going with this?"

"I believe I'm meant to help you find your Right Love." First toe dipped into murky waters, Cupid happily discovered he was still breathing—and Mia hadn't punched him.

"Heh, I've certainly had no trouble finding my *wrong* loves without any help." She was definitely not looking pleased. "And here I thought you actually had some potential. Silly Mia!"

"Please, believe me, Mia. I'd give anything to be your destiny."

"How are you so sure you're not? Ugh, did that sound as pathetic as I think it did?"

"You're anything but pathetic, and unfortunately, I am sure. It's kind of what I do, this love stuff."

"You do 'love stuff.'"

Cupid nodded as earnestly as he knew how.

Mia brought her fingertips to her forehead and rubbed. "I need to think." Cupid tried to wait patiently while his heart banged around inside his chest. "So, you want me to believe you're some kind of matchmaking expert, and you're going to help me find my Mr. Right, and this man will be better for me than you are?"

"Yes." Now they were getting somewhere.

"If you're some kind of scam artist, planning to extort large sums of money for this little 'service,' you should probably take a harder look around." A semi-hysterical cackle ended her rant.

"No, Mia, of course not. All I want is for you to be happy. Tragically, that does not involve being with me."

Taking in Cupid's defeated expression, Mia shook her head and sighed. "You, sir, are one wild ride."

Cupid held his breath until she spoke again.

"Okay, let's say I play along with your bizarre home version of 'The Dating Game,' and it turns out you're wrong. Can I have you back?"

Cupid allowed himself a smile and a little bit of hope. "Deal."

He probably shouldn't have, but Cupid drew Mia to him and kissed her mouth one last time.

30

BISTRO DU COEUR

"Tell me again where you found this Greg guy, and zip me, please?" Mia tried to ignore Q's soft, sad sigh and the feather-light touch of his hand one beat too long on her hip as she spun back around to face him.

"It's called Tinder. I've collected the responses over the last forty-eight hours and arranged a date with the man most likely to be your match."

"You found my date on *Tinder?*"

"Pan says it's the most efficient way to find the best prospects in your vicinity." *Pan.* Well, that explained it.

The sane part of her suspected she should have sent Q packing by now, but Mia couldn't see where she had anything to lose. Safety wasn't a real concern since Q's tether only stretched about fifteen feet. Any further, he claimed to not be able to judge the "rightness" of the pairing. Mia had no idea how this would all play out if she did, in fact, click with this guy Greg. The last guy she'd dated—and ended up marrying—would not have appreciated a shadow, especially one with an overprotective streak.

Then again, so what, really, if Greg got scared off? Q made a damn fine fallback plan. This seemed to be the ultimate win-win situation.

"Okay, just do me a favor? Let my mother go on believing you're actually my date. I don't think I could begin to explain this whole arrangement to her, and frankly, if I did, I'm pretty sure she'd talk me out of it."

"You look beautiful," Q replied, skipping right over her request. The tender compliment tugged on Mia's already frag-ile heartstrings.

She didn't know whether to kiss him or remind him she was only going out on this date for him. Settling on a sad smile, Mia grabbed his hand and dragged him out of the bedroom. "C'mon. We're gonna be late for my date."

The boys were lined up on the floor like three little birds on a wire, eyes glued to the *Goodnight, Sprout* show they only got to watch when Grams babysat. Mia gave the baby's bum a little pat through the sling of his bouncy seat. "Be good, Lukie. Night-night, Eli." Eli barely acknowledged her kiss on his cheek, but Jonah twisted around and linked his arms around Mia's neck.

"You smell fancy, Mommy."

"Yep, Q is taking Mommy out on the town," she answered.

Jonah's hands slipped away from Mia as he spun around toward Q. "G'night, Q." Joe waited with his arms in the air while Q stepped inside them and gave him a tight squeeze.

We don't get to keep him, Mia needed to warn them all, as if it weren't already too late not to get attached. Instead, she said what she could. "Night-night, Joe. You be good for Grams."

"He's always good," Mia's mom chimed in. "They're all angels."

"Night, Mom," Mia said. "Don't wait up."

"Good evening, Mrs. Franklin."

"Good night, Quentin, dear." Her mother flashed a smile

at Q and shot Mia an embarrassingly obvious wink. "Have fun, kids. Don't worry about us."

Mia suppressed her giggle until the door closed behind them. "Good night, Quentin, dear," she parroted in a voice sounding scarily like her mother's. Slipping past Q through the passenger door he was holding open for her, Mia added, "If she only knew you were my pimp."

Q's jaw dropped, and he didn't respond until he climbed in on the driver's side. "Pimp, am I? A man earning a hefty fee for selling the sexual services of others?"

"Hefty, huh? Abandoned, single mother-of-three has quite the steep street value, I hear."

"Mia! That's no way to talk about yourself."

"Whatever."

Q started up his car and coasted down the street. *Damn these hybrids*, it was way too quiet. Mia itched to turn on some music, even a damn talk show, but Q's knobs weren't hers to fiddle with—not tonight, anyway. Awkward conversation it was, then.

"So, can we talk about how this is going to work? If you're planning to sit and watch us all night while we eat, that's pretty creepy."

The tiny hammer pulsing against Q's cheek might have escaped the notice of someone less fluent in energy anatomy. "I'll be at a nearby table, close enough to feel your beat."

"You'll feel my 'beat'?" *Because that's not creepy at all.*

"If there *is* a beat, I'll feel it. But remember, we need two."

"Yes, right. The echoes." She was trying, honest, but all this talk about "right loves" and "echo beats" made Mia's head spin. Romance was for girls with time and imagination, not four mouths to feed.

Undeterred by whatever sarcasm might have seeped into her tone, Q nodded. "That's right. Just one is no good." His hand left the wheel and rubbed at his chest.

"Okay, say this guy isn't my perfect match. What if I like him anyway?"

Q shot her an anxious glance. "What do you mean?"

"I mean, what if I'm attracted to him? What if I want to . . ." Jump into the sack with the guy after one date? Now, there was a thought that never would have crossed her mind before Q dropped into her life. *See what happens when you break the seal?* "What if I want to spend more time with him?"

Stopped at a red light, Q rounded on her. The reflection off the windshield tinted his heartbroken expression with a garish smear resembling blood. "What would be the point?"

Right. If it were only for the meaningless sex, there would be no reason to choose anyone over Q. Oh wait, Q wouldn't sleep with her now. This whole situation held no joy for either of them. Mia sighed and folded her hands in her lap. "Never mind."

She searched for a safe topic but couldn't come up with anything that wouldn't be loaded right now, which really stunk because she'd wanted to tell him all about Eli and Jonah's bubble bath argument over who liked Q better and why. They drove the rest of the way to the restaurant in a stifling silence.

The car glided to a stop, and Q moved swiftly to open Mia's door. She took his offered hand and stepped out of the car, painstakingly avoiding his eyes. He retracted his support the moment she was vertical, as if touching her caused him physical pain.

"Good luck, Mia."

She gave his slumped body one final glimpse and immediately wished she hadn't. Forcing the defeat from her thoughts, Mia pulled in a deep, cleansing breath and stepped inside the vestibule. *This all better be worth it.*

A bud vase with a single red rose greeted Mia at the hostess stand as Frank Sinatra crooned at the perfectly staged volume. LED votives flickered on two-tops and cozy half-circle booths.

Good ol' Bistro du Coeur, Tarra's obligatory "romantic restaurant" and, unbeknownst to Q, the site of Asshole's cheesy proposal. *Great*, now she had a second man to push out of her head before her date showed up. Mia hadn't had the heart to tell Q, not after the countless hours of research he had already invested in this date.

"Please tell me you're Mia."

She started toward the honey-glazed voice to her right and happily noted the sleek chassis matched the purr of his engine. At least Q had good taste in men. Fit and tan, sharply dressed in dark jeans and a houndstooth check blazer, the blondish man in front of her waited with a hopeful lift of his eyebrows until she answered. "Greg?"

Their mouths widened into matching maybe-this-blind-date-won't-suck smiles, and Mia could've checked her lipstick in his perfectly straight, gleaming teeth. He offered his hand, and when Mia placed hers inside it, Greg set his other hand on top to seal the deal.

"It's *really* nice to meet you. Shall we?"

Greg nodded to the hostess, who seemed to have been awaiting Mia's arrival as well. Before falling into line between the hostess and her date, Mia peered back to check the entrance. No sign of Q.

How about paying attention to the hot guy pulling out your chair? Her date had actual manners, a definite plus and not necessarily something she would have expected of a Tinder hookup. Unlike Q, who somehow never seemed quite at home, Greg moved fluidly to his place across the table, swept his napkin into his lap, and studied the wine list as if he'd just stepped off the plane from Bordeaux. Then again, for all his suavity and *Esquire*-worthy clothing, Mia couldn't help noting her date lacked a certain *je-ne-sais-Q.*

Greg busied himself with the selection, but Mia caught him peeking over the thick leather binder more than once. "Would you prefer red or white?" he asked. "Wait, don't tell me. You're a champagne girl."

Mia flicked her white linen napkin open and draped it across her thighs. She hardly fit the label of "champagne girl" but couldn't find any reason to shatter her date's grandiose ideas. "I do love the feel of the tiny bubbles popping on my nose."

"Perfect," he said, setting the menu to the side and folding his hands on the table. "*Mia*. That's a beautiful name. Is it short for—"

Mia followed Greg's gaze to the figure who had materialized at their table. An awful grimace spoiled Q's face.

"Sorry," Q said simply. Mia had never seen him so twitchy and out of his element.

"Yes, we'll take a bottle of the Veuve Clicquot yellow label."

Q's head snapped up. "What?"

A prickle of heat crept up Mia's neck as the two men squinted at each other in confusion.

"Are you the sommelier?" Greg asked.

Things were about to get ugly. Mia could feel the gathering storm in her bones, but she didn't have the first clue what to do about it. What could possibly be the etiquette here?

Ignoring Greg, Q delivered his verdict. "He's not the one."

Mia narrowed her eyes at Q and gave him a tight shake of her head. Watching the whole exchange with a dropped jaw, Greg went from bewildered to furious before Mia could explain, not that she had a clue how she would have accounted for Q's presence. *Greg, I'd like you to meet my lover-slash-pimp.*

"What the hell is this?" Greg jumped up, shoving his chair away with a harsh screech against the wood floor. "You know this guy? Are you two trying to pull some kinky shit on me?"

With each question, his voice notched louder and angrier. "Fucking Tinder!"

Mia couldn't bear to watch as her date stormed off, the trailing breeze stinging like a slap across the face. The room tilted, and Mia clutched the sides of the table until she could find her center.

"Excuse me, miss." Another man appeared. "Is there a problem here? Is this man bothering you?"

The manager was not a big person, but he had a good head of steam going, and Mia had no doubt he was more than capable of throwing Q out on his ass and would have immensely enjoyed doing so. Mia considered the uneasy expressions of both men waiting for her verdict. Was Q bothering her? Why yes, he most certainly was. Thoroughly.

"No," she said. "We're okay."

"Perhaps the gentleman would care to be seated?" He gestured at Greg's chair while sending a crystal-clear message to Q: *sit or leave.*

"C'mon, Mia. We should go."

Yes, they should. Just probably not together.

31

CHILLY SWIRL

If their earlier silence was a cold breeze, this journey home was one of Demeter's winters. The only reason Mia let Cupid drive her home was the ruse with her mother.

"Can I at least get you something to eat before I take you home?" If Cupid couldn't fix things between them, he'd fill at least part of the hollow ache. Surely, Mia must be hungry too.

She folded her arms over her chest and harrumphed.

With a wistful sigh, Cupid passed the neon-lit Tarra Diner on the right side of the road and did his best to let go of the meatloaf fantasy that had already taken hold. "Are you planning to stay angry at me all night?"

Mia twisted in her seat, breathing fire from her side of the car. "All night? How about *forever*? Do you have any idea how humiliating that was?"

Cupid resisted the urge to smile. Harsh words, but at least Mia was speaking to him again. With communication, there was hope; the God of Love knew that much.

"Mia, I apologize, *again*." Cupid slid his hand across the

console hoping to reach one of hers, but they were locked in the tight grasp of her armpits. He drew back his peace offering and clutched the steering wheel instead. "Can we please talk about this?"

Mia's response was steady and detached. "As you put it so eloquently earlier, what would be the point?"

The point was he loved her so hard, every inch of him hurt. The point was he needed her not to despise him. The point was they were going to have to try again and again and again, if need be, until they found her match, or there would be no peace for either of them. But this was no time for logic.

"Please?"

After another few minutes of tortured silence, Mia relented. "Fine. I could go for some frozen yogurt."

"You could?" Cupid's downtrodden spirit flickered with new life. "Where does one find this yogurt?"

Mia turned slowly toward Cupid, and he couldn't resist the urge to meet her gaze. He promptly returned his focus to the road but not before registering the unmistakable affection in her eyes.

"Why is it impossible to stay mad at you?" she asked.

Figuring the answer had much to do with the strictly off-limits topic, Cupid responded with a relieved smile and a noticeable unbunching of his shoulders. Mia conceded a smile of her own, though hers held a definite reluctance.

"Take a right into the strip mall after the next light."

A "strip" mall sounded intriguing, but Cupid knew better than to let his mind wander. He'd been so careful the last two days, every second a torment of opposing forces: the scorch of his heart if he strayed too far from Mia's side versus the throbbing of his genitals, which only seemed to abate with distance and the yoga breathing he'd learned from Mia.

Cupid hated this whole terrible mess—hated his father, his mother, Hera, Hades, and most of all, himself—but he was no fool. Not touching Mia was basic survival. Pan had drilled it into him, finally. Cupid must absolutely and most scrupulously avoid doing the one thing that would temporarily release both his chest and groin from their gods-given afflictions.

He would pass this test. Mia would find her Right Love. All would be forgiven on Mount O.

As soon as he pulled into the parking spot, Mia threw open her door and took off at a furious pace. Cupid jogged to catch up and scurried around her just in time to grasp the large cone-shaped door handle. Unlike the romantic restaurant Cupid had so carefully selected using Zagat and Yelp, the yogurt shop screamed *cold* in every way, from the temperature to the bright lights to the snowflake motif repeated all around the icy blue walls.

"My gods, is that food squirting out of the wall?"

"*Shhh.*" She yanked on Cupid's sleeve, pulling him hard into her side.

The contact sucked his breath away. They froze, eyes locked and searching. With one simple kiss of their shoulders, two days of restraint were completely undone.

Mia frowned. "Q . . ." Her fingertips gathered in more of his shirt.

How easy it would be to surrender, and how incredibly selfish. Mia had worn that spectacular, body-hugging dress and strapped on those sexy heels and sprayed herself with fancy perfume for someone else tonight, for some stranger who might have turned out to be her Right Love. And that wide-eyed, wonder-filled, we-might-have-something-here gaze she was lavishing on Cupid right now? That, too, belonged to someone else.

"So, uh," Cupid started with a bumpy voice, craning his neck to indicate the bustle of activity around them, "how does this work?"

Picking up on his cue, Mia unfisted Cupid's shirt, took a small cup off the stack, and handed a large cone to Cupid. "Pick one or two flavors, fill up the cone, and we'll talk toppings when we get there."

Cupid nodded gratefully. "Which one's your favorite?" he asked.

She led him to the coffee-toffee-Oreo lever. "Hit me," she said, positioning her container under the nozzle.

Distracted by the sheer joy on Mia's face, Cupid failed to register the speed of the spurt until the thick coil flopped over the sides of her cup. "Shoot! Sorry!"

Mia giggled as Cupid threw the lever up and dove in to catch the excess. She bent forward and licked the sloppy mess from the palm of Cupid's hand. "All better."

Not from where Cupid stood. He closed his eyes and drew a deep breath into his lungs, visualized his diaphragm dropping, his chest expanding, and his erection softening—though the last was purely wishful thinking.

"What are you doing?" she asked. "Is that pranayama?"

One eye popped open and squinted at her. "Trying."

"Oh." The twinkle in Mia's eye faded.

Cupid shrugged. He didn't want to think about his problem, and he *definitely* didn't want to talk about it. With two careful pulls, Cupid filled his cone and proceeded to the toppings bar. Mia walked him through the do's (crushed Reese's and hot fudge) and the don'ts (fruit-flavored beads and gummy worms). Weighed and paid, they shuffled over to the least dribbled–on table.

Cupid squirmed on his plastic stool, actively ignoring Mia's hums and moans of pleasure across the table. He tipped his face inside his cone. The frozen version was a sweet surprise compared to the so-called Greek yogurt he and Pan had been eating for breakfast, and Cupid was momentarily distracted from his troubles.

"Taste?" Mia's spoon hovered under Cupid's nose.

His gaze shifted from the offered spoon to Mia's seductively puckered lips. "Are you trying to punish me?" he asked.

"I don't know. Maybe," she admitted. "I think I might've had the beat for that guy."

"You didn't." Cupid couldn't even acknowledge the storm of emotions he'd suffered over the possibility.

"You're so sure?" She backed down when Cupid shot her a scowl. "Okay, fine. What if he had it for me?"

"That is inconsequential."

"You're heartless."

"No, Mia. Anything but. A one-way beat is no good. Trust me."

She let out an exasperated groan. "Now what do we do?"

"Well . . ." Cupid reached cautiously for his phone, his eyes fixed on Mia's face. "Now, we try again. Mind holding this for me?" He handed his cone to Mia and swiped through several photos before choosing one with potential. "You seem to like blonds. I think we should try this one next." He turned the phone to show Mia the picture.

At first, she seemed less than impressed, but after staring at the picture, Mia changed her mind. "Sure, yeah, he's hot. We should probably line up a bunch of guys, don't you think?"

Cupid smiled back. "Really? I didn't think you would go for that. I'll set up five for tomorrow night."

Mia's smile flattened into an angry line. "*Seriously?*"

"Mia?" Cupid watched with horror as she flipped his cone upside down and stuffed it inside her cup.

"Take me home."

PEP TALK

"Wanna play *Call of Duty?*" Pan shot a guarded glance at the lump of god at the other end of the couch.

"Nope."

Cupid's answer didn't surprise Pan, but the way the guy had been staring at the screen without moving for the last hour was starting to freak him out. He looked like a character from one of those zombie shows. The effects of his sleepless night and anxiety-filled day would dissolve on their own in a day or two, but in the meantime, it hurt Pan to look at him.

Pan set down the controller with a sigh. If Cupid noticed him get up and grab two beers from the kitchen, it certainly didn't register on his face.

Handing off one of the beers, Pan plopped down next to him. "Here. Drink."

Cupid scowled at Pan, then at the beer, before lifting the bottle to his lips and tipping back his head. "I really hate beer."

Pan knocked his knee against Cupid's a couple of times. "It'll put hair on your chest."

"I already *have* hair on my chest." Eyes narrowed, lips curled in a full-on sneer, Cupid could almost pass for scary. "Dammit, Pan, how am I supposed to get through this night?"

What could he say? He sure as shit wouldn't have been able to watch the woman he loved test drive a bunch of other guys right under his nose. "I don't know, but I know you *can*. You have to. For Mia."

"Mia?" Cupid bolted off the couch, muttering more to himself than to Pan as he paced back and forth across the room. "Mia hates me. She hung up on me this morning." Purple-faced and short of breath, Cupid spun to face Pan, "Or have you forgotten?"

Pan slouched forward, his elbows sliding onto his thighs. "Nope, I remember." How could he ever erase that expression of sheer horror on Cupid's face or the way he'd glowered at his cell phone for a full minute afterward as if the phone had stabbed him through the heart?

Pan lifted his chin, peeking cautiously at his ranting, raving, distraught friend. *Stay objective,* Mercury would have counseled, but that advice amounted to a cork tossed in the ocean where Cupid was concerned. So much for professional distance.

Cupid paced to within a foot of the wall, pivoted, grasped a handful of hair, and repeated his relentless march. "Did I tell you she shut the door in my—"

"—face? Yes. Yes, you did."

"Aargh!" The pacing tapered, and Cupid came to a stop next to Pan. "You've got to teach me your tricks, Pan. I've never been rejected before."

"My tricks, huh?" Pan couldn't even be offended. "Come sit down. You're making me dizzy."

Cupid collapsed into the corner of the couch, downing the rest of his beer in one long swig. He tipped his face to the ceiling and groaned. The poor fucker barely had a chance to enjoy the ride before ending up as roadkill. Not that Pan was all that surprised. Experience had taught him if the gods bothered to toss you off the Mount, you were not about to ascend with a slap on the wrist.

"Okay. Mia's mad at you, but she's agreed to go along with the plan, right?"

"Yes. I'm picking her up at eight and taking her to the Ruby Lounge. Starting at nine, I have five solid prospects lined up in ten-minute intervals. By ten o'clock, she might have met the love of her life."

"More guys from Tinder?"

"No way. I spent four hours sifting through those guys who swiped Mia's Tinder profile. Would you believe most of them are only out for sex?"

Pan bit back a smile. "I thought you said that Greg guy was okay."

"Pfft!" A dark scowl twisted Cupid's face. "He was a phony Mr. Manners, ordering fancy champagne to impress Mia, biding his time before the pounce."

"Huh, so these guys you lined up for tonight, they're not after sex?"

Cupid lowered his gaze until it cut right through Pan. "Don't you think I know all guys want sex? At least these men have a chance of relating to Mia on a slightly deeper level."

"And where did you find this latest bunch of sterling gentlemen?"

"You're going to be super impressed."

"Wow me," Pan said.

"I found a dating site called 'OkCupid.' I think they might be channeling me."

Pan chuckled, his head shaking side to side. "A clear recipe for success."

"I filled out a questionnaire for Mia, and *poof!* Twenty-five matches. I narrowed it down to five. If these don't work out, I have another batch ready to go for tomorrow."

"Tomorrow?" Pan set down his beer and angled his body toward Cupid. "Look, man, you need to cool your jets. You can't keep hitting Mia with one man after the next without giving her any say in the matter. Even if you do get her to play along tonight—"

Cupid made an ugly sound and bolted up straighter against the back of the sofa. "She has to, Pan."

"Okay, yeah, whatever. So assuming none of these guys work out, because what are the odds that of all the places in the cosmos, her one Right Love would be living right here in this very town—?"

"Everyone's Right Love is within reach."

"*What?* Whoa. Are you saying you've stocked the pond?"

"Of course. Well, not *me,* per se, mostly Mother. How cruel would it be to populate the planet with seven billion people and not put a person's perfect match close enough to meet?"

"Everyone has a Right Love *that* close by?" An infinite lifetime of chasing, and Pan's own meant-to-be was close enough to touch?

"Yes, at some point in their lives."

Awed once again by the forces at work behind the scenes, Pan searched his friend for answers. "You don't think you could've imparted this little pearl of wisdom to me, say, a thousand years ago?"

"I probably could have, had I known you were *alive.*"

Ouch. Poor Q. That scar hadn't quite disappeared after all.

"Plus, just because you might bump shoulders with your Right Love at a crowded concert doesn't mean you'd know it at the time. If you had any idea how many people don't recognize the moment . . ."

"Ships passing in the night." A history of what-ifs scrolled through Pan's mind, all the moves from this Tarra to that Tarra. Had he already missed his opportunity? Was he doomed to live out the rest of his immortal life without his perfect match? Until a week ago, he'd had no idea such a thing existed; now, being deprived of his Right Love felt positively unbearable. "So that's it? You doze at the wheel for a split second, and you miss it? One and done?"

"I never said that." If Cupid weren't in such a miserable state, Pan might've punched the exasperating little fucker.

Somehow, love seemed even crueler this way, knowing it was right there within your grasp, more than once if the gods favored you. The puzzle pieces of Pan's grand understanding realigned themselves through this new lens, and he could only conclude how truly ill-equipped gods and mortals alike were for this enterprise called love.

"You'd think with all these perfect matches lying around, extramarital affairs and divorce rates would be a mite lower."

Cupid huffed. "Assuming the marriage is a true match, and fewer than two in a hundred are, Right Love is no guarantee of success. It's a foundation, but we both know the temptations that can gnaw away at even a divine union."

"Well, this is all quite cheery."

Cupid answered Pan's frown with a forced grin, picked up Pan's empty bottle, and strode to the fridge. "Don't get too low, my friend. The picture's not all bleak. As long as the coupling is reasonable, two people who aren't each other's Right Love can make it work over the long haul. Hell, they might even be convinced they're perfect for each other, and you'd probably agree."

Pan couldn't help mentally ticking off the happily-togethers he knew, turning them over in his head like a jeweler inspecting a diamond.

"The real tragedy, of course, is the unrequited beat," Cupid said.

"You mean, like yours for Mia?"

Cupid grimaced. "Yes, thank you, exactly like that. There's almost no chance for the afflicted party to escape without permanent damage."

"That sucks."

"Yep. Hello, devastation. And unfortunately, it's not all that rare."

The cold butt of a fresh beer tapped Pan on the arm, pulling him back to the moment. "Speaking of your problems . . ."

Cupid took a long drag, shivered, scowled, and repeated the process. "Right."

Though he hated doing it, Pan pressed him. "Let's say by some miracle, one of these next however-many guys you put her through is Mia's match. You'll step away gracefully, right?"

Cupid shot Pan an icy glare. "Now I have to be graceful? It's not enough I let her go?"

"I don't think the Goddess of Love is going to look too kindly on any interference at that point."

Another swig of Cupid's beer disappeared between his lips and past the bob of his Adam's apple. "I don't imagine interference will be an option. Once we find Mia the right guy, it'll be, 'Hello, wings; goodbye, mighty cock, and *yasou*, planet earth.'"

And there it sat between them, the first either had spoken the awful truth out loud. This happy reunion wasn't going to last forever.

"Nothing is certain with the gods," Pan offered, sounding lame even to his own ears.

Cupid twirled the bottle between his palms, staring off into the distance. "Just in case, we should probably say our goodbyes before I head out tonight." Craning his neck to study Pan, he added, "Don't you agree?"

33

RUBY LOUNGE

The failure of the fourth match should not have sparked even
a glimmer of glee in Cupid's heart, but it did, just the same.
Four men, algorithmically culled by a website that dared to
use Cupid's name, and not a single vibration to be found. An
ominous storm was gathering force. If the gods were to decide
Cupid wasn't giving his best effort, no telling how they'd twist
the screws. Worse yet, Mia might lose faith.

Still, without the finality of the echo beats, Cupid held onto
his hope that the gods would realize their mistake and make
Mia his for all eternity. As the night wore on, it sure seemed as if
Mia was leaning the same way. She seemed increasingly welcoming of each of Cupid's date-ending interventions, even rolling
her eyes this last time and muttering, "What the hell took you
so long?" before dropping her forehead onto the bar.

Cupid lifted his hand to soothe her, braced to draw his fingers through her silky hair when he remembered their rule: no
touching. He retracted his nearly guilty hand and shoved it into
the front pocket of his jeans.

"How are you holding up?" he asked the back of her head. "Can I get you another drink?"

"Mmhmm," she hummed, lifting her head, shoulders, and breasts off the bar. "I'm gonna need a *stiff* one." He might have heard Mia's remark as innocent if not for the teasing swipe of her tongue across her upper lip. *Oh, great. We're doing this again.*

Cupid had a stiff one for Mia, all right, ever since Jonah had opened their front door to reveal this evening's dress of destruction. The upper half covered even less skin than her yoga tops, and all that unavailable flesh called to Cupid in ways he was thoroughly incapable of ignoring.

Forcing his attention from her breasts, Cupid hailed the bartender, a nosy guy with beady eyes and a name tag that said Mo. Seconds later, a fresh gin and tonic arrived on a clean napkin, with a "What can I get you?" to Cupid.

"Oh, I'm not—"

"Come on, the least you can do is have one damn drink with me." The bartender's gaze followed Cupid's pivot toward Mia, whose lips curled into a frisky grin. "What's the matter? You're not okay, Cupid?"

A herd of buffalo charged through his chest before he realized Mia was only referencing the dating site. The stampede slowed to a trot, and Cupid drew a breath. "You know what, I will have a drink. Whatever she's having is fine." Now was not the time to get into a long consultation with the bartender.

"Yes," Mia snapped, "you should definitely have four guys in a row with another on the way."

Mo's eyebrows jumped into his gooped-up hair, and his mouth settled into a this-oughtta-be-good smirk. Cupid gave Mo a withering glare and waved him away.

"Are we having a problem, Mia?"

"Problem? Now, why would you say that?" Mia's head tipped

to the side at an exaggerated angle. *Shit.* He'd been focused on heartbeats and eye contact and not on Mia's alcohol intake. It struck Cupid for the first time that she had consumed a fair amount of liquor for someone her size—especially someone whose body was not accustomed to processing toxins.

Could she have downed a whole drink with each of the prospects—four guys in forty minutes? *Double shit.* Not that liquor would interfere with the vibrations, but a girl passed out on the bar seemed unlikely to make a great first impression.

Mo hustled back with Cupid's drink, horning in on their conversation as if he would be held responsible later for recalling it word for word. "Thanks," Cupid said, a scowl firmly in place as he tossed down a twenty and whirled around so his back faced the bar.

"To Cupid's last arrow," Mia toasted. Cupid's chest thudded once again, but he clinked glasses with her and downed a swig of gin and tonic. "And if this one misses, we send the chubby, flying crybaby home to Mama for a diaper change."

The alcohol had already reached Cupid's throat when the visual assaulted him. A sputter grew into a choke, then a cough, and a hot sting blasted up his sinuses.

"Oh shit, are you okay, Q?" Mia leapt off her stool and pressed her soggy cocktail napkin into his hand.

"I'm fi-i-i—" Another coughing fit strangled his answer.

"Hang on. Here, drink this . . . *slowly.*" The cool glass met his lips, and Cupid sipped at the ice water until the fire in his throat died down.

Glancing sideways at Mia, he clasped his hand over hers and gently lowered the water. "I'm, *uh-uhmm*, fine, thanks."

"*Are* you?"

Not even close, especially when she tipped her head like that and drilled deep inside his gaze. Lies were not a construct

Cupid had mastered yet, but his deflection skills were improving. "Evan should be here any minute now," he said.

Mia grimaced. "You really want me to do this?"

What he wanted to do was kiss her again like their first time in her kitchen, peel off her skintight top, and lick his way down to the miracle of her navel. "I'm sorry, Mia. There's no other way."

She blew out a sigh of frustration and folded her arms under her bosom, which only made everything worse. "No? Hmm, maybe you just need my scent, like a bloodhound. Hey, why don't I peel off my undies right here, right now," she said, smirking when Cupid's jaw hinged open, "and *thennnn*"—she poked Cupid in the chest with her finger—"you can tie them to your side-view mirror and drive all around Tarra, waving them around like a flag flapping in the breeze." Her eyes were wide with mischief and liquor. "Then all you have to do is find" . . . *poke* . . . "my" . . . *poke* . . . "panty echo."

The two sat locked together for several seconds, neither moving a muscle. Mia's little idea had every part of Cupid's body at full salute, a result she'd surely intended.

He gave his erection a discreet nudge and gently coaxed her fingertip off his chest. "Thanks for the creative input, but I don't think that's going to work."

"In that case," she said, "you better scram because I think my date's headed this way."

With an agonizing blend of anticipation and dread, Cupid located Evan. Tall, blond, and bright-eyed, Evan strode over toward Mia's tipsy grin with exactly the eager spring to his step Cupid would have expected. Evan's not-quite-perfect teeth somehow managed to form an endearing smile. The nauseating thought occurred to Cupid that these two would make great-looking babies.

"Oh, he's cute," she said to Cupid. "He's the football player, right?"

"Right." As he'd made more than obvious with that body-hugging shirt. "Don't worry, Mia. Once he gets close enough, I'll make this quick and get you out of here."

"What's your rush?" she asked. Cupid turned away from the rapidly approaching Evan to find Mia applying a fresh coat of lipstick. "I think I might like this one." Ignoring Cupid's dismay, she added, "What? Isn't that what you want?"

"No. I mean yes, of course, if he's the right—"

"Mia?"

Mia reached for the outstretched hand. "Evan." The name rolled off her tongue as if she were greeting Zeus Himself. Their palms met, and Cupid forced himself to push through his own confusing, conflicting emotions and focus on the beats. There it was—he hadn't imagined it—a resounding silence. He'd sort out his feelings later. Right now, he needed to get Mia away from this guy.

Wrenching apart their clasped hands, Cupid grabbed Mia's wrist, shook his head, and said, "Sorry, Mia."

"Sorry, my ass. I am having this date right now, mister, and you need to leave."

Sensing the man closing in behind him, Cupid threw a shoulder block that would have made Hercules proud. "Your date is over, and I'm not leaving without you." In the stare-down that followed, Cupid tightened his grip on Mia's wrist.

"Oh yeah?" Mia stepped into Cupid's body, pressing her icy drink against his chest and wafting a gust of sour breath across his cheek. Her eyes were wild, but no less alluring for their lack of focus. "If you're planning to dump me on my doorstep, thanks but no thanks. I am not in the mood to be alone tonight."

If Cupid didn't keep her company, other arms would hold

her tonight, arms Cupid himself had driven her into, arms that belonged to a man who did not have her best interests at heart. Behind the tough girl act were the saddest brown eyes Cupid had ever seen at close range. Only a man with a heart of stone could have possibly turned her down.

"I won't leave you alone tonight, Mia." Cupid wasn't sure what he'd just committed to, but he could not have been more earnest.

"Promise?" she asked, allowing the edges of her frown to ease upward into the beginnings of a smile.

"Uh, mind if I ask what's going on here?"

Mia's gaze shifted to the agitated man nudging his way around Cupid. "I'm so sorry, Evan," she said. "There's been a terrible mistake. My friend was about to take me home . . . and not leave me."

Before Evan could protest, Mia pushed past him, towing Cupid behind. The cool night air provided a welcome reprieve from the stale haze of failure, but the heat between them had only intensified. Cupid's no-touch rule had imploded at the worst possible time. Mia was shooting off pheromones as if she'd bathed in them, and all the logical arguments for not touching her made less and less sense.

Ignoring the cosmic consequences weighing on his heart even as Mia trapped him against the car door with that body, his personal agony and singular relief, Cupid succumbed with a deep groan, opened his lips, and drew her tongue inside. *So wrong.*

She flattened Cupid against the Prius, cancelling out his few working brain cells with a harsh grind of body parts that wouldn't take no for an answer, not that he offered it. Her fingers found his zipper; his breath hitched with each metal tooth unclenched. *Must stop her.*

"Oh god, oh god," she mumbled between deep kisses and gasps for air. She pressed her breasts to his chest. "Touch me. Please, Q, if you care about me at all, touch me."

Mia's need struck a chord deep inside him, surpassing any desire of his own or concern for divine retaliation. What kind of monster would refuse? His hand slipped between her soft thighs, found the warm valley. He rubbed the heel of his hand against the thin fabric. She bit down on his tongue and breached the opening in his boxers—reckless fingers meeting swollen flesh. *What could it hurt?*

Cupid moaned and burrowed beneath the silk, crazed with her desire on his fingers and her needy whimpers against his mouth. Mia rocked her hips, grinding against his hand while she pumped him furiously in return. *Hades, here I come.*

God and mortal yielded, but the Prius held its ground; tires straining to hold the vehicle in place, cold metal squealing with the pounding and rocking. Mia quivered and spasmed into his palm, tightening her fist and losing her rhythm. Maddened by her erratic strokes, Cupid pistoned wildly until three days' pressure uncorked in a spectacular release.

An insistent rumble against his ass cut through Cupid's bliss. *His phone.* He didn't need to see the picture of the buck on his screen; who else would call at the exact moment of Cupid's colossal orgasm? Delaying the reckoning would only make matters worse, and Cupid was fresh out of wiggle room.

"Sorry, Mia, I can't ignore this," he apologized as he answered Pan's call.

"What the FUCK have you just done?"

34

LUMP

Twin streaks of bright light arced across the truck's rearview mirror. Inside the parked Titan, Pan clenched and unclenched his fists once, twice, three times, as if rehearsing for Cupid's arrival. Despite the short ride to the diner, Pan's revenge fantasies had fully taken root—a punch to Cupid's stomach, perhaps; a knee to the nuts, *definitely*.

The Prius rolled to a quiet stop in the space to Pan's left. Glowing in the reflection off the dashboard, Cupid took his sweet time powering down the hybrid. The stalling spoke louder than had all of Cupid's objections during their brief phone call. *Oh, he's guilty all right.* Rage coursed through Pan's system like hemlock, paralyzing his heart and freezing out his affection for his oldest friend. Pan drew in one more set of choppy breaths, but the action did little more than remind him exactly how out of control he felt.

Cupid's anxiety filled Pan's nostrils even before Cupid stepped out of his car onto the makeshift altar for the slaughter. The irony nearly brought a smile to Pan's face: the lamb offering himself to the goat. *Very funny, you immortal fuckers.* Cupid's gaze dropped to the pavement, his hands retreated into his pockets, and he inched toward Pan's truck.

Pan threw open his door. His boots hit the asphalt with a purposeful *thunk*, and he opened his mouth to rip Cupid a new one. Before he could get a single word out, Cupid started spewing like a helium balloon stabbed with a pitchfork.

"I'm sorry, Pan. I swear, I didn't think it would hurt anything. We only used our hands. She was drunk, and I—"

"Stop it."

"But you know I wouldn't—"

"God*dammit*, Q! I said shut up."

Cupid shrank back, catching his upper lip between his teeth.

Pan spread his hand across the expanse of his forehead, rolling the pressure points at his temples with the pads of his fingers. "I can't think when you talk."

"Sorry," Cupid mumbled, looking away when Pan scowled at him again.

"We should go inside," Pan commanded, leaving the rest to play silently in his head, *so I don't beat you to a pulp.*

Cupid nodded, still working the puppy dog eyes but keeping quiet for once. This situation was dire, goddammit, and maybe it was about time Pan stopped shielding Mr. Innocent from the truth. It hadn't worked too well for either of them thus far.

"Y'know what? No. Gimme your fucking hand."

"Huh?" Cupid's forehead creased from confusion or fear; either worked for Pan.

He poked a finger at Cupid's wrist. "You really want me to reach into your pocket and get it myself?"

The hand was produced. Cupid flinched as Pan grasped him by the wrist and yanked him forward. "Ow."

Their hips slammed together, but Pan was in no condition to enjoy the contact. "Quiet."

Vibrating with rage, Pan tugged Cupid's arm around his back and locked their joined hands against Pan's spine. Cupid's shallow, labored breaths sprayed Pan's taste buds like droplets of dark ale: rich, bitter, intoxicating. Pan dragged Cupid's fingers down his back, drove them lower, under his belt, and—*fuck it, why not?*—inside the waistband of his boxers. Cupid tensed and fought the downward motion, but Pan outmuscled him, forcing Cupid's fingers to the growth on Pan's tailbone.

Cupid gasped. "What *is* that?"

Perhaps it was cruel to ignore the question, but Pan had a fucking right to be cruel. Flattening Cupid's hand against his skin, Pan traced the slope and fall of the stump, pressing firmly when Cupid tried to pull away. Beads of sweat gathered above Cupid's dark eyebrows; a vein throbbed at his temple. An onlooker might have mistaken their embrace as the prelude to sex. Someone standing close enough might have misinterpreted Cupid's erection as desire for Pan or construed Pan's lack of erection as disinterest. They all would have been wrong.

Cupid didn't move, barely breathed while the pieces clicked into place. "Your tail is growing back?"

"So it would appear."

Cupid's fingertips glided across the lump on their own, either unaware Pan had loosened his grip or perhaps serving his penance. "How long before it's . . .?" The question died with a piteous shake of Cupid's head.

Flaccid cock and tail bud be damned, Pan's resolve to hurt Cupid faded, which only made him more furious. "We need to focus on what *you* did, Q."

Pan glared at him until Cupid finally gave up and looked away, stroking the bump one last time on his way out of Pan's jeans, a tender sweep that weakened Pan's knees.

"I promise you, I did not sleep with her."

"I don't really think sleeping is the issue here," Pan pointed out.

"But my genitals were nowhere near her—"

"For the love of Zeus, would you please just stop? I have heard more about your dick in the week you've been here than all the other deities I've serviced put together."

Mentioning the beast made it impossible for Pan not to steal a glance, and he immediately regretted his wandering eyes. How unfair could things be? Yeah, he *so* didn't ask that question in his line of work.

"I'm *sorry*, okay? But I still don't see what my, um, has to do with . . ."

"My ass?"

"Yes."

Not nearly enough, Pan acknowledged with a rueful smirk. "Apparently, the Divine Council believes you might be moved to control yourself if they threaten to turn your old chum back into a goat."

"By the gods, Pan, I am sorry. I had no idea they would mess with you on my account." *Right*, because Pan had neglected to mention the minor detail of his impotence.

"Well, now you do. So keep it in your damn pants," said Pan, adding, "and don't invite company in there with it."

"Didn't mean to," he grumbled. "I just meant to pleasure Mia."

"In case you aren't aware, lover boy, Mia doesn't need you for that."

Cupid seemed to shrink an inch or two. Message received; remorse achieved. Nothing could be gained by further browbeating, and, frankly, the smell of warm apples and cinnamon wafting from the diner replaced Pan's hunger for revenge with a far more urgent need: pie.

The last of his toxic anger left Pan in a heavy exhale. "You hungry?"

Cupid cautiously lifted his eyes. "You're not going to hurt me?"

Pan huffed. *As if.* "Not right now."

Relieved for the moment, Cupid rubbed his hand across his belly as if gauging his need for food from the outside in. "I could eat."

Pan led his infuriating friend under the neon sign and inside the gleaming steel boxcar. The owner's daughter greeted them with a bright smile from behind the yellowing counter.

"Welcome in. Sit anywhere you like."

They slid into a booth just past a young, gooey-eyed couple who looked to be on their first date, taking delicate spoon swipes at opposite sides of an ice cream sundae. *Bet he leaves her the cherry.*

The waitress arrived at their booth and fixed a pair of starry eyes on Pan. "You boys know what you want?" She opened her mouth just enough to wedge the tip of the pen between her back teeth and flash him a glimpse of tongue.

Pan had been to this diner no fewer than fifty times since settling in this particular Tarra, and he'd been served by the owner's then-jailbait-now-barely-legal daughter at least a dozen of those. While the girl had always done a competent job with his food orders, their conversation had never progressed beyond side dishes and condiments—which suited Pan fine. "Apple pie à la mode, please."

"You want that hot, sweetie?" she asked, emphasis on the *hot*.

"Just the pie, not the ice cream. He'll have the same."

She giggled too hard as she wrote down Pan's instructions and glided away. While he would have liked to have been flattered, Pan knew the gods were pulling the strings. The proof was as close as the hump on his ass and the flaccid cock in his lap.

"How did you leave things with Mia?"

"Rather abruptly. Someone bleated?" Well, well, well. *Someone* was getting his sass back now that the threat of bodily harm was no longer imminent.

"At least you had the good sense to pick up my call. You really don't want to piss me off any further tonight."

"So I've gathered." Cupid picked up two corners of his white paper placemat, curled the edges under with restless fingers, and smoothed them out again. "Mia's impossible. This last guy, *Evan* . . ." Cupid wrinkled his nose as if he'd fallen face-first into a pile of manure. "She actually wanted to go on her date with him even though they weren't a match. How am I supposed to sit by and watch that?"

"Maybe you're not."

Cupid tensed. "You'd have me leave some unworthy mortal alone with Mia to pillage her body?"

The poor bastard wasn't going to appreciate the advice, but Pan gave it just the same. "Maybe she wouldn't be so damn horny for you all the time if she had another outlet."

"Now you're *really* being disgusting."

"I feel for you, Q, but Mia's a grown woman, and she doesn't actually need your permission to date. The less you're tempted to do whatever you two just did, the better off all three of us are going to be."

Cupid's gaze drifted to the spinning pie case on the counter, where it stayed fixed until their own slices arrived. A long, pensive silence and several forkfuls of soothing, apple goodness later, Cupid met Pan's eyes. "Fine, I'll try."

35

CONVINCING

What had seemed somewhat reasonable the night before turned into a snarl of doubt when Cupid actually had to follow through. Only the tactile memory of his fingertips rolling over Pan's tail stub kept him on task. He loved Pan like a brother, certainly much more than his own annoying little brother Anteros, and it killed Cupid that his well-meaning but obviously misguided actions were being turned so brutally against his best friend. Pan couldn't go back to the satyr life, not now. And Cupid sure as hell couldn't be the one responsible for it.

Two thousand years of Pan's absence had not dimmed Cupid's memory of the satyr's tortured existence on Mount Olympus. While Cupid had flitted about with a grown man's desires trapped inside his tragically pubescent body, Pan's situation held its own cruelty: a man's soul merged with the libido of a wild beast and a body that ostracized him from both worlds.

None of that stopped Cupid's heart from lurching when Mia answered his call, her warm, trusting voice stabbing even deeper at his innards.

"Hey, you. Am I gonna see you in class this morning?"

Class. Sweat. Skin. Heat. What Cupid wouldn't give to stand inches from a barely covered Mia as she stretched and posed.

"Um, no, sorry. I actually called to talk to you about your idea."

"My idea? *Eli, take that block out of your mouth!* Which idea might that be?"

"Uh, moving ahead with finding your proper match."

"Wait, you're not talking about tying my underwear to your—"

"Gods no." *And his erection was back.* Pan's plan to hold this conversation by phone was already paying off. At least this way, Mia wouldn't see how she affected him. "I think you should go ahead and meet the next bunch without me."

"Oh. We're back to that." Her voice fell, and along with it, Cupid's spirits. "So your line about not leaving me, that was just to pull me away from Evan? Or was it your twisted little way of getting into my skirt at the end of the night?"

Cupid had no loftier explanation to offer, giving Mia no choice but to take his silence as confirmation. Indeed, Cupid had become every bit the manipulative jerk she thought he was. Divine intervention, priapism, and heartache aside, nobody but Cupid deserved the blame for this almighty mess. A long, sad sigh filled Cupid's ear.

"This little game is really getting old."

"I'm sorry," he mumbled.

"Sorry? *Pshhh,*" Mia responded. "*Jonah, stop teasing your brother!* Good talk, Q. Know what? I'll take it from here."

He cleared his throat, hoping only his most altruistic intentions would reach her. "I'll email you the list of your next twenty matches in order of compatibility."

"Twenty?" Mia's harsh laugh sent a chill down Cupid's spine. "I haven't been on twenty dates in my whole life. Think I should see them all in one night?" The shape of Mia's voice narrowed to a sharp point, a steely spear meant to wound him back. "Oh, I know! I'll rent a room at the Tarra Arms and give each one a ten-minute roll. Then I'd figure out which one got my coochie vibrating, now wouldn't I?"

"Mia."

"Yes, I like this plan." Indeed, he could tell she did. Mia's words sliced deep, and Cupid bled with each new lash. "I'll call the motel and inquire whether they rent rooms by the hour. Let's see now, ten minutes times twenty guys, that's two hundred minutes. Round that up to four hours allowing for a double header or two . . ."

"Mia, *please.*"

"Please what?" Their conversation broke with the kind of rupture that feels like the two ends might never find their way to the middle again. "What do you want from me, Q?"

What *did* Cupid want? He wanted all this pain to end. He wanted his mother to stop punishing everyone around him for his failures. He wanted Pan not to turn into a goat. And more than anything, he wanted Mia to find her Right Love and live a long, happy life, even if his own heart would forever be shattered.

"I want you to be happy, Mia."

"But not with you."

A hammer pounded at the base of Cupid's skull. Around and around they'd gone, around and around they'd continue to go as long as Mia still held out hope she might still end up with Cupid. "No, Mia, not with me. Would you please do me the enormous favor of getting this over with quickly?"

"Sure," she huffed, "there's nothing I'd rather do than an enormous favor for you. Look, Q, Mom's sprained her ankle, so even if I wanted to continue being your guinea pig, my babysitter is out of commission until further notice."

"Isn't there someone else you can call?"

"Um, no. Despite recent evidence to the contrary, I don't go out much, and I don't have a stable of sitters. In case it's escaped your notice, I don't exactly have spare funds, plus Eli has serious separation issues. Sorry, seems like we're both shit outta luck."

"What if I stayed with the boys?"

Silence.

This was certainly not the role Cupid wanted to play in her life, but what else could he hope for under the circumstances? The stakes had never been higher. The next screwup would be his last.

"You want to babysit my boys while I go out on a date . . . or twenty?"

Her taunt flooded Cupid's brain with vivid pictures of a naked and writhing Mia, beneath forty hands and twenty mouths and body parts he couldn't bear to imagine. Despite his repulsion, Cupid knew better than to hesitate at this critical juncture. "Sure, why not? How hard can it be? Jonah knows how to do everything, right?"

"Jesus, Q. Jonah's five. The fact that you'd even suggest that should tell me everything I need to know."

"Then, *you* tell me what to do. I'm a quick learner; you've said so yourself."

Two or three seconds passed while Mia considered his offer. Cupid held his tongue and nurtured the seed of hope with all his might. When she groaned, Cupid knew he had her. "This is insane. You know that, right?"

Cupid tried to keep the smile out of his voice when he answered. "It'll be an adventure." Mortals loved adventure.

"It's already *been* an adventure." She sighed heavily into the phone. "I can't figure out what it is about you, but from the moment we met, you've made me disregard everything that makes any sense."

Cupid knew the answer, but he suspected Mia wouldn't welcome his insights. "That sounds like it might be a yes."

"God help me."

"Oh, that is *definitely* a yes."

Mia's tone eased as she fired instructions. "My rules, all the way. The boys need structure. They crave routine—especially since the asshole left. *Capiche?*"

"You're the boss, Mia."

"Have you ever changed a diaper?"

"No."

"Given a toddler a bath?"

"No."

"Do you have the slightest idea what to do if a baby is choking?"

He wanted to reassure her, but lying where the boys' safety was concerned would be inexcusable. Cupid lacked pretty much every qualification for the job. "Show me once, and I'll never forget."

"I truly must be insane, because I believe you."

"I won't let you down, Mia."

With the decision made, Mia barked orders as if she were Alexander the Great commandeering his troops. Cupid was the lone soldier, his mortal enemies, dirty diapers and bedtime. Cupid soaked up the details as if any one of them might become life or death—the boys' or his own. Throwing in a few "mmhmms" for good measure, he took feverish notes until Mia's litany slowed and eventually stopped.

"Be here at five. You can help me give the boys their dinner and baths. I'll supervise while you change Luke's diaper and get all three in pj's. How are we doing so far?"

"Fine."

"You're okay with all this? Things get messy sometimes; there might be tears."

"I'll try not to cry. Promise."

Mia's burst of laughter streamed through the phone like a banquet after a long, hard fast, and Cupid gobbled the nourishment into his ravenous soul. With fresh resolve to do this one thing well, Cupid said, "Mia, I can handle it. The safety of your family is my top priority. You know how much I care about your boys."

"I'll never forgive myself if something happens to them while I'm out on some fool's errand to find true love."

Cupid wanted to assure Mia that Right Love was no fool's errand, but that would've missed the point. "Neither will I," he answered most sincerely.

After a long pause, Mia set out the toughest of her conditions. "You need to promise me there will be no more interference with my dates. It's humiliating."

"I promise."

"And I don't want to hear about heartbeats and echoes. It takes all the suspense out of the awkward first date. Can you promise to keep that sh—*stuff* to yourself?"

"I'll do my best." He wanted to commit to her terms, but they both knew Cupid was lousy at holding back, especially where Mia was concerned.

"And I will not be judged," she added sternly.

How could he judge, really, when he was the one pushing her into the arms of all the other men? "Agreed."

The usual sounds of little boy chaos peppered the background while Mia weighed all the evidence. Cupid hadn't realized he'd been holding his breath until she delivered her verdict.

"I guess you're hired."

3 6

BABYSITTING

Self-discipline alone would not have been enough to keep Cupid from jumping to answer Mia's doorbell, but where resolve failed him, two little boys and a very comfortable, fat cat held him pinned to the couch.

"I've got it!" yelled Mia.

Cupid's shoulders twisted toward the voice tearing down the steps over the click-clack of heels. Tonight's outfit seemed a merciful choice: loose black pants and a long top that fluttered behind Mia as she rushed to greet her date. Her hand grasped the knob, and Mia fired a warning glare across the room. *Don't fudge this up for me.* With a boldness bordering on defiance, she pulled open the door.

Cupid wanted to look away, wanted to spare himself that moment of fated connection that might strike when their eyes first met, but he couldn't. What good would it have done him anyway? Because it wasn't what he saw but what he heard that made his blood run cold: *the beat.*

Holy Hera. Wait, was it one or two? He needed to get closer.

Scooping up a boy in each arm, Cupid sprang from the couch. Merlin spilled out of Cupid's lap but not before jamming his claws into Cupid's inflamed crotch.

"Unf!" Cupid doubled over like the jaws of a metal trap snapped shut, clutching the boys for all he was worth. Eli and Luke burst into giggles as Cupid staggered to Mia's side.

She stepped out onto the stoop toward her shell-shocked date. "We were just leaving," she said in a tight tone clearly meant to end the conversation. "Goodnight, boys."

Mia's stern glower should have silenced Cupid, but he had more pressing worries. The beat, definitely one-way—and coming from Mia. *Shit.*

"I need to talk to you," Cupid said. "It's urgent."

Mia balled her hands into angry little fists. "Not. Now."

Cupid stole a glance at Mia's date and nearly lost his balance again. Tall and devastatingly handsome with a healthy crop of dark waves on top—the resemblance was unmistakable. The first guy she picked for herself was the mortal duplicate of Cupid, and for *him*, Mia beat?

"Uhh"—Mia's date jerked his chin toward Cupid—"who's this?"

Mia thrust her hip between the two men, creating a tragic chain of mismatched signals—Cupid beating for Mia, Mia beating for the Cupid lookalike, her date beating for no one.

"He's Q," Jonah answered.

"Q! Q!" Eli echoed, bouncing his tiny bottom up and down against Cupid's arm.

"Boys, quiet!" she snapped, effectively silencing the chorus of Qs. "He's the *babysitter*." She sounded like someone else, someone Cupid didn't know. Cold, detached, finished.

If her date had the sense he was looking in the mirror, he did not appear threatened by the lowly babysitter. "Ah, cool."

"And those are my boys, Jonah and Eli, who promised to be good." Cupid caught the heat of Mia's warning though she aimed her words at Jonah. "Mommy and Reese are leaving now."

Reese. Cupid hated as he had never hated before.

"Bye-bye, Mommy and Reese." Jonah's sweet voice shattered the icy resolve Mia had meant for Cupid. Her sons had only gotten caught in the crossfire.

An ache settled in her eyes, a mother's regret. Cupid shivered as Mia stepped inside again, spreading her arms to embrace the sons Cupid was hugging. She took her time with the silent amends, breathing each one into her lungs, dropping tender kisses on their freshly shampooed heads.

"Mommy will see you tomorrow. Be good for Q." Shifting her sad smile to Cupid, Mia whispered, "Don't wait up," pivoted toward the door, and hooked her arm around her date's waiting elbow.

Cupid forced his feet to stay put, hugging Jonah and Eli a little tighter as the click of the front door finalized Mia's departure.

"Mommy go?" asked little Eli.

"Yes," Cupid answered. "Mommy go." *Mommy walked into a giant mess of heartache, and I couldn't do one thing to stop her.* "Who wants to watch *A Bedtime Story?*"

"Me! Me!" Both little boys bounced in Cupid's arms.

"Okay, little monsters, let's get you settled in front of the TV."

Cupid made an exciting ride of their trip back to the couch and tossed them into the cushions with carefully delivered chaos. The moment Cupid hit the cushions, the boys burrowed in on both sides, filling his arms and lap. Even Merlin forgave Cupid, after issuing a long warning yowl, and wedged himself between the warm bundles of boy.

The television droned on, hypnotizing the boys but failing to take Cupid's mind off Mia's heart. By now, she and her date would have arrived at Bombay Palace. She'd be sipping chai tea, falling deeper and harder for Reese. He'd be soaking it all in—*who wouldn't?* A beautiful, enthralled girl, aching to fill the hole Cupid himself had hollowed out.

The vision persisted: Mia clinging to this Reese with all her heart, shunning the Right Love the gods had in store for her while some unworthy *kopanos* stole her affection and her devotion without offering Mia an equal share in return, trapped forever in a futile struggle to win Reese's love like a fig tree straining to produce fruit in the shade.

And what about these sweet, innocent boys? Should they have to settle as well? Hadn't there already been enough of that with their father? Even if Mia could unravel herself from this relationship, would any of them fully recover?

This is my fault, all of it.

Helplessness turned to agitation; guilt became determination. Only one conclusion made any sense. He couldn't let Mia spend another minute in that man's presence. Better to endure her wrath now and save them all from a horrible fate.

Cupid was no fool; this was a huge risk. Mia would be angrier than ever, maybe even angrier than she'd ever been at "the asshole ex." If this backfired, Mia might well push him away for good, and where would that leave them?

Mia would languish in unrequited misery or wander aimlessly from one bad relationship to the next. Pan's tail would grow back, followed by hooves and horns. He'd be a pariah on Earth, doomed to live out the remainder of his days exiled to the woods, cut off from the human contact he craved. His heart would blacken toward Cupid. As for Cupid, he and his shattered soul and useless, permanent erection would be locked forevermore in this Limbo-on-Earth, never to be desired again, never to return home to the life he knew or the people who once loved him, without the comforts of the palace or the amusement of his arrows. Alone with his conscience for all eternity.

The answer was clear: he could not fail.

Before Cupid could talk himself out of it, he gathered all three boys into Mia's car along with a responsible supply of diapers, juice boxes, snacks, and enough toys to keep them all occupied. The older two clambered into their car seats while Cupid fastened the baby in and double-checked the security of Luke's straps, grateful for once for the blasted belts.

"Great job, Eli. What a good boy you are."

"Me too?" asked Jonah, pulling his seat belt across his lap and clicking it in place.

Cupid leaned across the seat to ruffle Jonah's hair. "Yes, you too. You are a huge help, Joe."

Jonah beamed. "Grams never takes us out at night," he told Cupid with wide-eyed wonder.

"I thought we could all use an adventure," Cupid answered.

The controls of Mia's Subaru bore little resemblance to his Prius, but Cupid had no trouble finding the buttons to adjust the seat and mirrors as Pan had taught him. The engine roared to life and settled into an uneven rumble immediately drowned out by the stream of kids' music pouring out of the speakers and attacking each of Cupid's jangled nerves. He reached for the knob to turn it down but thought better of it when Eli and Jonah started singing along.

According to the car's computer, Cupid had twenty minutes to come up with some story to justify taking three little boys out for a late-night drive, interrupt Mia's date after swearing he wouldn't, and embarrass her in public this time. He'd have to tell Mia what he'd heard, one beat with zero chance of ever being reciprocated. He would have no problem describing for her how that particular sting would develop into a fiery sword searing her heart. With each mile the car closed in on Mia's location, the familiar agony gripped Cupid's heart more fiercely.

The red light gave Cupid a chance to catch his breath. Three more blocks, said the GPS, and he'd just about worked out what he needed to tell Mia if she gave him a chance to talk before taking her boys and kicking Cupid out of her life for good.

He exhaled deeply as the light changed to green, then stepped on the gas and eased into the intersection. A sharp horn blared to their right. Cupid jerked his head toward the huge truck barreling toward them. Headlights blinded him. Instinct took the wheel, swerving away from the truck into oncoming traffic.

Skidding tires. Blaring horns. The squeal of brakes strained beyond capacity. Shattered glass and the sickening gnash of metal against metal.

Silence.

37

CRASH

Reese's car screeched to a stop inches from the yellow police tape. Mia threw open the door, ducked under the tape, and sprinted toward the rescue workers clustered at the center of the scene. Adrenaline flooded her system. The fight or flight question wasn't even a dilemma—Q was a dead man. But first, she needed to hold her boys.

"Miss. *Miss!*" One of the patrolmen jumped in front of her, arms spread wide. "You're going to have to wait behind the—"

"Those are my babies in there!"

"Okay, gimme one sec." The officer kept both eyes on Mia while speaking into his shoulder. "I have the mother here . . . yes . . . okay," he said, then nodded to Mia. "I'll take you in. Please, mind your step."

Mia followed the uniform into the thick smoke. Even through her tightly cupped fingers, she tasted ash. Sloshing through puddles and dodging car parts burnt beyond recognition, Mia repeated her mantra—"They're okay. They're okay. They're okay."—into her hand until the words lost their meaning.

The officer guided her around the massive truck, lying on its side like a wino sleeping off a binge as firefighters doused the hissing metal. Mia tried not to look, but the incinerated door confirmed what she already knew: the driver of the truck had not survived.

"They're okay. They're okay."

At last, she reached the heart of all the buzz, and there stood Q, holding Eli and Jonah in his arms as he had in her living room not an hour earlier.

"Mommy!" Eli cried, lunging from Q's arms into his mother's.

"My baby!" Mia pulled him to her chest, and the flood of tears broke free. "You okay, E?" She loosened her grip on the boy to thoroughly inspect him for bumps and bruises. *Nothing,* as Q had reported. Mia peppered her son's forehead and hot cheeks with grateful kisses.

"Mommy, we did a spin!" Jonah scrambled out of Q's arms and rushed to Mia's side.

"You sure did, bug." She dipped down to gather him up in her other arm.

Fixing an icy glare on Q, she asked, "Luke?"

At least the selfish fucker knew better than to make excuses or move any closer. "He's fine, Mia. He slept through the whole thing."

Keep your cool. "Where . . . is . . . my *baby?*"

Q pointed over his shoulder. "In his car seat. We didn't want to disturb him."

"You didn't want to *disturb* him?" The insanity of his remark tuned Mia's pitch to a piercing howl. "You might've thought of that before you took him out of his crib and drove him into the middle of an *eight-car pileup.*" Mia elbowed Q out of her way.

"Mia, I'm so sorry. I—"

She spun and cut him off. "Don't."

Bent to peer through the car window, Mia confirmed Lucas was safe and sleeping soundly. Her forehead dropped to the heated glass, and she drew in a deep breath. And another. The acrid tang burned a path down her throat and into her lungs. Fury made room for relief, and hot tears flooded her cheeks.

"Ms. Barnes?" A gentle hand landed on Mia's back. She drew in one last shaky sob before peering up into the eyes of yet another official type wearing an expression that said, *it's been a long damn night.*

"Yes?"

"Ma'am, my name's Lieutenant Goode. You're Ms. Barnes, correct? The mother of these three boys?"

Mia nodded, fully ready for the officer to voice all the self-recriminations she'd been playing through her head since Q's call had interrupted her date ten minutes ago—the longest ten minutes of her life. *How could you have left your boys with a man who was so clearly unqualified to make responsible decisions?* But if that's what Lieutenant Goode was thinking, he kept his thoughts to himself.

"We need to get you and your children out of harm's way just as quickly as possible."

"Absolutely. Yes, of course." Problem was, Mia couldn't get her brain to work past the mismatch of her two hands versus three children with all their paraphernalia. "I'm sorry, I can't . . ."

"Ms. Barnes," he said calmly, "time is of the essence. Perhaps Mr. Arrows could be of assistance with the children?" The lieutenant's gaze slid carefully to Q, then back.

Sensing his opportunity, Q stepped forward and opened his arms. "I'm here."

This wasn't the moment to turn away help, no matter her feelings. Mia simply could not manage the two older boys *and* Luke *and* all three car seats on her own. Without a word, Mia transferred Eli and Jonah to Q. The boys, trusting as ever, latched onto Q as if he'd been a fixture in their lives for years, not mere days. Working as quickly as possible, Mia slipped into the back seat and drew Luke into her arms while Lieutenant Goode climbed in the other side and unbuckled the car seats.

"The diaper bag's up front," Q called back to her, "in case they need a snack or something." A *snack*. What they needed were their warm, safe beds. If Jonah didn't have nightmares for weeks, it would be a miracle, and who knew what kind of trauma Eli would suffer down the road?

Mia bit back the rage she couldn't express with a baby in her arms, a toxic smoothie of anger, guilt, betrayal, and bitter disappointment churning in her belly. Where was all that therapy when she really needed it?

"If you're ready, ma'am?" Under different circumstances, the sight before her might have at least inspired a grin: the strapping, authoritative lieutenant with a car seat grasped in each hand, a booster seat tucked under one arm, and the brightly striped diaper bag slung over his broad shoulder. "I'm going to lead you all out of here. Ms Barnes, I want you to keep your eyes glued to my back and stick as close to me as you can. Okay? And Mr. Arrows, you hold tight to those boys and stay right behind Ms. Barnes. Everyone got that?"

Lieutenant Goode waited for them both to nod, then squared his shoulders and set a course through the ruins. Mia's focus caught on the diaper bag bouncing against his broad back, its cheerful burst of color as out of place amid the disaster as sequins at a funeral. She tried not to jostle the sleeping baby, but as they neared the police tape, Luke was jarred awake by the commotion of shouted questions.

"Can you tell us what happened? Who caused the accident?"

Mia scanned the scene for the first time, squinting into a

sea of flashes popping against the eerie haze. Luke whined in her arms.

"How is it possible you survived unscathed? Are you a professional driver?"

"What's your name? Are you the father?"

"Are you two estranged? Who was that man who dropped you off?"

"Have you been drinking, sir?"

Goode picked through the throngs and pressed forward. Mia followed the bouncing diaper bag. Beyond the crush of the crowd, the lieutenant drew them into a huddle. "Unfortunately, we won't be able to release your car for several hours. Is there someone I can call to give you a ride home?"

Mia spun toward the general direction Reese had dropped her off. "I think my date might be around here somewhere." Her date, a good-looking, *normal* guy whose company she had actually been enjoying.

Goode reached for the radio at his shoulder. "What kind of car was he driving?"

Between her first-date jitters and the ugly scene with Q before she'd left home, Mia couldn't even be sure of the color of Reese's car, let alone the make. "Uh . . ."

"Can you describe what your date looks like?"

The easiest way to describe Reese was standing right in front of her. "He looks like *him*." Mia jutted her chin toward Q, who acknowledged her comment with a tight grimace. "Y'know what? Never mind," she said. "There's no way his car would fit all the kids' seats anyway." And as much as she hated to admit it, Mia had a pretty good idea her date hadn't stuck around for the horror show that was her life, not that she could blame him. Still, she'd felt something for the guy, and that made her even angrier at Q.

"Why don't I give you a lift?" said Goode. He seemed like a decent sort, but then, if there was one point this evening had hammered home, it was that Mia was truly the world's crappiest judge of character. Though to be fair, the universe had been sending that message for quite some time now.

Mia studied the name on his badge, the gold bar on his collar, and the trustworthy look in his eyes. If this guy wasn't a safe bet, she might as well throw in the damn towel for good. "Thank you. That's very kind of you."

"Sure thing, ma'am. I can fit you all in my squad car if you two don't mind a tight squeeze up front."

"That's no prob—" started Q.

"Oh, no. It's just the four of us," Mia said, answering Q's hurt expression with a harsh glare.

The officer followed Mia's gaze to the man who had nearly killed her children. "Sorry, I thought . . .?" God only knew what Q had told the police about their relationship.

"Mr. Arrows is definitely not coming home with us. *Ever.*"

Cupid's head slumped forward, and he pulled both boys tighter to his chest.

"I see," answered the officer, who seemed to be trying to work out their strange dynamic. "In that case, my car is just over here."

He led them to a black-and-white cruiser. Cinderella could not have been any happier to see her coach. *Just let me make it home and put my babies to bed.*

The lieutenant organized the car seats in back and stepped aside for Mia and Q to settle the boys inside. "Try to ignore the whole police car aspect if you can," he said, but Jonah had already connected the dots.

"Mommy, can we put on the siren?"

Mia clicked the belt into place across Jonah's seat and gave him a peck on his sweet little nose. "I don't think your brothers would handle the noise too well right now, Joe." His sleepy pout tugged at Mia's already brittle heartstrings. "Don't you think we've had enough excitement for one night, kiddo?"

Jonah's little brain worked back through the evening's events until a smile stretched from dimple to dimple. "We had a big adventure."

Mia chuckled. "A little too big, bug." *Waaay too big.* Her chuckle bloomed into full-blown, maniacal laughter by the time she climbed into the passenger seat. *Loony bin, here we come.*

Hold your shit together, Mia. Your boys are counting on you, and you're all they have.

Mia closed her eyes and pulled in three deep breaths, releasing each in a loud, practiced *whoosh.* Centered and feeling a bit more in control, she opened her eyes to a scene that nearly unraveled her all over again. Lieutenant Goode and Q were having an intense conversation, which ended with the lieutenant extending a handshake and a shoulder squeeze that seemed to say, "Good man."

I cannot swallow any more tonight.

The lieutenant shot Mia a sympathetic smile as he slipped into the driver's seat. He twisted the key in the ignition, and the headlights threw an otherworldly spotlight into the fiery haze. Q threw an arm up to shield his eyes, but he didn't look away.

She shouldn't have met his gaze, but Mia feared she might miss her last chance to see the man she'd grown so fond of, the enigma who'd burst into her life and tossed all her carefully organized balls into the air. The man who'd thrilled her as no other man had ever come close to doing, whose outrageous ideas about love and destiny had raised her hopes and wrecked her. The man who, despite using terrible judgment in putting her children in harm's way, had somehow managed to navigate an eight-car pileup without a single scratch on her boys or even her car. Mia should have cemented him in her memory as the larger-than-life superhero with the Q on his chest, not contaminated her last impression by taking in the broken man exposed by the harsh blaze of the headlights.

The bright eyes that had danced with such childlike joy squinted back at Mia, desperate and defeated. The endearing, confident grin was replaced with a dejected frown. The miraculous body that had awakened hers with unspeakable pleasures was no more than an empty, beautiful husk.

She had no idea, really, who this person was or where he'd come from, but Mia knew for damn sure she would never again meet anyone like Quentin Arrows.

38

TOWN HERO

Cupid perched at the edge of Pan's couch, hands folded between his knees in what might have been a prayerful pose if he'd ever once met a god worth beseeching. Meanwhile, Pan's method of viewing the TV coverage was pacing an even deeper rut in the carpet while taking turns yelling at the reporters and Cupid.

"Under the radar, I told you. How is this under the radar?" Pan cradled his head with both hands as if it might blast off his neck.

Though Cupid survived the crash, he was deeper in the stew than ever—with Mia, with the gods, and now with Pan. "I've apologized at least twenty-five times. I feel horrible, Pan. I don't know what else to say."

"Quiet! I need to hear this."

"*Have you seen the aerial footage yet?*" the reporter asked TV Cupid. "*Can we cut to the live copter feed?*"

The grisly matrix of twisted metal came into view as the propellers chopped up the smoky clouds over the accident scene.

"*Wow,*" said TV Cupid.

"I feel sick all over again," said live Cupid. His stomach lurched once more just to back up his story.

"*Exactly. Our collision experts tell us there was a 0.06 margin for error, and you navigated through without a dent. It's almost superhuman.*"

"Oh shit," Pan muttered.

Cupid's attention snapped to Pan. "What?"

"The gods do not appreciate any references to the divine. It raises their hackles."

"*I learned that from the Speed Racer app.*"

Pan groaned and squeezed his temples. "Please tell me you didn't also announce you learned to drive just last week from a video game."

"No, Pan. I told you, I was cool."

The reporter threw an arm around TV Cupid and smiled at the camera with two perfectly matched lines of chalk-white teeth. "*Well, folks, you heard it here first. Mr. Arrows saved the day, thanks to Speed Racer. I dare say, I will be buying this game for my two teenagers. Sadly, we've learned the truck driver was DOA at Tarra General, but thanks to your, no offense, freakish reflexes, eleven adults and six children walked away from this tragic scene unscathed. This town owes you a huge debt of gratitude, Quentin Arrows. Back to you, Brent.*"

Pan clicked off the television and collapsed with a heavy sigh next to Cupid.

Gratitude was the very last thing Cupid deserved. If not for his long string of misdeeds, Mia's boys would have been snug in their beds and not at the center of the wreckage. For that matter—

No! The enormity of his guilt landed squarely on Cupid's chest like one of his stepfather's anvils.

"Pan, you don't think . . ." Cupid's voice faltered, but his anxious tone had already caught Pan's attention.

"What?"

"Did that truck driver die because of me?"

"No, Q. That is *not* on you."

Cupid wanted to believe him, but the note of desperation in Pan's voice undercut his emphatic delivery. Perhaps Pan was feeling a little bit responsible himself.

"Please don't start lying to me now. I know I've made a lot of mistakes, but a man's life is . . ." Cupid's head shook side to side, picking up momentum until his entire upper body was swaying. "I could never forgive myself."

"Whoa." Pan gripped Cupid's shoulders and held him until he settled. "Q, you know how this works as well as I do. Clotho spins the thread of life for each newborn, and Lachesis determines its length. When that life has run its course on Earth, Atropos cuts the thread."

"Yes, but even the Fates can be overruled by Zeus. What if Atropos was ordered to cut that man's string tonight because of *me*?"

Pan set a gentle gaze on Cupid, but what could he say, really? If they were meant to know the truth, Mercury would have delivered it. The rest was pure conjecture. Pan's grip loosened, and his hands fell away from Cupid's arms.

"We can't change what's happened, and it won't help to dwell on what we can't understand." He offered Cupid an encouraging smile. "Besides, you're the town hero tonight. If anyone else had been at the front of that line of cars when the light turned green, there definitely would have been more deaths."

"Mia sure doesn't see it that way. I don't think she'll ever speak to me again." The word "goodbye" hadn't passed between the two of them, but even blinded by the headlights, Cupid recognized the haunted look in Mia's eyes for exactly what it was.

"Well, we both know that is not going to happen." Good ol' Pan. Right back to business.

"I don't see what any of this still has to do with me. As fudged up as tonight was, I did bring Mia together with her Right Love." Saying it out loud caused Cupid's heart to spasm all over again. It wasn't the directional pulse that had repeatedly led Cupid back to Mia, but the out-of-control beating of a heart forced to accept the finality of the soul-crushing truth: there would be no happily ever after for Cupid with Mia, not ever.

"Right. That cop who drove her home," Pan said.

"Yes." Mother had followed through on her promise to provide Mia's true mate, choking off the last breath of Cupid's fantasy that perhaps, if he exhausted every other possibility, Mia might somehow beat for him after all. "So, I've fulfilled my punishment, and I'm done, thank you very much."

"Need I point out the obvious?" Pan answered Cupid's defiant scowl with an equally stubborn eye roll. "Okay, I guess I do. You are still here; ergo, your work here is not done."

"The gods mean to exact a heavier price from my heart?" *What's left to take?*

"Apparently, there is more to your task than simply facilitating a meeting."

"*Simply?*"

"You told me before that Right Loves don't always recognize their moment. Do you know if either of them felt something?"

"There is no way Mia could have acknowledged any beat with all I put her through tonight. Plus, she was already beating for her stupid date."

"Your clone?"

"What's a clone?"

"The lookalike, the guy she chose because she couldn't have you."

"Yeah, him." Cupid's nose wrinkled. "*Reese.*"

"What about the cop? Do you think he got it?"

"I can't say I was really paying attention to the lieutenant's *feelings*," Cupid said, the words raising a sour taste in his mouth, "but I seriously doubt even the lowest of low would've been thinking about his love life at a time like that."

"Fair enough. We have to assume neither has a clue what's going on," Pan said. "If it's your job to make sure these two ships don't pass in the night, what's your next move?"

"You didn't see how she looked at me, Pan. She's not exactly going to be begging me to come over for a consultation."

"Well, *somebody's* gotta get my car from her house."

Cupid stared at Pan for several long seconds. "I hate you."

Slapping his hand down onto Cupid's knee, Pan answered. "Don't shoot the messenger, bro."

"I don't see any wings on your shoes . . . *bro*."

"Would you like to feel my tail again?" Pan asked brightly.

No, Cupid hardly needed the reminder of how everyone around him was suffering because he couldn't seem to carry out his assignment. Cupid bowed his head and moaned.

"Look, Q, I know this sucks, but you're positive this Lieutenant Goode is the guy, right?"

"Yes, the beat could rival your snoring."

"Funny," Pan deadpanned. "Then you don't have a choice. You just have to make it happen this time. You might not get another chance."

"Yeah, no pressure there." Cupid clutched his chest.

The two men rose, awkwardly close and neither pulling away. Pan wrapped an arm around Cupid's shoulders and drew him in for a hug.

"Hang in there, man. We don't know how this will end."

39

GOODBYE

With the clarity of morning's light, Pan understood he'd made a terrible mistake. He should have insisted Cupid get a decent night's sleep rather than matching him beer for beer while rehashing the highlights of their unnaturally long childhood. Even as the vapors of the late-night hours bled into early morning, Pan told himself *just one more story/beer/hour* until the sun eventually rose.

To say Pan had mixed feelings about this morning was perhaps the biggest understatement of the century. Bottom line, neither man had a choice. Their little slumber party was a lovely parting gift from the gods, but Pan knew better than to imagine there might be more where that came from.

Cupid's mission was clear. The moment was now.

The two men eyed each other across the kitchen counter while they loaded up on coffee and courage. Cupid's fingertips traced a familiar circuit over his heart, slowly at first, then faster as his signal grew more intense. Pan watched silently until the inevitable could no longer be cheated. "We should go."

Cupid answered, "Okay," with a quiet resignation that plucked Pan's last heartstring.

They set off wordlessly in Pan's Titan. Swallowing over a lump the size of a small country, Pan watched Cupid dial the number from the lieutenant's business card.

"Hello, this is Quentin Arrows, from last night . . . Yes, I might have some new information for you. Would it be okay if I stopped by the station? . . . Okay, see you in about—" Cupid glanced at Pan, who mouthed the missing number "—eight minutes. Goodbye, Lieutenant."

True to his word, Cupid strode into the squad room eight minutes later with Pan glued to his side, where he had every intention of staying. The lieutenant opened his office door and stepped out to greet them. Clearly, Goode lacked Cupid's panache—*who didn't?*—but the lieutenant had a genuineness about him, something that struck Pan as sturdy, and he liked that for Mia. Maybe Aphrodite wasn't completely off her rocker.

"Thank you for coming in, Mr. Arrows." Goode offered his hand to Cupid, and after a pause that lasted one beat too long for Pan's sanity, Cupid reached out and shook it.

"Everyone calls me Q," he replied. "Lieutenant Goode, meet Pan."

Goode shifted his attention to Pan and seemed to be puzzling out who he was in the grand scheme of things. "If you'll excuse us, please, Pan, I'd like to speak with Mr. Arrows in my office."

Oh, hell no. "We're a package deal." Without waiting for an invitation, Pan followed Cupid through the doorway into the lieutenant's office.

Goode registered surprise, but he recovered admirably. Of course the professional investigator would know how to school his features. "Have a seat, then, gentlemen."

"How were Mia and the boys when they got home?" Cupid asked before his butt met the metal chair.

"She was remarkably calm, actually."

Cupid's face lit with pride. "She's very centered."

"You said you had some information for me?"

The abrupt change of subject drew a frown from Cupid. His fleeting stay on earth had not afforded him the lieutenant's skill at concealing his emotions. Probably for the best. Dishonesty didn't play well where Cupid would soon be returning.

"Yes. You asked me last night about the truck driver, and I couldn't . . ." The rest of Cupid's words caught inside his throat, and his shoulders slumped as if sitting up required too much effort.

Goode leaned forward ever so slightly, sliding his folded hands a few inches closer to Cupid. While Goode's subtle gesture of support didn't go unappreciated by Pan, Cupid was still *his* responsibility as long as he still walked the earth, though that window was squeezing shut before Pan's very eyes.

With a reckless disregard of their previously established boundaries, Pan placed his hand at the back of Cupid's neck and worked his fingers into the knot of muscles. "Take your time," Pan whispered. He clapped Cupid twice between the shoulder blades before moving his hand back where it belonged— in his own damn lap.

Cupid lifted his head, half smiled at Pan, and cleared his throat to address the lieutenant. "After I had time to let things sink in a bit, I remembered a few more details."

"I'm listening," Goode said.

Cupid's gaze drifted to the wall behind Goode's chair as he dredged up the painful memory. "The headlights blinded me at first, but then the truck drove under the traffic light, and for a split second, I caught this look of sheer terror on the driver's face. He slammed on the horn and threw the steering wheel hand-over-hand like a dog chasing its tail. The truck lurched and skidded hard, and that's when he started to tip."

Pan cringed but held his tongue.

Goode cut in with a follow-up question. "Would you say the driver seemed fully alert and was attempting to stop the vehicle?"

"Yes, and when he realized it wasn't going to stop, he . . ."

"He intentionally flipped it."

"I believe so," Cupid answered quietly.

Goode tapped his folded hands on the desk. "Your statement corroborates the physical evidence: tread marks, angles of impact, other eyewitness testimony, and such. There wasn't much left of the, uh"—he paused and shot Cupid an apologetic glance—"body after the fire, but with your account and the tox screen coming back clean, we can cite faulty brakes as the cause of the collision. It may not sound like much, but it should bring some comfort to the driver's widow. She can lay her head on the pillow at night, knowing her husband died a hero."

Cupid took in the information with a sober nod. The mention of the widow wouldn't help Cupid rest peacefully, that much Pan knew for sure. For all his god-concierging, Pan had to admit he was basically impotent when it came to shielding Cupid from the harsh realities of divine justice, not that he'd done such a bang-up job shielding himself this time.

"I'm sorry I can't tell you more. I had to look away at that point because cars were coming at us from every direction," Cupid added quietly.

"And that's when you pulled your Racer Q maneuver?"

Pan snorted. "More like Chimchim." Cupid shot Pan a confused look.

Note to self: teach Q about cartoons.

P.S. on note to self: too late.

"I don't know if you two have heard yet, but they're calling this the 'immaculate protection.'"

Pan shook his head and groaned. "Shoot me now." Cupid was many things, but the son of a virgin he most certainly was not.

Goode's penetrating gaze shifted to Pan. "You don't think Mr. Arrows deserves the accolades?"

"Of course he does, but the media gave all the credit to a video game, which is completely irresponsible. My friend here happens to have the reflexes of an Olympic athlete."

"Oh yes?" Goode swung back to Cupid. "Which sport might that be?"

"Archery," Cupid blurted.

Pan shot Cupid his best shut-the-fuck-up glare. The lieutenant's intuitive skills rated higher than the average mortal. Curiosity was his day job, and he had the stripes to prove he excelled at it. Cupid's flimsy cover story wouldn't take much effort to unravel, and who was more likely to tug at just the right thread than a suspicious cop? Their best bet was putting Goode onto Mia's scent sooner rather than later. Love was a highly potent distraction.

Goode leaned back in his chair, tenting his fingers under his chin. "I am inclined to agree with you about the media. Mr. Arrows, Q, last night, you mentioned you were babysitting for Ms. Barnes. Is that your full-time position?"

"No, I was just helping out. Her mom usually stays with the boys, but she wasn't available."

"So, you have no problem with Ms. Barnes dating other men?"

He asked what, *now?* Pan's antennae shot up. *Oh, how very unprofessional of you, Lieutenant Goode.* Pan bit back a grin.

"Nope," Cupid replied. "In fact, I was encouraging her."

"Encouraging?" Goode shifted to the edge of his chair. "Is that what you were doing when you set out to interrupt her date?"

"I needed to tell her something."

"Wouldn't most people use a telephone in that situation?"

"She wouldn't have answered. She was angry with me." *Poor, fudged-up Cupid.*

"And why was that?"

Surely, Goode knew his questions were inappropriate, yet he pressed on with a dogged determination as if fully expecting to be cut off at any moment. Pan liked him more and more. Cupid, however, squirmed in his chair like a kid caught with his dick in his hand.

"Despite a rigorous selection process, Mia's date turned out to be—"

"A douchenozzle." Pan couldn't help himself.

The lieutenant cracked his first smile, the crinkles at the edges of his eyes settling into well-worn ruts. Serious when he had to be, Lieutenant Goode also seemed like the kind of guy who could knock back a case of Bud and share some laughs with his pals when he was off duty.

He opened the case folder and ran his index finger down the page. "Reese Harris, fitness model," Goode said, his voice dripping with scorn. "The guy just couldn't resist those cameras last night."

Cupid's frown deepened. "He wasn't my choice for Mia."

Lifting his gaze from the page, Goode continued his interrogation. "I see. Does Ms. Barnes normally seek your approval of her dates?"

"It's complicated."

Pan guffawed, covering his outburst with a faked cough, but Goode was laser-focused on drilling for answers.

"Complicated how?"

Cupid fell silent and glanced at the whiteboard on the side wall. Pan held his breath and stared straight ahead. This was why they were here, basically all the marbles.

"Lieutenant, Mia and I are not together."

Pan turned his head, just enough to catch Cupid's profile. The signs of struggle were obvious to someone who'd known Cupid since he was a chubby little cherub: the unnatural set of the jaw, the tension across the bridge of his nose, the tightness in his voice.

Goode's demeanor softened at once. "But you wish you were?"

Cupid hesitated again before answering with a sad shake of his head. "We can't be."

"I'm afraid I don't understand."

The awkward silence returned. From the jaw-gnashing visible to Pan, it appeared Cupid was grinding his teeth into dust. Pan could no longer sit idly by and leave his best friend to twist in his noose.

"Babe."

Cupid pivoted toward Pan's unexpected endearment. Without another word, Pan placed his hand palm-up on Cupid's knee. You could've heard a pin drop in the next county while Cupid shifted his gaze to the invitation and watched, seemingly incredulously, as his own hand spread out over Pan's and curled into the waiting spaces. Pan's eyelids touched down for the brief millisecond he allowed himself to melt into the intimate contact, even if it was purely for show.

"Lieutenant, I'm . . . Pan and I are . . ." Cupid cleared his throat and met the grin spreading across Goode's face. "Mia and I are just friends."

"Yes, I used my police superpowers to deduce that."

Pan squeezed the hand Cupid was still letting him hold, and a reluctant smile lifted one side of Cupid's mouth. *Fuck*, he wished he could tell Cupid how proud he was of him right now. Stepping aside for another man to take his place with the only girl he'd ever loved? That shit took some serious balls.

As bold as he'd been with his questions earlier, Goode was almost shy now. "So, uh, is Ms. Barnes serious about this Reese character?"

Not surprisingly, Cupid bristled on the subject of Reese. "Just until the right man comes along."

"Huh." Any second now, Goode was going to ask Cupid to pass Mia a note: *Do you think I'm cute?*

Pan turned up the heat. "Are you throwing your cap in the ring, Lieutenant?"

"Oh, uh . . ." Goode fiddled with the folder again, then smoothed his hand down the length of his tie. "I hadn't really . . . maybe?" He glanced up, looking very much like a man who'd just stepped in front of an oncoming train.

Pan squeezed Cupid's hand, then jerked his chin toward Goode. The affirmation would be stronger coming from Cupid, who caught on like a champ.

"I think that's an excellent idea."

Goode squared off his shoulders and sat taller in his chair. "Yeah?"

"Sure," Cupid said.

"So, you know Ms. Barnes fairly well, then?"

"You could say that," Cupid answered. "Mia could really use a nice guy in her life."

Goode allowed a hopeful little smile to curl the edges of his lips. "Good to know. I'll make a plan to check up on her in a week or two, after this whole incident is behind her."

"I have a better idea," Cupid said. "Pan was just about to drop me at Mia's to pick up my car and attempt to apologize. To tell you the truth, Mia doesn't really care for Pan—no offense, *babe*—and I think she'd take much more kindly to the situation if you drove me."

Ouch, but playing concierge to fallen gods didn't always allow Pan to be Mr. Nice Guy. *Whatever.* As long as the Olympians were pleased with his performance, Pan could deal. Meanwhile, Goode was warming to the concept.

"Hmm, I was actually going to send a patrolman out to the house this morning. Ms. Barnes' car has been released, and she'll need a ride to the yard to pick it up."

"I'm sure Mia would be very touched if you decided to follow up personally," Cupid suggested.

Goode leaned forward, practically whispering even though nobody was around. "Can I be honest with you guys?"

"Absolutely," Cupid answered earnestly.

"Ms. Barnes is, uh, a bit out of my league, if you know what I mean. I would really appreciate any intel you're able to share."

"Tell you what, Lieutenant," Cupid said. "Why don't I give you some pointers on the way?"

Lieutenant Goode stood and straightened his cap with great care. "I would be much obliged."

This little scene was winding down, and Cupid's ascension was likely to follow. This was the end of the line for Pan. Time for goodbye.

Man up. Don't make this any harder for him than it already is.

Pan rose, pulling Cupid to his feet right along with him. They stood mere inches apart, toe-to-toe, hand-in-hand, eye-to-eye. Tenderness swelled like a sudden wave, nearly pulling Pan under. His love for Cupid was the purest love Pan had ever experienced, not that Pan hadn't entertained plenty of impure thoughts toward Cupid, but his heart was noble. Despite what it had cost him, Pan had done everything in his power to keep Cupid safe. Only one task remained, the hardest one: letting go.

No words would have been adequate to mark this monumental goodbye. At least this time, Pan could take comfort there were no lies between them.

"Dammit, Q, I don't want to say goodbye to you again."

Fuck.

It was just meant to be a hug. One long-ass bear hug to last both of them, well, all of eternity. Maybe if Cupid's moist eyes hadn't caught the light, Pan wouldn't have come undone so spectacularly.

Pan's free hand wrapped around Cupid's neck, tugging him close, but instead of the do-si-do their cheeks were meant to dance, Pan forced a head-on collision even Cupid's reflexes could not prevent. Or maybe he wasn't trying.

Noble flew right out the window. Pan pressed his open mouth to Cupid's lips, and Cupid kissed him back. One needy tongue met the other. Teeth clashed. Grunts were answered with growls more suited to beasts of the wild than two civilized gods.

"Guys, no offense or anything, but you're sucking all the oxygen out of my office."

Whoops.

Cupid placed his hand on Pan's chest as he broke their kiss. Breathing hard, Cupid gave Pan a grave shake of his head.

Pan flinched as if he'd been punched in the gut. "Yeah, okay," he answered, stealing one more kiss before pulling away. "It's been amazing, Q."

Goode stood up and slapped Pan on the back. "Not to worry, Pan. My driving record is impeccable."

40

ECHOES

The first news truck arrived before six a.m., jarring Lucas awake a full hour ahead of his normal schedule. Like dominoes, Jonah and Eli followed. There would be no coaxing the boys into her bed this morning, not with the media circus going on outside. That's what happens when you live in a town with a news cycle about as quick-moving as a glacier and a bunch of bored housewives angling for another glimpse of the hot hero and the stunt-double dinner date. Theories of a scandalous love triangle were quickly gathering steam.

"Joe, come away from the window, please."

"But, Mommy, that man who picked you up last night is here."

"Oh yeah?" Mia grinned despite herself and carried Luke over to the window. Inching a sliver of curtain out of the way, she snuck a peek at Reese as he trotted up her walk. *Yep, still hot.*

And he'd come to check on them. The gesture warmed her, especially since there had been no word from him last night after he dropped her off at the accident scene. Frankly, she'd begun to lose hope that he cared at all, which actually stung a bit since he inspired a flutter kick behind her rib cage . . . and there it went again. *Could this be my beat? Could he be the one? Wouldn't Q have told me?*

Wait, is that what Q was trying to tell her last night? With all the madness and anger and relief last night, Mia hadn't even paused to wonder what the hell Q was trying to accomplish, dragging her kids out to interrupt her date. Now she would never know.

Well, screw that and screw Q. So, Mia had married epically wrong. She was smarter now; she could solve this puzzle herself. In the meantime, she might as well enjoy the view.

This guy rocked the white V-neck—the thin cotton straining just so across his pecs and hugging a set of biceps that belonged on the cover of *Men's Health.* And the dark denim clinging to his thighs? GQ material. Mia had no trouble conjuring a rear view from her many years of experience with the human form, not to mention an ogle she might have enjoyed on their too-short date last night. The sexy aviators were a nice daytime touch although his dazzling blue eyes did not need accessorizing.

Mmm, someone's a morning person. This guy Reese was one of those rise-and-shiners who hit the pavement with a forward spring in his step, the kind of person Mia used to be before she turned into a single mother of three.

The vultures swarmed him, shoving news station logo microphones in his face and pacing backwards with video cameras in hand to capture every inch of his death-defying approach to her front door. Mia wanted to spare him, but what could she do? Run outside in her bathrobe? *Wonderful. I'm in my bathrobe.*

She briefly considered a mad dash for clothing but could never have made it upstairs and back before the ravenous mob devoured her new beau. Taking cover behind the front door, Mia peered through the peephole, primed to rescue Reese with

a perfectly timed opening of the escape hatch. He shook off
the last of the parasites, jogged up the steps, raked his fingers
through his thick, dark waves, and . . . whirled around to face
the crowd?

He raised an arm, calming the bloodthirsty mob. Through
the fisheye peephole, Mia watched his arm descend. Reese delivered some statement she couldn't hear, the reporters hanging on
his every word as if he were the freaking president holding a
press conference in the Rose Garden. He tapped his knuckles on
the door when he finished speaking and posing for the cameras.

Mia yanked open the door, grabbed Reese's elbow, and
pulled him clear before slamming the door behind him.

"Morning, beautiful," he said, planting a kiss on Mia's lips.
Swoon. "How's everyone doing today?"

"What the hay were you doing out there?"

He shrugged it off. "Giving the crowd what they want."

"And what's that?" Mia couldn't decide if she was more pissed
off or shocked. Sorting out her emotions was confusing enough,
but all the extra beating made the job impossible.

"Sound bites. Did you know we're trending on Twitter this
morning?"

Definitely leaning toward pissed. "I don't want to trend anywhere."

"He who rules social media rules the world." Reese slipped
one arm around Mia's shoulders and stretched the other way out
in front, angling his phone toward their faces. "Mind if I take
an *ussie?*"

Did he have to feel so damn good against her side? Why
did he smell like a sandalwood forest sprinkled with cinnamon?

"Yes, I mind!" Mia threw her hand up to cover the phone.
"In case you haven't noticed, I'm not dressed."

Reese turned his head, and for the first time since arriving, really looked at Mia. Covering his smile with a pretend itch on his upper lip, he gave Mia a sheepish, "I, uh, honestly didn't notice. Smoking hot robe though." Shifting his gaze to Luke, he asked, "How about I just Insta the baby instead?"

"Cheese 'n' crackers! No pictures." Mia swaddled Luke in her arms and spun him away from Reese. "No tweeting, no trending, no Instagramming. My family is not a photo op."

He raised his hands in surrender. "Okay, okay. It's not as if you aren't all over the news anyway. They're saying your babysitter saved a whole bunch of lives."

Mia sighed. "Lives that wouldn't have needed saving if he'd stayed put to begin with."

"Mommy, Q is here!"

Speak of the devil.

"Jonah Barnes, I told you to get away from that window."

The boy scrambled down from the back of the couch and grabbed the knob just as the doorbell rang. Before Mia could stop him, Jonah swung the door wide open. The media hounds erupted with a roar of shouted questions. The last person on God's green earth Mia wanted to see this morning was Quentin Arrows, but she only had one hand free, and she used it to pull Jonah from the line of fire.

"Come in!" she shouted not very nicely from behind the open door. "Hurry up."

A handful of yellow tulips rounded the corner first, accompanied by an uncertain, "Umm?"

"Nice try," Mia said, as a teddy bear bigger than Eli came into view, "but it's not going to—*oh*, you're not Q."

"No, ma'am," said the officer who'd driven them home from the accident scene. "Lieutenant Goode? From last night?"

Momentarily stunned, Mia remembered herself a beat later and gave the door a shove.

"Ow." Q stepped around the door, rubbing his elbow as he stole a cautious glance at Mia. "Hello."

"Q!" Jonah ran for him, and Q scooped him up as he kicked the door closed. Eli toddled over and wrapped his arms around Q's leg. *Damn him for making my boys love him.*

Mia clasped the collar of her robe and pulled both sides together around her neck. "What are you doing here?"

"Lieutenant Goode brought me by to pick up my car."

"Your car is *outside*," she said. "And since when are you two so chummy?"

"Begging your pardon, Ms. Barnes." Juggling the stuffed animals in his arms, Lieutenant Goode yanked off his cap and smoothed down his thick brown hair. "Mr. Arrows was down at the station, answering some questions about the collision. When I told him I was headed over here, he mentioned needing to pick up his car. I certainly apologize for any inconvenience."

"Inconvenience? Mr. Arrows is more like a plague."

"Mia, can I please say again how—" Q's focus shifted to a spot just beyond Mia's shoulder. "Hey, what do you think you're doing?"

Mia whirled around just as the flash went off.

Reese checked his phone and grinned. "Great shot. Smooth move on the stuffed animals, Lieutenant. Wish I would've thought of that."

Belly flutters or not, Reese was an asshole—and a dangerous one. "Please delete that photo," Mia said.

"C'mon, Mia, you're being oversensitive," Reese said, tucking his phone inside his back pocket.

Q started toward Reese, but Lieutenant Goode wedged his body between them. Despite the teddy bears and tulips, the lieutenant managed to strike a menacing pose. "Ms. Barnes asked you to delete the photo of her children."

Reese rolled his eyes dramatically, plucked his phone out of his jeans, and poked his finger at it a few times. Flashing the screen at Mia, he swiped both directions until she nodded. "Happy?"

"I'll be happy when you leave." The quake in her voice frustrated Mia as much as admitting yet another failure in picking men, especially in front of an audience. And it didn't help that her stupid heart was still doing the samba for the creep.

Reese brought his hands to his sexy little hip flexors. "Seriously? You're kicking me out?"

"The lady asked you to leave, far more nicely than I would have," said Goode.

Reese rounded on the lieutenant. "Dude, what are you gonna do? Throw a teddy bear at me?"

Goode shook his head and regarded Reese with an expression of practiced patience. "No, sir, the stuffed animals are for the *actual* children," said Goode. "You were leaving."

Reese's smug grin finally vanished. "It's been real, Mia."

She flinched as the door slammed shut behind Reese's perfect ass.

"I really dislike that guy," Cupid muttered under his breath.

Lieutenant Goode eased out of his bad-cop stance. "Are you okay, ma'am?" he asked in that soothing tone she recognized from last night.

"Yes, I'm fine. Thanks for the assistance."

"That's what we're here for, ma'am." Mia couldn't be sure, but she thought he might have blushed. "Oh, and I have some teddy bears to deliver."

He turned toward Jonah, who'd been riveted to the whole scene from the safety of Q's arms. "You're Jonah, right?"

"Mmhmm."

Handing him the biggest bear, Goode said, "This is for your extreme bravery last night in a very scary situation."

Jonah's face lit up as he squashed the bear between his chest and Q's. "Thank you."

"You're welcome. And this one," he said, squatting to hand Eli a smaller bear, "needs lots of love. Can you take good care of him, Eli?"

"Yes!"

The lieutenant gave Eli a pat on the shoulder. "Attaboy."

Mia couldn't decide if she was more impressed Lieutenant Goode had bothered to look up all her boys' names or that he'd gone to the trouble of bringing each one a gift. And there was something especially sweet about the way he was saving those tulips for last.

Hmm, yellow tulips. Now, I wonder who could have suggested that.

Jiggling the miniature teddy bear in his outstretched hand, Goode inched toward Mia and the baby, silently seeking her permission to approach. She loosened her tight hold on Luke and turned him toward the bear. Luke reached out and pulled the tiny, floppy ear into his mouth. The lieutenant responded with a wide, easy grin. Good cop had a nice smile.

Mia's heart took an unexpected flip as Goode presented her with the tulips. "And these are for you," he said.

Wow, his eyes have little gold flecks that sparkle when he smiles. Mindful of all the eyes trained on them, Mia responded with a whispered thank-you.

"I'm just glad everyone's okay," he said. "Also, your car is ready, so if you all wouldn't mind riding in the squad car again . . . I believe *somebody* wanted to turn on the siren?" He gave Mia a little wink as Jonah climbed out of Q's arms and scrambled over.

"Yes, me, me! Can I, Mommy?"

She gave the lieutenant a grateful smile. "Sure, bug, but I really need to—" Suddenly, the idea of mentioning a shower or even drawing attention to her flimsy robe felt way too intimate.

"Q, may I have a word with you, please?"

"Of course." Q practically tripped over his own feet skipping to Mia's side. "What can I do for you?"

"I need to get dressed."

His forehead crinkled in confusion. "You want me to come upstairs and help you?"

Because who wouldn't want to reopen that gaping wound?

"No. Would you stay—down here—and watch the boys?"

If Q was disappointed, his eager smile was a convincing mask. "Of course, Mia. I'm honored you'd trust me again."

Mia passed Luke into Q's arms. "The man standing on the other side of the room has a gun. Do us all a favor, Racer Q; don't make him use it."

41

ASCENSION DAY

Cupid's day was getting brighter by the minute, not even counting the fact that Mia was showering just upstairs, an image he pushed from his mind. Repeatedly.

Mia's sorry excuse for a man-choice was out, never to be invited back, while Mr. Right Love was slowly but surely melting the ice around her heart. And there sat Cupid, apparently back in Mia's good graces, on the floor of her great room with her boys, building a pillow fort for their new teddy bears. This bonus time with all of them was a series of sweet agonies: the baby venturing away from Cupid, only to crawl back into the security of his lap minutes later; Eli wedging his diapered bottom into the narrow space between Cupid's knees, casually making himself at home; the widening of Jonah's intense, Mia-green eyes every time a new idea popped into his little head. This little family had become Cupid's gravity, the ballast that kept him from flying away, and Mia's renewed trust in him—armed guard aside—was a gift Cupid would never take for granted.

"Mommy, look what we made!"

Cupid's head swiveled toward the staircase, where Mia sat, perched on one of the upper steps, silently observing the scene below. "How long have you been sitting there?" he asked.

"A few minutes." She made no move to stand. "I didn't want to disturb the moment. Everyone looks so happy."

Cupid's heart split down the middle—at least, that's how it felt—as if half of him would stay here with Mia and the boys when he had to leave, which could happen any second now.

"Come on down," Cupid said. "You should be a part of this."

Mia gave him a tender smile, stood, brushed off her bottom, and skipped down the stairs. "Where's Lieutenant Goode?"

"He went outside to pull the car up. He didn't want you and the boys to have to brave the mob."

"Mommy, look! We made a bear house," Eli called from under the blankets. Mia dove under and tickled Eli until his wild kicking knocked the roof off. Jonah jumped on top, and the three of them rolled around in the mess of pillows and blankets and giggled until they were gasping for breath.

Lost in the happy scene, Cupid didn't notice the soggy bear leaving Luke's pudgy fingers until it hit him in the nose. "You wanna play too, Lukie? Huh? Huh?" Cupid rolled onto his back next to Mia, tossed Luke into the air, and caught him with a silly jiggle and peck on the nose. Luke's squeals and baby belly laughs started a second round of giggling, and soon Mia was holding her stomach and sighing. The boys went to work rebuilding their house around the grownups lying side by side.

Cupid seized his chance to apologize. "I was wrong to drag the boys out last night, Mia. I hope you can find it in your heart to forgive me."

She flipped onto her side and propped up her head in her hand. "God, that guy Reese was such a tool. You tried to warn me, but I didn't want to listen."

Cupid itched to hold her hand, but it was both too soon and far too late for all that. "It's not your fault, Mia. You were beating for him."

She rolled her eyes and grimaced. "I really hate my stupid heart."

"Tell me about it." Cupid didn't realize he was rubbing his heart until Mia gave him a sympathetic smile. They were in this stew separately and together, united in victimhood against their common foe, Love.

"Oh, Q," Mia started with watery eyes, "of course I forgive you."

His thank you caught in his throat, and all that came out was a choked whisper.

"I'm taking a break from men for a while," Mia said. "I need to get my life back."

Cupid tamped down his panic and rolled toward Mia, mirroring her modified side plank. "Please don't let one bad experience throw you off track."

"One?" Mia huffed. "Q, this isn't even a track I wanted to be on, remember? Sure, my life was kind of boring before I met you, but the boys and I were doing okay. Now, it's all . . . well, it's nuts. I believe last night was the universe beating me over the head with a sledgehammer. This isn't good for the boys, and frankly, it's not good for me."

Earth girls still confused him, but Cupid had learned enough to know Mia needed to come around to the lieutenant on her own terms. Until then, Cupid needed to do everything in his gods-given power to make sure Goode didn't get too far away.

He leaned in and brushed his thumb along Mia's cheek. "Try not to give up on Love, Mia." *Gods*, he loved her so much it hurt. Wanted her with every inch of his body and soul. What he wouldn't give for one last, quick kiss—

The doorbell was a bucket of cold water dumped not a

moment too soon. Jonah charged to the door, teddy first. "Joe, wait!" Mia yelled, jumping up and overtaking him before he could turn the knob. "Only grownups open the door, remember?"

Mia peered through the peephole before opening the door. Lieutenant Goode stepped inside and pulled off his cap. "You need a childproof deadbolt on this door," he said. "I'd like to stop by with my toolbox and take care of that for you, if that would be okay?"

Mia's hands went to her hips, but Cupid could see the tiny grin planted on her face. "I have my own tools, Lieutenant, and I assure you, I'm not afraid to use them."

He nodded with great reverence. "I believe you, Ms. Barnes."

"Would you please call me Mia?"

Even from his spot across the room, Cupid saw the tips of the lieutenant's ears turn pink. "Well, unless you also have a spare deadbolt lying around, *Mia*, I'd like to pick one up for you and stop by, say, Saturday . . . to install it? I'd do it sooner, but that's my next day off."

She backed down, tilting her head and smiling. "Okay, sure. Thank you."

"Thank the gods," Cupid muttered under his breath—or so he thought.

Mia turned and gave Cupid the murderous shut-up glare he'd received so many times from Pan. The lieutenant glanced back and forth between the two of them, released a deep sigh, and replaced his cap. "All right, then. The squad car's out front, and I've taken the liberty of installing all the car seats, so whenever you and the boys are ready."

"Okay. Give us a minute?"

"Of course." Lieutenant Goode strode to the front door where he took up his post like one of the palace guards, far enough out of earshot to afford Mia and Cupid some privacy but not too far for Cupid to hear the echo beats lining up with Mia's in perfect synchronicity.

As if the gods needed to drive home the point Cupid was the odd man out—and would, in fact, *always be* the odd man out in Mia's life—Cupid's heart endured an erratic stream of sharp stabbing pains that might have been Hades himself, jabbing his pitchfork around Cupid's inner chambers for sport. Cupid rose from the floor, scooping up Luke in one arm and pressing the baby against his aching chest.

Mia sprang toward them on tiptoes, barely containing her glee. "What I said earlier about taking a break?"

"Mmhmm?"

"Not that I'm asking your opinion or anything, but if I *were* . . ."

Cupid raised his eyebrows. "You want my opinion?"

"Maybe."

Cupid shook his head, chuckling. "Are you actually going to take my advice this time?"

"Q, *please*." She set her palms together in front of her belly as if to do a *Namaste*. Mia's measured monotone was poor camouflage for the inner storm gathering momentum. "Is . . . he . . . *my* guy?"

Well, there it was, wasn't it? Cupid's Big Moment. The love of his life, searching his eyes with all the hope and faith she possessed, asking him to confirm that another man was, in fact, her divine match.

"Yes, Mia. That is your man." Oddly, it didn't slice him open to send Mia into the arms of another man. How could it, when her face radiated pure joy? He'd witnessed enough heartbreak to know his pain would come soon enough. When it did, it would all be worth it. For this.

Mia teared up, and her smile brightened and spread as Cupid

told her the rest. "The two of you are beating so hard for each other, I can't hear myself think."

"*Really?*" Mia patted her heart and giggled.

A searing pain filled Cupid's chest, and he rubbed furiously with his free hand. "*Owww.*"

"Oh my god, Q? Are you okay?" Mia asked, scooping Luke from Cupid's arms.

"I'm won—*ahh*—wonderful."

"Breathe, Q. We need an ambulance. Lieutenant, call 911!"

"No! Please, no." There wasn't a hospital on the planet that could relieve Cupid of his pain now. This was the gods ratcheting up his suffering so he could live out the rest of his days in unendurable misery.

"Mommy, is Q all right?" Jonah and Eli scrambled into Cupid's view near Mia's feet, as did a pair of shiny black shoes belonging to Lieutenant Goode.

The throbbing spiked more violently than ever, making it impossible to draw a breath. Ravaged and weak, he swayed off balance and was set right again by the firm hand of Lieutenant Goode. Fearful of setting off a fresh episode, Cupid drew a shallow breath, then another and another, until he could straighten up, thanking the lieutenant with a brief nod.

"We should get you checked out," said Lieutenant Goode, his fingers spread over the radio strapped to his shoulder.

Cupid held up his hand and breathed more deeply, cautiously experimenting with the fragile equilibrium. The piercing agony appeared to have flattened into a uniform ache, painful but bearable.

"I'm okay," Cupid said, smiling as best he could at Mia, whose face looked as white as her bed sheets. Cupid reached down to high five Jonah and Eli. "Really, I'm good."

As good as I'm going to get, Cupid realized with a start. The weeklong siege that had knocked him off the treadmill had come to a resolution of sorts. Cupid's heart would be permanently afflicted with unrequited love for Mia—his new reality and his own private Tartarus.

With the moment of ascension upon him, Cupid had no time for a long goodbye. "Mia, I've got to go. Please don't take this the wrong way, but I'm not sure if I'll be able to see you again."

Mia stepped back, cradling Luke against her chest. "Oh." She shot Cupid a glance heavy with pity. "I understand."

"No, I . . . I want you to know if I don't come back, it's not because I didn't want to. Okay?"

"Sure," she answered softly.

Damn, I thought my heart was all done twisting. "You'll explain it . . .?"

"Of course." Mia glanced at Jonah and sighed. "We'll all miss you, but I'm starting to believe we'll be okay." Eyeing Lieutenant Goode, she added, "Maybe even better than okay."

"I know you will." Cupid gave Mia a brave smile, leaned in, and kissed her on the cheek. "Be happy. You all deserve it."

Mia grabbed his arm before he could pull away. "So do you, Q. I can't believe I'm about to say this, but thank you. For everything."

Lieutenant Goode cleared his throat. "Q, would you like me to escort you to your car?"

The crowd of witnesses. The car. What the hell was going to happen when he vanished from behind the wheel? Would he go crashing through the roof of the Prius?

"No, but thank you." Cupid offered his hand to Lieutenant Goode. "Take care of them, Lieutenant. They're very special to me." A man of few words, Goode answered with another of his solemn nods.

Cupid squatted down and pulled Jonah and Eli into a hug. "Bye, guys. Be good for your mommy."

Jonah squeezed him tight, then pulled back with wide-eyed excitement, his pupils darkened bullseyes. "Did you hear, Q? We get to turn on the siren!"

"Sounds like you're off on another great adventure." *I'm going to miss you all like crazy.*

Goodbyes hurt. Cupid set his sights on the door and didn't look back.

42

LEAVING MIA

"GODDAMMIT, FATHER, TALK TO ME!"

The release felt mildly satisfying, though Pan's outburst would accomplish nothing. The messenger of Mount Olympus wasn't summonable. He dropped in at the whim of the gods on high, not their lowly servants on earth.

Mortal gadgets with their "up-to-the-minute" news were laughable compared to oracles, but Apollo was "unavailable" as well, so Pan did what any demigod would do in his position— paced like a madman in front of the TV and swore at his cell phone every two seconds. This time, Pan couldn't be angry at Cupid for not calling; surely, he had his hands full right about now *if* he still walked this Earth. Pan couldn't bear to think about the *if not.*

Some friend you are. You'd rather have him stay and be tortured. For what? Pan slowed his pacing as the memory of their kiss slammed him for the billionth time.

"Let's cut over to the Barnes residence. Can you tell us what's happening, Nancy?"

"Yes, Brent. We're watching Reese Harris exit the house."

"Fuck me," Pan fumed. "The little shit came outside to make another speech?"

"Just to remind our audience, Mr. Harris is the fitness model who reunited Mrs. Barnes with her three little boys last night."

"Fitness model," Pan huffed. "My goddamn hero."

"He appears to be heading toward his car."

Pan stepped closer to the screen. *Huh.* "Where's your smug smile now, you arrogant bastard?" Unless Cupid had somehow ascended without being noticed by every media outlet in Tarra, he and Lieutenant Goode were still inside with Mia. Pan had no way of knowing what to think about that.

"There's movement again at the front door. Let's cut back to the scene and listen." Lieutenant Goode slipped out the door and checked the security of the lock before turning to the hungry crowd.

"Why are *you* leaving?" Pan yelled at TV Goode. "Why is he leaving, Q? And why are *you* still inside? God *damn* you, Q. God damn you all. YOU BETTER HAVE YOUR PANTS ON!"

Pan eyeballed his phone, still not a fucking word, and paced and cursed some more. A terrible habit, this pacing, and the wool rug was no match for his size twelve canoes, as evidenced by the rut paralleling the coffee table. With a passing thought that sickened him, Pan imagined furrows of hoof prints instead. Working up a full head of steam now, Pan stroked the ungainly nub at the top of his ass crack.

"Thank you ever so much, you selfish prick." Speaking of pricks, Pan wondered if his own would ever work again.

"Lieutenant Goode! Lieutenant Goode, can you tell us what's happening inside the house?"

The officer pushed forward, a man on a mission. *"I'm going to need this crowd to disperse so I can bring the cruiser right up front. We don't need anyone else getting hurt."*

The camera zoomed out to follow Goode jogging to his car, then inching his police cruiser up the street so as not to maim the idiots standing in his path. Goode exited the car, skipped up the walk to the front stoop, pushed the bell, and struck an official-looking pose in front of Mia's door. Seconds later, he was swallowed up inside the house.

"Well, all right, then," Pan said to no one in particular, allowing himself a breath of hope. Drained from his sleepless night and the exhausting responsibility of Cupid's welfare, Pan slumped into the sofa, tossed his phone onto the cushion beside him, and rubbed his eyes. He wouldn't have traded places with Cupid for anything, even if it meant living with a broken pecker and regenerated tail, though truly, those things were no fun at all.

"Come on, Q. Get these two lovebirds together and get the hell out of there."

"The man known as 'Racer Q' is leaving the house."

Pan bolted off the couch, heart pounding as if he'd just run a marathon. If this measly TV coverage was to be his last glimpse of Cupid, Pan wouldn't miss a second. Not that Cupid was easy to track once the paps swarmed him with their cameras and mikes and obnoxious questions.

"How are the boys? Is Ms. Barnes still angry with you? Do you feel like a hero?"

"Get the fuck out of the way so I can see him!" *Shit.* Pan couldn't read Cupid's expression, but he sure didn't see a smile. Could Cupid have failed again? Had Mia booted him, maybe for good this time?

Fuck, fuck, fuck, fuck! Pan rocked on his feet in front of the TV, bobbing and weaving as if he might improve his view. Cupid didn't speak to anyone, just set his chin toward the ground and pushed through the hordes until he reached the relative safety of the Prius. The bastards pressed their microphones into the windows and beat on the glass.

The car started forward. Only Cupid could have success-fully woven through the maze of gawkers without injuring any-one, though there were a few he could have put a dent in without drawing any tears from Pan. The Prius shrank into a mere blip and eventually disappeared. With a weary sigh, Pan clicked off the news and paced some more.

He really hated feeling so goddamn useless. This wasn't at all how Pan had imagined things ending between them. But then, he'd never expected to see Cupid again at all, certainly not this excruciating blend of innocence and hotness that made Pan want to both protect him and fuck his brains out.

And I've done neither.

Wallowing wasn't helping, and pacing only got him more worked up. He threw himself onto the couch again, closed his eyes, and succumbed to the memories of intimate *almosts*, end-ing with their goodbye kiss. And he was stiffening. Surely that was inappropriate right now. *What the—I'm hard?*

Pan plunged his hand inside his jeans to verify what friction had already told him. *I'm hard.*

Lifting his voice toward the gods, he cried out, "*Efharisto!* Thank you." Pan slid his palm up and down his glorious erection, temporarily setting aside his anguish to enjoy the resurrection.

Wait, does this mean . . . ? Lifting his hips off the cushion, Pan reached inside the back of his jeans and slid his fingers down his tailbone. No more nub! Just the same hairy, *human* ass he'd known and loved since he fell to earth and landed on it. Much delighted that his lump had repositioned itself in front, where it could be so much more useful, Pan celebrated for one jubilant moment—*Cupid's done it!*—before taking in the full implication of his return to status quo.

Cupid is gone.

Pan ejected his hand from his pants with a guilt-laden groan and shuffled to the kitchen for a beer. He yanked open the refrigerator and reached for a Sam Adams as Connie Francis belted out Pan's newest ringtone, "Stupid Cupid."

"Holy shit!" Pan slammed the refrigerator door and sprinted across the room, diving onto the couch for his phone. "Q? You're still here?"

"Yes," came the shell-shocked answer. "You are too?"

Tears sprang from Pan's eyes. "Of course, buddy. Where else would I be?"

"I don't know, I . . . I'm confused." *Jesus*, the guy was a wreck. "I think I did it, Pan."

Pan's heart raced a mile a second, painfully aware every word might be their last. "I'm so proud of you, Q. Where are you, exactly?"

"I'm not sure. I pulled over somewhere. I'm afraid to drive. What if I, you know, just vanish into thin air while I'm driving down a busy street? I don't want anyone else to get hurt."

"Q, listen to me. That's not how this works."

"How *does* this work?"

"They'll send Mercury to retrieve you somewhere you won't be seen by mortals." The thought of it broke Pan's heart all over again. He would have given anything to be there for Cupid, but the gods weren't big on emotional support.

Silence followed, then a small, sad, "Okay."

Fuck, he hated this job sometimes. "So, you just left Mia's? I watched the whole thing on TV."

"Sorry about that, Pan. I couldn't help it. They were all over the place when we got there."

"Forget it. It's not your fault," Pan said, hoping his assurances could offer Cupid some measure of comfort. "How are you feeling?"

"At the moment they crossed their Liminal Point, it felt like I took a dozen thunderbolts directly to the heart, but now it's more of a constant ache, like I got beat up from the inside out. I'm going to miss them all so much, Pan."

"Yeah."

"Lieutenant Goode promised to take care of her and the boys now. They're just at the beginning of everything, but it's been a long time since I've heard such a perfect echo."

"The Right Love," Pan said. "You really did it, buddy."

More silence.

"Pan, if I did what the Council wanted, why am I still here?"

Pan pulled the phone away from his head to check the time. Nearly five minutes had passed since Pan's happy, south-of-the-equator discoveries. The slowest retrieval he could remember had taken just over three minutes. *Huh.*

"The gods must not be ready to send you home."

"What? Really? I'm staying?" The lift in Cupid's voice tore a fresh hole in Pan's heart. An extended tour of duty was no cause for celebration.

Pan found himself pacing again. "If you don't ascend today, that only means they're not done fucking with you."

"Oh."

"Yeah."

A long pause. "What should I do, Pan?"

"Come home."

43

GETTING VERTICAL

Cupid woke to the harsh beating of a fist against his bedroom door.

"Go away. I'm sleeping."

Pan burst into the room, bolted straight for the windows,
and yanked open the blinds. "It's four o'clock in the afternoon.
You haven't been vertical in three days. Your ass is gonna get
flabby if you don't get off it soon."

The bed creaked as Pan flopped down next to Cupid. His
bulk offered a small creature comfort but did little to ease the
raw throbbing in Cupid's chest. He groaned and pulled a pillow
over his eyes.

"You're lying. My body will go right back to how it was before
whether I stay in bed and starve myself or stuff my face with
every nasty kind of junk food in your kitchen, so you can just
kiss my flabby ass."

A low, booming laugh shook the bed. "You're developing
quite the potty mouth."

Cupid squinted one eye open from beneath the corner of

the pillow. "Flabby ass, potty mouth, who could possibly care? I am going back to sleep."

"No, you're not." Pan gripped the covers and threw them across the room.

"Hey!" Cupid thrust the pillow over his privates and shot up off the bed. "What the *fuck*, Pan?"

A wide smile stretched across Pan's face. "Hallelujah. We're not using 'fudge' anymore. At least one part of you is back to normal even if your internal clock is shot to hell."

"It's not just my clock, Pan. That whole heart guidance system is gone too. Like someone switched it off."

"Someone did," Pan answered, jabbing a finger toward the ceiling.

"Well, how am I supposed to know what to do now without any direction?"

Pan shrugged. "I guess you can do whatever you want for now. What *do* you want to do?"

Cupid brought his fingertips to his chest and rubbed. "Nothing."

"Nuh-uh." Pan shook his head. "No more doing nothing. This room smells like a festering wound. You need a shower, and we both need a decent meal. I'm afraid to leave you alone, and if I don't get out of this house soon, I swear, I will blow the roof off."

"I'm sorry, Pan, but I'm not ready to go out."

"I understand this is hard, Q. I've nursed a broken heart or two myself, and it is the suckiest of all sucks. It feels like you'll never feel good again."

"How could I, without Mia?" Cupid asked, his voice breaking on the name he hadn't allowed on his lips since their final goodbye.

"Look, I can't make any promises involving forces beyond my control. Who knows what the gods have lined up for you next?

BETH C. GREENBERG

All I know is you're still here, and you need to get back into cir-
culation while you still can."

"Don't you mean while *we* still can?"

Pan opened his arms. "Okay, yes. I'll admit, I'm eager to
take advantage of my restored manhood. Is that so terrible?"

No, there was nothing terrible about Pan's manhood except
it, too, seemed to be off limits to Cupid. He swallowed hard and
shook his head while Pan railed on.

"There's one thing we can count on: the future is uncertain.
I, for one, would like to take this opportunity to celebrate our
little intermission for as long as it lasts and surround myself
with hot bodies, preferably of the hard, male persuasion."

Hard. Male. So that's where Pan's pent-up desire had crash-
landed.

No wonder, after their dramatic goodbye at the police station. Their unexpected kiss had caught Cupid entirely off guard,
but *oh*, the yearning of Pan's last, stolen nip. The memory had
provided a reassuring, albeit confusing, lifeline more than once
during Cupid's bedridden grieving.

The pillow shield was starting to feel grossly inadequate.
This conversation needed to end.

"Fine. Where do you suggest we find these hot bodies?"

Pan grinned. "You go clean up. I'll take care of the rest."

Cupid waited for Pan to leave his room before tossing away
the pillow. The old goat was right; this place stank. Cupid
opened the window and left the winds to their work.

The hot shower washed away days of grit and caked-on
tears. Some God of Love, crying like a baby over the girl who got
away. Cupid was no different from any of the other poor suckers
pierced by his gold-tipped arrows. His immortal heart would
beat forever, but that didn't guarantee the absence of pain. No,
that was a privilege Cupid had surrendered the day he shot his

arrow into Cerberus. He could no more regain his immunity to love than he could take back his virginity.

Did Cupid regret his actions, inciting the ire of the First Lady of the Mount and the God of the Underworld? Handing Ares the long-awaited excuse to discipline his wayward son? Shaming Aphrodite in the eyes of her peers, putting her in a position where she had no choice but to punish him? Those things weren't good. Neither was the hurt Cupid had unwittingly inflicted on Mia along the way, building up her hopes only to dash them again and again. Nor did he feel good about how Pan had suffered in all of this.

With all those tally marks piling up, Cupid should have regretted his actions. Wasn't that the whole point of consequences? How could he though, when the alternative was a monotonous life of watching everyone around him fall in love while he floated along in his impermeable bubble, free from harm but blind to the glory of love?

He whom Love touches not walks in darkness. At once, he understood the inscription tattooed down his spine.

Would Cupid have preferred love's tender caress to the chokehold that besieged his heart? A happy ending instead of this misery? No question. But would he choose to erase recent events and return to the not-knowing, the darkness? No, thank you. No matter that his insides were a pit of snarling snakes depositing venom into every chamber of his heart. The burning continued day and night, awake or asleep, never letting him forget the love he had known so briefly and lost forever. His punishment, but also his revelation. A wound he could bear, knowing he'd delivered Mia into the arms of her Right Love.

He scrubbed the shampoo through his hair and took extra care with the razor blade around the contours of his chin and cheeks. When he finally stepped out of the shower, he at least looked and smelled presentable.

True to his word, Pan took care of the decisions, driving Cupid to an "out-of-the-way spot" for dinner—a nearly deserted, refurbished train station where they could more or less be themselves. Two friends out enjoying a couple of thick, juicy steaks.

"Nothing like a good slab of beef to put the color back in a man's cheeks," Pan said cheerfully. "You were starting to get a little pasty."

"I guess that's what happens when you eat nothing but ramen for three days." Cupid finished off his wine, and Pan swiftly refilled their glasses. "Are you trying to get me drunk?"

Pan's gaze met Cupid's. "Just relaxed. I want you to have a good time tonight."

"I'm trying." Despite his best efforts, Cupid couldn't help but wonder what vegetarian dish Mia was serving the boys tonight and whether the lieutenant had joined them. "Are you sorry I'm still here?"

Pan's head snapped up. "Of course not. Why would you ask me that?"

"I don't think I could be worse company."

A gentle smile eased the corners of Pan's mouth. "Sure, you could. You could be lying in bed, pissing and moaning and stinking up my house." Pan waved his fork through the air. "Stop trying so hard, man. You're fine. However you are, for however long you're here, I will gratefully take your company. Okay?" With a hearty wink, Pan stabbed another piece of meat and placed it between his lips.

"At least I have one friend down here," said Cupid.

Pan leaned forward, a glint of mischief in his eyes. "You haven't been paying attention, my friend."

He thought he had this time. "To what?"

"Don't look now, but every female in this place—and maybe that one guy at the bar—is hot for you. The God of Love is back, baby."

4 4

WANTED AGAIN

"Welcome to Versailles." Pan waggled his eyebrows and pushed open the ridiculously ornate doors. "So," Pan yelled over the pounding sex beat, "what do you think of Tarra's one and only male dance club?"

For starters, there are an awful lot of men, was Cupid's first thought. The dance floor was an enormous circle, ringed by a series of connected, mirrored archways. At the center, a glittering crystal monstrosity of a bar rose two stories above the dance floor.

"Looks like Narcissus threw up all over the place."

"Hahaha. C'mon, let's hit the bar." Pan slapped a hand onto Cupid's shoulder and steered him through the crowd of hungry stares. "What are you drinking?"

Wine was for dinner, and alcohol was for *serious* action, according to Pan.

"Hmm, I feel like something fancy." Expensive-looking bottles with etched designs stood in colorful rows, awaiting their big chance to be poured by deft-handed bartenders in bowties and black leather thongs.

"Two Ketel One dirty martinis," Pan said to the nearest bartender, a cute blond boy who seemed barely old enough to serve drinks.

Pan rested his elbows on the bar behind him and gazed up at a dancer wearing what looked like Cupid's boxer briefs, only briefer. Nothing subtle about this place, but then subtlety wasn't exactly the goal. A burst of high-pitched laughter across the dance floor caught Cupid's attention.

"Why are there women here?"

Pan leaned in and still would have had to shout if not for Cupid's superhuman hearing. "It's mix night. Whatever you're in the mood for, you'll find it here tonight."

Whatever *was* Cupid in the mood for? After three days of licking his wounds, Cupid felt he might be able to tolerate being wanted by someone other than Mia, but that was as far as he'd gotten.

"Two dirty martinis for two dirty boys."

Cupid and Pan spun around and picked up their drinks. "Here's to a night out with my best friend in the cosmos," Pan said, setting his mouth near Cupid's ear before adding, "and two sets of working equipment."

They clinked, and Cupid took a cautious sip of his salty drink. "I can't believe you never told me your . . . equipment was broken."

"It's not exactly something to brag about. Bad enough I had a tail."

A sweat-soaked, skinny young man tapped Cupid on the shoulder. "Did someone say 'tail'?" he asked with a cute wiggle of his hips.

"Thanks, but we're having a drink at the moment," Pan answered.

The man glanced at Pan, shrugged, and moved backwards until the crush of dancers absorbed him.

Cupid locked eyes with Pan. "So, Pan . . ."

Pan lifted a lazy brow. "Hmm?"

"That was quite a kiss at the station."

"Oh." Pan looked away first, swirling the spear of olives around the edge of his glass as if missing a spot might have dire consequences. Throwing back his head, he lifted the plastic sword to his mouth, plucked off the bottom olive with his tongue, and washed it down with a gulp of martini. "Sorry."

Cupid nudged his elbow into Pan's side and waited for Pan to return his gaze. "Really?"

A little smirk lifted Pan's mouth at the corners. "Maybe not entirely."

"Maybe not at all," Cupid answered, taking another sip of his drink. "Not that I minded or anything."

"Yeah, didn't taste like you minded."

"You're a good kisser."

"You're not terrible yourself." Pan's lips parted. His nostrils flared ever so subtly. All that carefully restrained passion seemed to be leaking out like the contents of Pandora's urn. "But then, if Cupid can't kiss, we're all in trouble."

A blush filled Cupid's cheeks, and he cooled off with a sip of his drink. "I thought we agreed we weren't doing that."

Pan released a heavy sigh. "You're absolutely right. I shouldn't have kissed you. I'd only meant to throw Lieutenant Goode a few hints—holding hands, googly eyes, that sort of thing."

"That was pretty smart." Cupid grinned at his friend's ingenuity. "So, all of your grave talk about responsibility and reckless joyrides and why we shouldn't . . .?" He finished the sentence with a jut of his chin.

"Yeah, well." A pained gaze flickered from beneath Pan's blondish-red lashes. "All of a sudden, it hit me you were really leaving, and I was about to lose you *again*, maybe for the rest of our eternal lives this time. I might've gotten a little carried away."

Pan had taken a terrible risk, and his body language right now—dilated pupils, flushed cheeks, racing pulse—screamed he would willingly take the plunge again. If anything, the pull was even stronger now that Cupid's full potency had been restored.

Freed of his obsession with Mia, Cupid could have succumbed to temptation as well. Anyone could see what made Pan stand out from the sea of men at Versailles: rugged bone structure and broad shoulders, the alluring combination of mossy green eyes and thick, auburn hair, the way he strode through the crowd with the virility of the god of the hunt. On top of all that, Cupid had the inside track on the glint of mischief in Pan's eye, the easy, disarming smile, and the soul of the wild beast that lurked just beneath the surface of the man. And it didn't hurt that Pan was fully aroused and completely absorbed in Cupid alone.

"You know, Pan, I wasn't so keen on losing you again either."

Pan angled his body toward Cupid. "Oh?" Was he fishing or just being dense?

"What do *you* think?"

Pan's mouth lifted in a lopsided grin. "I think you were understandably sidetracked by a certain girl we're not talking about tonight and more than a little anxious about what was about to happen to you."

"True enough. When I was driving away from Mi—*her* house, leaving behind all the people I loved so much, everything came roaring back. That awful day they told me you'd died. It felt as if someone had cut off my right arm. And then the other day, when I thought I was about to evaporate into the clouds and return home again without you, I—"

Pan spun his martini glass on the bar, fidgeted with the napkin, anything to avoid meeting Cupid's eye.

A week ago, Cupid might've pounced on the situation. No

question, he'd exhibited a lack of judgment with Mia at times—
many times. But try as he might to convince himself it would be
okay to mess around with Pan right now, something bigger than
Cupid's sexual urges had taken control of his behavior. *Huh,
who would've ever thought I'd be the mature one?*

"No matter what happens now, Pan, we've found each other
again, and you're still my best friend. I don't want to mess that
up for a few minutes of physical pleasure."

"A *few?*" Pan's eyebrows popped up to meet his unruly bangs.
"Pshh. I don't know who you've been talking to."

The two friends exchanged wicked grins.

"I can't imagine Cheri would complain about your stamina."

Pan huffed. "Not while everything was working properly."

"Is that why we're here in this testosterone palace, then?
Because Cheri dumped you? This is my fault, isn't it?"

A soft smile danced in Pan's eyes. "Don't sweat it, Q. My
tastes fluctuate, and I enjoy a wide range of partners. Right
now, I have a taste for men. Is that your fault?" Pan's half-lidded
gaze came to rest on Cupid's mouth. Cupid's lips parted; Pan's
did the same, forcing a puff of desire to Cupid's tongue. "Yeah,
that's on you."

How easy it would be to lean in and steal another kiss and
ruin everything.

No, Cupid wouldn't do that. Instead, he grabbed Pan's wrist
and gave it a tug. "Dance with me."

Pan set his empty glass down on the bar and let Cupid
drag him into the crowd. The two were instantly absorbed by
the writhing mob: a cute boy for Cupid, a muscle man for Pan,
one behind, another in front, hands everywhere. It felt good to
be hard from raw desire and not some hideous curse. Mostly,
Cupid was happy because Pan was enjoying himself and, from
the looks of things, getting exactly what he needed right now.

The melody shifted, but the bass pounded on. A strobe light kicked on, throwing the whole place into a giant, slow motion, black-and-white circus where nothing felt real. Fists punched up through the crowd. Heads whipped side to side, throwing off ropes of sweat. Strippers gyrated in floating cages, making love to invisible partners, inspiring a hundred fantasies. Anything was possible.

The stranger behind him yanked Cupid's T-shirt out of his jeans and slid the fabric up over his belly and chest. Greedy for the skin-on-skin, Cupid raised his arms to help the shirt off when he was seized by a terrible, crushing pressure inside his ribcage. He doubled over in agony.

Pan rushed to his side, thrashing away the bodies in his path. "What happened? Did that guy hurt you? I will rip his fucking nuts off."

"No." Cupid clutched at his chest though he knew it wouldn't help. "It's my heart."

"Fuck. *Now?*"

Cupid moaned.

"Let's get you out of here."

Pan practically carried him off the dance floor. With a menacing glare, Pan emptied the nearest bar stool and gently lowered Cupid onto it.

"You guys all right?" asked the bartender. "Someone having a bad trip? Should I call security?"

"We're fine," Pan answered gruffly. "My friend needs a glass of water and a little air."

Pan squatted and placed his hand on Cupid's knee. "Talk to me. What's going on?"

"Throbbing. Starting again."

"Wow, they sure didn't give you much time to recover. Sorry for asking, but is it Mia again?"

BETH C. GREENBERG

"No, not Mia." *Huh*, the name didn't feel like razor blades on Cupid's tongue this time.

"Okay, that's good, I guess." Pan passed him the water. "Here. Drink up. Breathe."

Cupid sipped at the water, then brought the cool glass to his chest. It offered absolutely no relief. "I'm sorry, Pan."

"What? Stop that. Wait"—Pan slapped a hand over his heart—"it's not *me* this time, is it?"

"No. It's not you. I just really wanted us to have fun tonight."

"I did, Q. I had a fucking blast. Now stop worrying about me."

Cupid groaned again. "This feels worse than last time."

"Yeah, they tend to ratchet things up. The important thing is, you know what you need to do."

Oh yes, Cupid knew. As soon as he could breathe again, all he had to do was follow the tracker in his chest straight to the truest love his heart had ever known.

CAST OF DIVINE CHARACTERS

AUTHOR'S NOTE: The primary name (all uppercase) for each divine is consistent with the narrative of the "Great Syncretism," an invented departure from Greco-Roman mythology. The character snippets offered here are based on canon; where multiple stories exist within the classical sources, I have chosen my favorite version.

APHRODITE (Venus): Goddess of love, beauty, and fertility. Rose fully formed out of the foam (*aphros*) floating around Uranus's castrated genitals. Married to Hephaestus, bore four children to Ares, including Cupid.

APOLLO: God of light, music, prophecy, and medicine. Twin brother of Artemis.

ARES (Mars): God of War. Son of Zeus and Hera, brother of Hephaestus, "biological" father of Cupid.

ARTEMIS (Diana): Goddess of the hunt, protector of new brides. Twin sister of Apollo.

ATROPOS: One of the three Fates ("allotters") responsible for spinning men's fate. Clotho spins the thread of life, Lachesis determines its length, and Atropos cuts the thread with her shears.

CERBERUS: The vicious three-headed hound of Hades, guards the gates of the Underworld to prevent the dead from leaving.

CLOTHO: One of the three Fates (with Atropos and Lachesis), Clotho spins the thread of life.

CUPID (Eros): God of erotic love. Illegitimate son of Aphrodite and Ares.

DIONYSUS (Bacchus): God of wine and ecstasy.

HADES (Pluto): Ruler of the Underworld. Brother of Zeus and Poseidon.

HELIOS: God of the sun. Crowned with the aureole of the sun, he emerges each dawn driving a chariot drawn by four winged steeds and descends in the far West at each day's end into a golden cup that bore him back to the East.

HEPHAESTUS (Vulcan): God of fire and forge. Blacksmith and divine craftsman. Son of Zeus and Hera. Married to Aphrodite, stepfather to Cupid.

HERA (Juno): Queen of the Gods. Sister and wife of Zeus. Famous for her ill temper.

HYPNOS: God of sleep. Rises into the sky each night in the train of his mother Nyx.

LACHESIS: One of the three Fates (with Atropos and Clotho), Lachesis determines the length of the thread of life.

MERCURY (Hermes): The gods' messenger. Father of Pan.

PAN (Faunus): Demi-god of the wild, protector of the herd. Satyr (half man, half goat). Son of Mercury (and in one version, Penelope, wife of Odysseus).

ZEUS (Jupiter): Ruler of the gods. Married to Hera, yet father of many, *by* many—divines and mortals alike.

To get your free, full-color, downloadable guide to the mythology of the Cupid's Fall series, visit:
www.bethcgreenberg.com/mythology-guide

ACKNOWLEDGMENTS

Publishing a book is a daunting enterprise I never could have undertaken on my own. I am grateful to so many people for sharing their wisdom, talent, and enthusiastic support.

It all began with a certain fandom (you know who you are) for giving me the bright idea that my wild imaginings might be worth writing down and sharing. To my worldwide network of fandom friends, thank you for enabling, encouraging, and loyally following my writing journey here. To my *First Quiver* beta readers—Jean, Veronica, Adèle, Lisa, Qwen, and Shelley—thank you for bravely taking the earliest looks at this story. To Susan Atlas, my ever-editor, "last eyes," and true partner in words, thank you for lending your wisdom and your warmth to the editing process; I so appreciate that the rules are always only our starting point. To the crazy-talented Betti Gefecht, thank you for putting your whole heart and soul into drawing this gorgeous cover with your very own loving hands, for injecting the process of creative collaboration with pure joy and (almost) never saying no, and especially for gifting me with the title "Lady Pestershire," which I will cherish always. To Maria, some day we will meet, and you will show me your beautiful country; meanwhile, thank you for helping me sort out Cupid's Greek-speak. To Shay Savage, Melanie Moreland, and K Evan Coles, thank you for going first and so generously sharing your lessons learned from the publishing world. To Kate, thank you for inspiring Mia, my fierce Mama Bear, and allowing me to borrow from your love story. To

Jayme and Sandy, I miss you both and so wish you were here for this journey. To Cupid's Street Team, thank you for helping to spread the word and cheering me every step of the way. To all who hung out in a certain pumpkin patch in the ether and read my words when I was just beginning to find them, thank you so much. You might never know how much you mean to me.

To the community of writers I discovered through flash fiction writing, thank you for teaching me so much about story and critique and sending words out into the world. Mostly, thank you for modeling high standards, positivity, and dogged determination. Carrie, thank you for your encouragement but even more than that, your honesty. Di, thanks for always answering the call for help and teaching me just enough to be truly dangerous.

Thank you to Henri Lazaridis for an insightful manuscript consult in the early drafting and to GrubStreet instructor Kate Racculia for an extremely useful novel revision course after round two. To Brad and Lauren, thank you for reading and sharing your honest feedback. Thank you to Dominic Wakeford for your copyedits and reassurance and to Domini Dragoone for the book's beautiful interior design.

To my mother, thank you nurturing my love of books with a million trips to the Children's Room at the Akron Public Library and for your steadfast encouragement and pride in all my writing endeavors. Dad, I wish you were still here to see that I kept on doing what I was doing. Guess what—it's done! To my book group (of 23 years!), thank you for keeping that interest in good stories burning bright and for hosting my first "live" author appearance. To playgroup, the original Group Therapy, thanks for helping me celebrate every milestone along the way. To Rachel, thank you for always making time to ask and listen and care.

To my miraculous daughter, Lindsay, thank you for modeling the act of fearlessly sharing your story. You are my hero every day. To Jeffrey, my beautiful son who surprised me one day with a completed manuscript of your own, your title is now stamped on the spine of my books: Isotopia Publishing. I miss you every day, and I can feel you cheering me on from above.

Last and never least, to my amazing husband Larry, who is always the best part of every character I write, thank you for taking Cupid into your heart.

ABOUT THE AUTHOR

BETH C. GREENBERG earned an accounting degree at the Wharton School of the University of Pennsylvania, which she is putting to excellent use writing modern-day mythology. She lives outside of Boston, where she and her husband are occasionally visited by their daughter and grand-dog Slim. *First Quiver* is her debut novel and book one of the four-book CUPID'S FALL series.

COMING SPRING 2021,
FROM ISOTOPIA PUBLISHING:

INTO THE QUIET

BOOK 2 OF THE *CUPID'S FALL* SERIES

Read on for a preview...

The second time Cupid's heart revved up should have been easier, and in some ways, it was. He recognized the stabbing pain in his chest right away, and he had a general sense of what was expected of him.

But Cupid wasn't particularly eager to relive the Mia experience—except for that one exceptionally nice part just before he blurted out he loved her, then realized there was no echo beat and vomited up his dinner. Also troubling, this signal was already stronger than the first, more of a piercing throb even through Cupid's drunken haze. The gods proving, yet again, they weren't messing around.

Cupid forced himself off the bar stool. His knees buckled, sending him floorward. Pan's firm hand closed around his arm, steadying Cupid as he'd been doing in one way or another for the past ten days.

"Easy," Pan said, his voice raspy with concern.

Cupid dragged in a deep yoga breath, exhaled slowly, and nodded gratefully at Pan. "Okay, I'm ready." He sure hoped he sounded braver than he felt.

"Don't you think you better put your shirt on first?"

Cupid's gaze dropped to his bare chest. *Right.* That pretty boy he'd been dancing with had tugged it off him. Cupid turned toward the dance floor, one giant, tangled organism pulsating under the purple lights. "It's buried in there somewhere."

Pan tapped his nose. "I'll be right back. Don't move."

Cupid had nearly wrapped his head around the here-we-go-again when his shirt came flying at his face. "Thanks," he said, pushing his arms through the sleeves.

"Lead on," said Pan.

"You're coming?"

"Of course. My ass is on the line, too, or have you forgotten already?" Truthfully, Cupid's Worthy-tracking system left little room for distractions, despite how hard Cupid had been working to put Pan's ass out of his mind before his awful motor started up again.

"Fine. This way." Off they went, Cupid's relentless heart-compass guiding the way and Pan trailing tight on his heels. Judging by the intensity of the churning in his chest, whatever Cupid was meant to find was right here in this club.

So intent was Cupid on following his heart, he nearly crashed into a raised platform that placed a dancer's gold-covered bulge exactly at eye-level. An impressive set of white feathered wings fanned out from the dancer's shoulders and somehow fluttered gracefully while the lower half of his body popped and gyrated at his audience.

Pan licked his lips and stared, mouth agape. "*Wow.*"

"He's all yours," Cupid replied. "He's not the Worthy."

But Cupid was close; he could feel it. The signal pulled him along the edge of the stage and into a flock of wild women, screaming and stuffing money into the dancer's pouch. *Not this one, nope, nope . . . boom!* Cupid stopped short, and Pan—distracted by the slicked-up, writhing angel on stage—slammed into Cupid's back, ramming him into the new love of his life just as she was tucking a bill inside the dancer's thong.

The woman grasped at the fabric to regain her balance, but the measly garment was no match for her downward velocity. The pouch gave way, spilling money and genitals, before Cupid could manage to grab the falling woman around the waist. A collective gasp went up around them—with Pan's enthusiastic, "Oh *hell*, yeah!" loudest of all—before the angel could tuck himself and his tips back inside.

"Oh gods, I'm sorry," Cupid said, relaxing his grip around the goddess in his arms as she regained her footing. "Are you okay?"

She blinked up at him with a shocked pair of hazel eyes set into a deep blush. "I . . . I honestly don't know." She rattled her head, shaking a tendril of spun gold across her cheek.

Without thinking, Cupid reached in and gingerly tucked the loose hair behind her ear. The two sets of eyes locked, and neither would let go of the other, dazzle-*ee* meeting dazzle-*er* and vice-versa. She melted his insides with every shaky breath passing between her lips.

"Take your time," Cupid said, finding himself in no rush to go anywhere or do anything except exactly this. "I won't let go until you're steady." *Until you know how much you want me, too.*

Racing pulse, dilated pupils, dry mouth. Need poured off this woman in hot, dangerous waves—waves that had already pulled Cupid under.

She raised her hand to wipe the beads of sweat from her brow. Two rings dwarfed her left hand: a diamond the size of a robin's egg with a solid band below. Married.

"Hey, what's—" Pan stopped cold. "Oh boy. Q, we need to talk. *Now*."

Barely registering Pan's presence, Cupid answered him with a dismissive, "Call me." About to hoist his precious love into his arms, carry her to bed, and pleasure her for the rest of his days, Cupid remembered his circumstances and the horrible ordeal he'd gone through with Mia. Distilling his beloved's heartbeat from all the rest, Cupid listened with all his strength. Try as he might, even placing an ear to her chest, he could find no echo beat to match his own.

In that terrible moment, Cupid understood. The goddess in his grasp was not his Right Love after all; she was his next torment.

Visit cupidsfallseries.com for ordering info.